IT TAKES *Three* TO TANGO

Dance Lovers Collection
Book 2

JEM WENDEL

Published by Larking About Press

Edited by Jenn Green and SJ Buckley

Cover designed by Stephanie

Cover photo: Enrico Berni, Mattia Sala, Miguel Gallego

ISBN: 978-1-916758-32-2 - Trade Paperback

It Takes Three to Tango

Dance is the language of life—and love—that brings three wounded hearts together

Rafe: Jilted at the altar, he's on his Barcelona honeymoon—alone—when he finds refuge in a dimly lit tango bar. Constantin: His bar is all he has left of the one great love of his life, until a handsome stranger awakens a need to connect. Florencio: A lonely foreigner whose judgmental father sent to Spain to discover the contents of his elderly aunt's will.

One tumbledown bar. Three hearts in need of repair. One dance floor where all they need is the common language of dance—and a whisper of silk—to find forever.

Note: *It Takes Three to Tango* is book two in the Dance Lovers Collection. The books in this series are standalones and can be enjoyed in any order. Contains a bi-awakening, age gap, second-chance, forced proximity romance set against the backdrop of Gaudi's Barcelona.

Ideal wine pairing: a dark, passionate red blend.

"I think you've stolen my dance partner," he says, his voice low. "I rather thought he was ours."

IT TAKES

Three

TO TANGO

Dance Lovers Collection

Book 2

JEM WENDEL

Author's Note

Thank you for reading It Takes Three To Tango. While completing Not Strictly Ballroom and throughly enjoying writing about dancing, I came across an Instagram reel of three men dancing the tango. I knew then I wanted to write that story. Thank you to Enrico Berni, Mattia Sala, Miguel Gallego for the inspiration and for letting use your photo.

It Takes Three To Tango wasn't easy. To take three men who are strangers, set it in a country different to my own and with a language that I don't speak very well was a challenge. But I love these guys so much and I'm glad I got to tell their story.

One song that came to me while I was writing It Takes Three To Tango, was I Could Have Danced All Night from My Fair Lady. Sadly I wasn't able to secure the rights to directly include the lyrics in time, though they are intimated within the text. The song feels particularly appropriate for my own journey in writing this book - I was spreading my wings and trying a thousand things.

Content Warnings: Mention of death (historic and side character.)

This book intended for adult readers. It contains scenes of

sexually explicit material between male characters. If this is not for you then please do not read my books.

Language Notes

It Takes Three To Tango is written is British English which means that some words are spelled differently - such as s in the place of z as in apologise. Similarly u is used such as in colour or favourite. Practice/practise - both are used in British English depending on if they are being used as a verb or a noun.

Also in some cases, different grammar rules are followed.

There is also a smattering of Spanish throughout the book, where possible I have made sure this can be understood, either as a direct translation or through the character's thoughts. It is a pet hate of mine when phrases are given in a different language but no translation is provided.

Época - Gotan Project
Pequeña - Joel Tortul
The First Time Ever I Saw Your Face - George Michael
Balada para un Loco - Aquiles Delle-Vigne
Look at Me - Carrie Underwood
Todo Es Amor - Romántica Milonguera
I Could Have Danced All Night - Frederick Loewe, Marni
Nixon, André Previn, Warner Brothers Studio Orchestra
Kiss Me - Sixpence None The Wiser
Sex on Fire - Kings of Leon
Libertango - Tango Bardo
Distant Sun - Crowded House
Corazon Loco - Antonio Machin
All My Happiness is Gone - Purple Mountains
Somebody's Me - Enrique Iglesias

Queremos Paz - Gotan Project
Esta Noche La Luna - Osvaldo Jorge Maciel
Vivir Mi Vida - Marc Anthony

Dedication

For everyone who has the courage to spread their wings and
try a thousand different things

Chapter 1

Rafe

It was the need for shade from the hot sun that sent me down the shadowy alley shortly after midday.

It was the desire to slake my thirst that made me enter the small bar with the curious name and soft music.

It was the hypnotic voice of the singer and the sensuous movements of the dancers that kept me there until after midnight.

What brought me back the next day I have still to discover, and yet here I am, my book unopened on the table as I sit sipping coffee and trying not to contemplate the disaster that is my life.

Here I can pretend, just for a little while, that everything is all right. That I still have a job and a career, that I still have someone who loves me, and that I'm not in Barcelona, on my honeymoon—alone.

I've spent a lot of time over the last week beating myself up that it's my fault Loretta left me at the altar—not literally, thank god, the embarrassment would've been too much. But she called the whole thing off the day before. Two days before, my publisher, her father, had cancelled my contract. Apparently, literary novels don't sell anymore, and I said I wouldn't write a cosy mystery in a market saturated by celebrities. So here I am, nursing a broken heart and a broken life.

The music, the singing, the language forming the backdrop, foreign to my ears and all the more exotic for it, anchor me to this place. It feels timeless. I hardly register that coffee has been replaced by wine, and the waitress has placed a couple of plates of tapas—that I barely remember ordering —in front of me. The hours pass, though I can't account for them.

A glass landing heavily on the table startles me. It takes a second to get my bearings and I focus on the dark liquid almost sloshing over the side, watching it settle into a calm ripple before lifting my eyes to the source.

The singer stands across from me and sets another glass on the table. He's tall and broad, dark-featured with heavy brows and full lips, probably around forty or so. But it's his heavy-lidded eyes that grab most of my attention. I stare into a chasm, the edges lined with desolation. They're striking, and I'm momentarily adrift in their tragic beauty.

I realise I'm being rude, but I also have no idea what he's doing here. Blinking, I look around at the bar, now empty of customers.

"Oh, I'm sorry. You're closed." I hadn't noticed everyone leaving, so wrapped up in my own thoughts.

"*Quédate, por favor.*"

"I'm sorry, I don't speak Spanish. *No hablo español.*" I've pretty much exhausted the extent of my foreign language skills.

His mouth twitches slightly and he switches to English.

"Stay. Please." His richly accented voice is perfect, causing fleeting chagrin that I never bothered to learn Spanish. He settles into the chair opposite and I look around again.

"Are you sure? It's late. I don't want to put you to any trouble." I'm babbling, but I've hardly spoken to anyone all week. I feel ill-equipped to be good company, even if he does intrigue me.

"I don't want to drink alone." He pushes the glass closer to me and picks up his own. He nods to my glass, and I grasp it. The message is clear, and I don't want to appear rude. He briefly swirls the liquid in his glass before holding it aloft.

"To not drinking alone." I start to laugh, but it dies on my lips as his eyes capture mine, and he doesn't look away as he downs the drink in one. I watch, fascinated, as he wipes his mouth with the back of his hand. I raise my glass and echo his words.

The alcohol hits the back of my throat, searing a path. Rum. I don't usually take it neat. I cough and splutter, trying to compose myself instead of looking like the uncouth English guy who can't speak the language or knock back a drink.

His mouth twitches again, but he doesn't comment as he reaches for the bottle and refills the glasses. I think I'll just sip the next one.

He reaches into his pocket and pulls out a packet of Marlboros. He offers one and I shake my head.

"I don't smoke."

"Very wise. It's a filthy habit." That doesn't stop him taking one out, flipping the top of a Zippo, and lighting up. He carefully places the lighter down on the table, takes a long drag, and exhales, gesturing to my book with the hand holding the cigarette.

"What are you reading?"

"*The Shadow of the Wind.*" I'd thought it somehow

cultural to read a book set in Barcelona while I was here, but now as I say it, I feel gauche.

"Zafón?" He nods. "Good choice. I have it in the original if you want to try it."

Whilst his approval feels like I might have passed some sort of test, I stare at him, trying to work out whether he's joking. I already told him I didn't know much Spanish. But his face is impassive, as if learning a new language was something you did every day.

"What brings you to Barcelona?" The question is casual enough, but there's a dark intensity to his eyes, and I wonder if he's asking about Barcelona in general or what brings me back to his bar.

In any event, I'm not going to share my pathetic story with a stranger, so I shrug.

"I've never been here before. I wanted to see some Gaudi." Both statements are true, so it doesn't feel like a lie. And wanting to see the Casa Milà and the Casa Batlló were some of the reasons I wanted to visit this beautiful city. Though I've done exactly zero sightseeing so far. I wince internally at the fact that my insistence we come to Barcelona might have contributed to Loretta's accusations, thrown at me on the afternoon she left.

You're so boring Rafe, all you ever do is work.

"A regular tourist then," he says and takes a drag on his cigarette.

I feel like he's mocking me slightly, or at least dismissing me, and I blurt out,"Not really. I've been here a week and haven't seen anything yet." Now I just sound like a fool. He doesn't respond, just continues to regard me with a curious expression. The seconds stretch and I feel it might be one of those moments where he's deliberately leaving a silence for me to fill. Well, I'm not going to just prattle out anything to embarrass myself. I need to change the subject.

I take a sip of the rum, allowing it to slip down smoothly instead of burning my throat. It occurs to me I'm accepting after-hours hospitality from a guy and I don't even know his name.

I read the sign behind the bar: La Casa de Valery. Valery's House.

"Are you Valery?"

His expression shifts, almost like someone has flicked a dimmer switch.

He picks up his lighter, turning it over and over in his fingers. He takes another long drag on his cigarette, exhaling slowly with a sigh.

"Valery was my husband. He was my world."

Damn, I've gone from not wanting to embarrass myself to making him uncomfortable. I really am bad at this, being in company.

Another puff of his cigarette.

"I loved him and would've followed him to the ends of the earth. In the end, I just had to follow him here."

"You're not from Barcelona?"

He shakes his head. "No, I'm from Gran Canaria. Valery went there for a holiday." His face softens and his eyes are far away, in a bygone time. "I hardly left his side for the month he was there; I was besotted, and so was he. When he returned, I came with him."

He gestures round the bar with his hand, careless of where ash is falling.

"This was his dream, to have a bar. It was all he talked about. We spent a long time saving up for it. But he never got to see it."

He picks up his glass and downs the rest in one gulp, his eyes dark and brimming with a deep hurt.

"What happened?" My voice croaks, and I take a gulp, forgetting to sip. I swallow past the burn.

"He got sick . . . cancer. Three months. That's all we had . . . three months." Bitterness laces his words. "I watched him turn to dust in front of my eyes."

"I'm so sorry," I say. It's the usual thing to say, but I know it won't touch the side of his grief. His mouth forms a tight line as if he's heard it a million times and it brings no relief.

"It took me a year to finish saving up, to open this place. To realise his dream. All of it, it's for him."

He sits back, his face expressionless, like telling his story has wiped him clean of emotion.

I look round at the bar, seeing it as the tribute it is, seeing the effort that's gone into making it a vibrant and lively place.

"I think that's the most romantic story I've ever heard."

When I look at him again, the bottomless sadness is back.

I yawn, tiredness catching up with me. He stands.

"I should lock up. It's late."

I understand my dismissal, but I don't have the energy to be annoyed. I can see he wants to be alone.

I say goodnight and take my leave.

It only occurs to me, back in my hotel room as I get undressed for bed, that I still don't know his name.

Chapter 2

Constantin

I bolt the door and lean my head against it, taking deep breaths. I will the memories to go away, but it doesn't work, it never works.

Images of Valery play through my head like an old family movie and I know there's nothing I can do but let it run. Memories of the time we met, that carefree summer when life was full of light and love, along with sea and sand. When we dreamed big and loved even bigger. When I would have followed Valery to the ends of the earth, long before he went somewhere I couldn't follow him.

I push off from the door and go back to the table. A part of me says to put the rum back on the shelf, but I know how this will play out—the same way it always does—so I pour another glass and sit down, lighting another cigarette.

The images are replaced by those of us building our life here in Barcelona. Valery working in bars and me singing in them, being careful with our money, saving everything we have. The evenings off when we'd walk the streets, usually making our way here. Valery would always stop and look up at the old three-storey building for a while before turning to me with a light in his eyes, and declaring that this would be ours someday. The day I asked him to marry me, on my knees on the dragon stairway at the Park Güell, a place we visited often. I believed myself to be the luckiest man that had ever lived when he said yes.

The last set of memories are the ones which bring the most pain. Valery becoming sick, and the useless hope we clung to that everything would be well, that it was a short-term illness, until the day of the diagnosis. We married shortly after, foolishly thinking that the universe couldn't split up two people as in love as we were, that it couldn't be that cruel. But life doesn't work that way. I close my eyes to blot out what I know is coming next, but it just heightens the tightness in my chest. It hurts too much, the loneliness and the loss of a future we will never get to have. You'd have thought that after ten years, the pain would have diminished, and in a way it has, as these days I can draw breath without the loss stabbing me through the heart. But sometimes, when I talk about Valery, it brings it all back up.

Smoke hazes round me as I pour another two fingers of rum. I knock this one back, the scorching in my throat matching the sears on my soul.

A flash of annoyance that the memories had been evoked plays through my thoughts, but I tamp that down. It wasn't the guy's fault, he was just being polite.

Why did I invite him to stay and drink? That's the curious part of all this. I'm not in the habit of asking people to drink with me. In fact, in all the years since I opened the bar, I've only done it on a handful of occasions when the thought of being alone became too much to bear, and then they were usually staff, musicians, or acquaintances. Never with a stranger. Admittedly, he was a very handsome stranger. If his light brown hair and pale skin didn't mark him as northern European, his awkwardness and politeness did. His English accent had sent shivers up my spine. He looked serious, a scholar or academic maybe, though not nerdy or delicate. But none of this explains why I targeted him. Why, when the bar was closing, did I grab a bottle of my finest rum and invite him to stay?

Maybe it was something in the way he tilted his head that drew my attention as I glanced across the room. Or it could've been the look in his eyes: as if life had beaten him, and he was sure there was more to come but couldn't do a damn thing about it. I don't know if these can properly describe the pull I felt tonight, the need to connect with him somehow. Not that it worked, as I ended up practically kicking him out, and now here I am, drinking alone and wallowing in self-pity.

I know from experience that no good can come of this, so I stub out my cigarette and stand. It's time to go to bed.

Habit ensures that I empty and clean the ashtray so the smell doesn't linger. Smoking isn't allowed in public places, but I figure that with it being after hours, it isn't public anymore. I leave cleaning the glasses until the morning, though.

I lock up and take the stairs to the two-storey apartment above the bar. My home. Technically, it has two floors, but the upper one, a sizable loft space, is largely storage and I rarely go up there. It was going to be our bedroom . . . mine and Valery's. Another project he had grand plans for. One day, after he'd decided this was *our* building, but before it had come on the market, he'd talked the previous owner into letting us have a look around. He'd stood in the large loft and, with his usual ebullience, described exactly how we should have it. A plan that was refined over the following months until I knew every detail. When I finally secured the building, a year after Valery left me alone in this world, the bar I could create for him—that part of his vision I could do. But not the bedroom. I was unable to stand the oppressive weight of sleeping alone every night in a space where we were supposed to celebrate our love. So, I remain living all on one level and sleeping in a smaller bedroom.

I run the tap for a glass of water, hoping it means I won't wake up feeling like I've drunk several glasses of rum. The pipes grumble, a reminder I need to get the plumbing looked at, especially as the damp patch on the wall seems to have grown slightly. Maybe tomorrow.

As I pull my T-shirt over my head, the stranger's handsome face comes back to me, or rather, how his honeyed eyes had looked like liquid gold when he'd told me that running the bar was romantic.

I have no idea what he meant by that, but the way he said it stirred up memories I needed to be alone for. We only get one chance at love in this life, and I don't need a reminder that I've had my turn.

I slip between the sheets, enjoying the coolness, just perfect now in spring, before the heat of the summer renders sleep almost impossible. There was a lost look in his eyes, and I wonder if there's more to his story than he told me. As I drift off to sleep, I wonder if he'll come back to the bar again. The thought fosters a small seed of hope that he will. After all, I never got to ask his name.

Chapter 3

Florencio

"Bye Auntie, I'll be back later." My hushed tones still seem too loud in the quiet room. I glance at the prone form in the bed and then at Juana, my great aunt's housekeeper and now, I suppose, her nurse. She shakes her head, her mouth downturned in sadness and resignation. I've only been in the country for a few days, but I'm learning the patterns of the house. Some days, my aunt has times of lucidity and energy, and some days not. This is one of them.

Unable to face a long afternoon and evening by myself, I decided to explore the city.

I've never been good at solitary confinement, so it feels wonderful to get out of the house for a while.

The problem isn't the house itself—as it's a large mansion split over several floors and has plenty of space—but the zero stimulation it provides. Built in the 1920s, it's stunningly beautiful, just like its owner, my aged great aunt. And just like its owner, its beauty is faded, reminiscent of livelier and more decadent times. Now, the past is an opaque filter which can be viewed but not lived in. Like looking at a photograph of a long-gone Hollywood star, it belongs to another era.

Leaving behind the hushed oppression of a building waiting to exhale, I choose to walk down the hill from the mansion and into the city, needing the freeing nature of movement. I doubt I could walk back up, though. I'm not used to hills back home in Buenos Aires, where it's flat. When I get to the centre, I follow La Rambla for a while, enjoying the wide tourist street of boutiques and restaurants. I select an outdoor table at a cafe for a coffee and a bout of people-watching while I rest after the walk. The weather is warming up, whereas back home in Argentina we'd be heading into winter. Maybe spending the summer in Barcelona won't be such a bad experience after all.

I'm not sure how long I will be here, but no one argues with my father. I remember him summoning me to his office —a rare occurrence, as I'm not usually welcome at his work. I'm the son he tries to forget unless it's convenient to remember me, like now. He'd held a letter in his hand. That in itself was odd, I mean, who writes letters anymore?

"I've had a letter from Aunt Estrella's solicitor." He brandishes the thick cream sheet of paper as if showing exhibit A. "She's dying. You will go to her."

"What? Me?" Incredulity and surprise sends my voice loud and squeaky and my father visibly winces. I know who he's referring to, of course. We all know of Aunt Estrella—or rather, his Aunt Estrella—we've just never met her. She left Argentina a long time ago, even before my father was born. And whilst he's met her a few times, as far as I'm aware, she's not returned for over thirty years.

"She is family, so someone needs to be there." His voice holds

no emotion. Maybe it's hard to feel anything for someone you've not seen for a long time. But then again, this is my father; emotions are not something he's familiar with. Myself, on the other hand . . . It's one of the reasons we don't get along.

There's no point saying that he should be the one to go, or that I actually have a job and commitments here in Buenos Aires. His mulish expression shows me that arguing would be useless.

"Your flight leaves in four hours."

"Papa!" The name slips out and my father looks up sharply. I was twelve when my father said I was no longer to call him that. It was to be only Padre or Señor. But I've been caught off guard. Four hours is barely enough to get home, pack, and get to the airport. I thought I might have a day or two, at least some time to make other arrangements for my classes.

My father's expression softens slightly. Anyone might think it's with affection, but I know my father better than that.

"Florencio, you are the best person to go to her. She will like you." A rare compliment, even if it is backhanded. He pushes an envelope across the desk to me, no doubt containing my tickets. He keeps his hand on it and looks me square in the eye. "We're all she has." And with those last four words, my father reveals himself and what he's asked me to do.

Before I continue exploring the city, I snap a photo and send it to my sister, knowing exactly the reaction it'll get. I'm rewarded with a message of her outrage within a few seconds. That I can no longer be at my sister's beck and call is one of the few kicks I'm likely to get out of this whole assignment. I can't be her unpaid childminder if I'm thousands of miles away. I love my nieces, but that's not the problem. It's the way my sister always drops those duties on me when she knows

I'm not teaching, as if I don't have anything else in my life except to be there for her.

I open a browser on my phone and look up gay bars and clubs, discovering a whole area in the Eixample district, cutely called Gaixample. That's definitely somewhere for me to visit another night, maybe find a hookup or two. After all, no one said I couldn't have any fun while I'm here, so I fully intend to. Things are looking up. For now, though, I decide to explore the old town some more, heading past the Cathedral and the Picasso Museum, making a note to come back another day. I follow the ancient winding streets, enjoying the old buildings and quiet reverence past the Basílica de Santa Maria del Mar, Our Lady of the Sea. I stand for a while, staring at its gothic beauty.

Music catches my attention. I can't mistake the sound of the bandoneón—tango music. It is unexpected, as flamenco music is more common in Spain. Tango is infused in my soul, and the familiar sound of it creates a wave of longing to be at home, to be dancing and teaching. Like a magnet, my body is pulled towards the source of the music. It's coming from a small bar, set away from the main streets and down a cool alleyway. La Casa de Valery . . . sounds intriguing. When I enter, a sense of rightness settles over me. Standing at the bar, I look around, and it's easy to see why—I could be back home in Buenos Aires. The bar isn't big, but larger than it looks from its unassuming outside. A long bar runs along one wall and there are at least a dozen tables and chairs. To one side is a dance floor with enough room for several couples to dance comfortably. The lower half of the walls are all wood-panelled, and the upper half is painted cream but covered in an eclectic mix of paintings and photographs, all tango related.

It has a timeless quality, almost as if it could have been

transported out of Argentina and dropped into Spain a century ago. What's more surprising is that it's busy. Nearly all the tables are occupied, and the dance floor already has a few couples. The music is provided by a bandoneón player, a violinist, a flautist, and a guitar player. An upright piano is pushed against one wall of the dance floor but is not currently being played.

There's a small unoccupied table close to the dancers, so I take a seat and watch them. I think of the lessons I had to cancel and the two club owners I've let down at short notice by being here. I hope there's a job for me when I return home. Not that my father views it as a proper job, which is really why I was the one chosen, the one member of the family who could be spared. It doesn't take long before I'm itching to get up and dance.

I watch as one of the couples sits back at their table. The woman doesn't look like she's ready to stop, but the guy is paying her no attention. On a whim, I stand and ask her to dance. She smiles like a vixen at her partner, who looks daggers at her for a minute, but she pays him no heed and eagerly steps onto the dance floor.

Maria, I learn, is probably nearly twice my age, very elegant, and a good dancer.

"Your partner has nothing to fear from me," I tell her and she laughs.

"I know, but it won't hurt for him to stew for a little while." She smiles, and the next time we pass the table, she draws just a little closer to me. The guy is practically apoplectic, so after the song finishes, I take her back to her seat. I don't want to be in the middle of an argument or risk the wrath of her bullish partner.

I need a drink, so I place my order and sit back at my table. The music starts up again, and this time the guy with the guitar sings. I relax, content to people-watch for a while. My eyes are drawn to a photograph on the wall behind the bar. It's a picture taken of a happy-looking couple on a beach. I recognise one of the guys as the singer in the tango group, but I don't see the other one. He looks older now than in the photo, and the joyful, carefree look is gone. His dark brows seem drawn, weighed down like life is a difficult weight to bear. Strangely, it suits him, almost more than the joyous look from the photo. It adds a gravitas to his handsome, dark face. But what strikes me the most about him is his voice. It's deep and reverberates in my bones. It makes me want to move, want to dance. He sometimes closes his eyes and then the song takes on a more soulful air. More than once, he flicks his eyes across the room, and I follow his gaze to where a guy is reading a book. The man is gorgeous. He's definitely *not* Spanish, his skin is too pale, but it's perfect for his light brown hair. He's wearing gold-rimmed glasses, which give him a scholarly air. Yes, he's definitely rocking the sexy professor look. If he notices the attention on him, he doesn't look up or acknowledge it. He seems completely oblivious to what's going on around him. I envy him his focus and his beauty. With the singer's rich tones coursing through my body, I make my way over to the handsome stranger. When I get closer, I see the book he is reading is English, though the author was Spanish.

"Would you like to dance?" I ask, speaking English, reasoning that unless he is trying to improve his language skills, he's English.

It takes him a second to notice my presence and that I've spoken.

"Hmm?" He blinks a couple of times—he obviously hadn't heard me. I almost feel sorry for disturbing him, but it was worth it to have his light brown, almost gold eyes on me.

"Would you like to dance?" I repeat.

His brow knits together for a second, and he answers with a frown. "I'm . . . err, straight."

The unexpected answer makes me snort.

"Cariño! I asked if you wanted to dance with me, not if you wanted to fuck me!"

Chapter 4

Rafe

"Oh shit! Sorry!" I blurt, wishing the earth could actually open up and swallow me. My cheeks burn and I'm sure I'm a horrendous puce colour. "I didn't mean it like that. I—"

What *did* I mean? It dawns on me that my first reaction was to think the guy was hitting on me. Have I just been homophobic? Damn, I hope not, because I'm not, in any way. But I don't know many gay people and there are certainly none among my close friends, not that I have many of those either. I don't even know if the guy is gay. It's not like he has a neon sign above his head. I messed up talking to people yesterday, and today doesn't look any better. Maybe I should've stayed in my hotel room. But I like it here, I find it calming, though I'm trying to not catch the eye of the owner. I'm still embarrassed about yesterday.

Luckily, the guy looks amused rather than upset.

"I . . . I've never been asked to dance before," I finish.

"Really? Now that does surprise me," he chuckles.

"Look, I'm sorry I was rude. Please let me buy you a drink?" I feel it's the least I can do.

He flashes a brilliant smile and sits down at my table. "Well, if you insist." I signal to the waitress and order a bottle of wine.

I pour him a glass and he takes a large swallow. Then he looks at me with an appraising air. "That is *good* wine. Apology accepted."

"You sound surprised," I laugh.

"That you know good wine?" He frowns slightly. "I guess I am a little. I'm sorry, too."

"Apology accepted." I raise my glass, and he matches me, both of us taking another drink. "I once wrote a book that centred around the wine industry, so I did a lot of research and a lot of wine tasting."

"You're a writer? How exciting." His eyes sparkle.

"Not really. It's a lot of looking at a blank screen, wondering how to get the words in your head to form into recognisable and coherent squiggles."

He laughs again as if I've said something witty instead of just venting my frustrations. Writing is rewarding, and it's the only thing I know how to do. But it's a hard slog, and right now, with no contract, I might never sell another book. The thought is certainly demotivating. I'm sure it would make my family happy too. My parents thought I should have gone into a more stable career, like being a solicitor or an accountant, but I don't want to think about that right now. Here I am in company for the second day in a row and for only the second time since I arrived here.

"Are you famous? Have I heard of you?" he asks, leaning in a little closer and whispering. "Are you here incognito?" He looks around furtively, like maybe some sort of paparazzi or fan might appear at any moment, and he should be on the lookout. Watching him slightly lightens the heaviness I've felt for a week, and I chuckle.

"No, nothing like that. I doubt very much you've heard of me. I don't think any of my books have been translated into Spanish."

"Tell me anyway, and I can tell all my friends I've met you."

"Okay, I write under the name Rafe Rowell."

He pulls back a little and scrutinises me for a minute. He scrunches his nose slightly, something I don't think I've seen another guy do before. It's kind of cute, which is a word I've never used to describe a man before. *Huh.* It's probably the wine kicking in. I've been sitting here drinking slowly and reading for several hours, making myself comfortably numb.

He gives a little shake of his head.

"Sorry, I've got nothing." He looks genuinely apologetic.

"I don't think most people in the UK, or the States for that matter, would know who I am either." I have a small readership in the US, but I'm hardly a household name. "The way I'm going, I'll probably fade into obscurity, anyway." I hadn't meant to give anything away. I don't want to bring the mood down. I cast my eyes down and sigh. A warm hand rests on my arm.

"I'm sure that'll never happen; all books deserve to be read." He gives my arm a squeeze, and I lift my head to look into his eyes. A fleeting recollection of the rich red-brown of the conkers I used to play with as a kid passes and is gone. His soft expression watches me with no judgement.

"Thank you for saying so." The reassurance of a stranger casts my life and family in stark contrast. I press my lips together, his kindness almost overwhelming me, and I blink back the tears that are threatening to form. I desperately try to think of something to say, needing to change the subject before I find myself spilling the whole of my sad story. I look down to where his hand is still on my arm.

"You know, if you're going to touch me, you could at least let me know your name."

He smiles, showing a row of white teeth. "It's not always necessary or desirable to be that familiar." He withdraws his hand, though, and takes another drink.

Oh . . . Oh! It takes me a few seconds to understand he's referring to hookups. Not something I'm familiar with, but the wine emboldens me.

"And what about in this case?"

The corners of his mouth twitch and he looks like he's about to speak. I'm interested in hearing what he'll say since he's managed to surprise me more than once already. Another voice cuts in.

"I wanted to apologise for yesterday. I didn't mean to kick you out." I look up, straight into the face of the guy from yesterday—the bar owner.

I catch the eye of my drinking companion; his eyebrows are somewhere up near his hairline, and he's giving me another of his appraising looks.

"It's fine." I make an open gesture with my hand. "It seems to be the day for apologies, so please come and drink with us."

It's only then that I realise the music has stopped and people are leaving. I'm not sure how it got so late.

"Oh, it's closing time." I'm a little disappointed as I don't feel like leaving yet.

"You can stay a while longer and so can . . ." He turns to address the other guy.

"Florencio," he replies. "Florencio Delgado. My sister calls me Florrie. You may not."

I'm sure I see the serious mouth of the older guy twitch slightly as he bows his head. "I am Constantin Marin."

They both look at me. I guess I should introduce myself. "Rafe Alderson."

"Give me a minute. I'll just need to check on the staff and lock up." He turns and heads towards the bar where the waitress is clearing up.

"Soooo." Florencio draws the word out and smirks. "He kicked you out last night, *and* he didn't know your name? Colour me intrigued."

I laugh. "I'm sorry to disappoint you. It's not nearly as exciting as you'd think. I'd never met him before last night."

"Well, that just sounds *more* exciting. Come on, tell me all." He leans a little closer and glances over to where Constantin is talking to the other musicians who are packing their instruments away. "He is very handsome, isn't he? I can see why you stayed."

"Oh, no! It's nothing like that. He asked me to stay for a drink and I had nothing else to do. We talked for a little while and then he seemed to become sad and wanted me to leave." I wasn't going to disclose his story; that was for Constantin to decide who he told. As for handsome, I don't know. I haven't thought about it. I guess he is. I can appreciate that other guys are good looking, can't I? Florencio is looking at me as if I'm lying, a smile playing on his lips.

"Look, nothing happened," I protest. "I had a drink, and I left. And anyway, I told you, I'm straight." I have no idea why I needed to blurt out that last bit again, but Florencio's expression turns to full smugness.

"Mmmm, I've heard that one before."

Chapter 5

Constantin

When my eyes landed on the guy from yesterday, the air felt lighter and the room was brighter somehow, which is ridiculous. Here in the bar, the lighting is the same day in and day out, so I don't know *why* it seemed that way. I guess it's because I was afraid I'd scared him away. I was quite abrupt with him last night. Most days, I can cope well enough, but for some reason, last night, sharing my story with the stranger made it feel raw again. I thought time would heal the grief, but it hasn't. It just makes it easier to bear. That is, until something reminds me of the future I can never have with Valery, and then it catches up with me. I push the thoughts away, determined to not go through it again.

I help the staff finish clearing up for the night and lock the door after them. I glance over to where Rafe is sitting, talking with the other guy, Florencio. At first, I was a little annoyed that Rafe wasn't on his own when I went to apologise earlier. Had I wanted to talk to him alone? Had I wanted him to myself? That's a curious thought that I might unpack later. Was it a wise decision to ask them both to stay? I spend far too much time on my own, and I don't make great company. This could be a chance to finally crawl out of my shell and engage with the outside world. I could do with trying to make some friends.

On my way back over to their table, I choose a bottle of wine. It's one of my favourites and I feel like sharing. Also, staying off the spirits might be a good idea.

They both look up, stopping their conversation as I pull up a chair and sit.

"Don't let me interrupt you," I say as I apply myself to opening the bottle.

"Do you know Rafe here is a famous author?" Florencio smiles widely and I watch Rafe's brow crease.

"No, not famous at all. Barely known, really." His expression is painful, as if he'd rather not talk about it.

Instead, I pour us all some of the wine. I watch as Rafe lifts the glass and peers at the wine before giving it a swirl and bringing it up his nose to sniff it. I catch the eye of Florencio, and he's smirking slightly, almost as if he knew this would happen. Rafe takes a sip, leaving it there for a minute, and he even closes his eyes for a few seconds.

"That's a damn fine Rioja," he says. "Where's it from?"

He reaches for the bottle, picking up his glasses from the table, obviously needing them to read the label. They suit him and give him a kind of dishevelled teacher look. I can see him spending hours writing, peering down at the words he creates, his focus totally consumed by it.

"It comes from a small vineyard my cousin Luis Eduardo owns just on the edge of the Navarre region," I enlighten him, and he turns his attention to us, becoming aware we're both watching him, our own wine glasses untouched.

"I—" He puts the bottle down. "Sorry, was I being a wine bore? I get told I am all the time."

"I'm not sure you can be one of those in Spain. I'm just not used to seeing our wines being appreciated by . . . outsiders."

I grimace, wincing at my own words, wishing the biases we acquire didn't rule us unconsciously.

"I've already made that mistake tonight." Florencio laughs, picking up his glass and taking a hearty swallow. "He's forgiven me, so I'm sure he'll forgive you too."

"I actually like surprising people." Rafe is smiling, much to my relief. "I forgive you." He raises his glass and nods before taking a drink.

"Gracias."

He tips his head with a small smile, and I realise I've answered in Spanish.

"Sorry. I—" I start to explain.

"It's fine. It's actually one of the few words I do know, so I understood."

I turn to Florencio. "So, you're from Argentina, correct?"

He currently has his glass to his lips, so he makes a flourish with his hand.

"Wait, you know where he's from? You just met." Rafe pulls back slightly in surprise.

"You must have the same with your English dialects," I explain.

"Well, yes, of course. I've not really thought about that for other languages."

"And you can always tell an Argentinian," I add with a slight smirk.

"¡Que maleducado!" Florencio slaps a hand on his chest, but his smile is wide.

Rafe's brows knit together as he stares off into the distance, his bottom lip caught between his teeth. I watch transfixed as he chews it slightly, remembering too late that we were excluding him. I'm about to apologise again, but he speaks first.

"I don't know it, but contextually, I guess you were being a bit rude towards Florencio, and he was mock offended."

"That's exactly it. Well done. It translates as 'how rude.'"

His warm smile is genuine and causes the corners of his eyes to crease slightly. He repeats the phrase. "*Que maleducado*. I like that."

He says it a few more times quietly to himself, as if committing it to memory, before taking another drink. "You say your cousin owns a vineyard?"

"My mother's family is from the Rioja region, so most of her family is involved in the wine industry. My grandfather owns one of the largest vineyards in the area, and it's been in the family for a long time. My cousin didn't want to sit around and just wait for his legacy, he actually had an interest in cultivating grapes and making his own wine. He set up his own vineyard in Navarre. He studied the area carefully, trying to find the right terroir. That's the combination of altitude, the soil, the correct side of the mountain so it gets enough sun, and all the environmental factors that affect the grapes." Rafe nods in understanding. I guess he knows something about wine if he's already familiar with the term. "It makes for very good wine," I conclude.

"It does." Rafe takes another drink as if to agree with his point.

"Your family's vineyard though, which one is it?" Rafe leans forward a little, his eyes shining in interest.

"Castillo Otero."

He sits back, his eyes wide and his mouth slightly open. "You're part of the Otero wine family?"

I shrug. I'm not that close to the maternal side of the family. I find them too caught up in their own success, too haughty for me—overbearing and annoying. My mother felt the same, which is why she moved away to Gran Canaria as soon as she could. It's also why my cousin wanted to set up on his own. He's the only one I can stand for any length of time and is the closest I have to a brother.

"I feel I should apologise." Rafe's mouth forms into a slight grimace. I can't imagine what he means.

"I wrote a book a few years ago. Although it was mostly set in England, it was based on the wine industry, so there were elements of Spanish vineyards. The Otero family . . . your family was one of the ones I studied. I might have formed some characters on them. I'm not sure I was wholly complimentary." His face creases, and he looks like he might have painted them all as devils, which, to be fair, wouldn't be too far from the truth.

"Well, if you made them self-centred narcissists who think of profit above all else, then you'd not be far wrong," I reply blithely.

Florencio emits a loud snort, nearly spitting out his wine.

We both turn to look at him.

"Sorry," he says when he's recovered. "I thought you were talking about my family there for a minute."

I'm suddenly curious about the witty Argentinian.

"So what brings you to Barna?" I ask Florencio, using the familiar term for Barcelona. His face, sunny one minute, clouds slightly.

"My father sent me." He says it so flatly I'm not sure if he's joking or not.

"He can do that?"

"Were we not just talking about families?" he huffs. "If your father is Antonio Delgado he can."

Ah, even I've heard of him and his media empire. Florencio might not have been far wrong if he was comparing the behaviour of our families.

"Why did he send you?" Rafe asks. "For business?"

Florencio snorts again. "Like he'd trust me with anything like that." He reaches for his glass again, twirling the stem in his fingers. When he speaks, his voice is cold and expressionless. "No. My father heard his aunt is unwell and probably won't live too much longer. An aunt he hasn't seen for thirty years or more. He decided now was the time her family should visit and that family should be me. He dressed it up to be because I would be the most suitable. What he really meant was that because everyone else is part of his business, I was the one who could be spared. It didn't matter what I was doing. I was given four hours' notice to get on a plane." He lets out a long breath as if he'd needed to get it off his chest.

"Well, is it not good that she has some family with her?" Rafe says quietly.

"Oh, please!" Florencio exclaims. "My father doesn't care about that. He is her only family, but all he cares about is that she isn't leaving his inheritance to a cat shelter." He takes a deep swallow of wine as if he needs to wash a bad taste out of his mouth.

"And is she?" Rafe's mouth quirks at the corners slightly and Florencio shrugs.

"I don't know, and I don't care. She can do what she likes with her money. My father doesn't need it. She's not at all what I expected from the stories I've been told of her. I wish I'd met her sooner, before she became sick."

This time, when I lock up after they've gone, I'm not plagued by memories. There's no anticipation of them barrelling into me and being forced to relive them all again. Tonight, my head is calm and I feel at ease, something I haven't felt in a long time. So long that it almost feels unfamiliar, and it takes me a moment to identify it. I realise I've enjoyed the last hour, talking to Rafe and Florencio. Rafe is smart and interesting, surprising me with his knowledge of my maternal family. Florencio is witty and doesn't take himself too seriously, though I feel there's a lot more to the pretty guy than he lets on. Pretty? I'm not sure where that came from, but I have to concede that Florencio is *very* pretty. He has dark eyes and lashes coupled with a stunning set of cheekbones above a wide mouth and a ready smile. Rafe's beauty is earthier, with his soft brown curls and amber eyes. I don't even know why I'm thinking of them like this. I have no right to, and I usually barely notice how anyone looks—I certainly haven't for a long time. They're just interesting, friendly guys. That's it. Neither of them live here, so at some point, sooner or later, they'll head off back to their own countries. I might as well enjoy their company while I can.

I run some water into the washbasin, ignoring the even louder grumbling from the plumbing, and stare into the mirror on the wall. There's an old guy looking back at me. When did I get old? When did I start showing some grey hairs? Tiredness adds creases to skin that was once smooth. With my thick brows and heavy jawline, I'm not pretty— never have been, though I've been called handsome. Valery said I was as rugged as the rocks at Guayedra beach back on Gran Canaria. But now, in contrast to Rafe and Florencio, I look old, tired, and heavy. Nothing appealing that anyone would be interested in. I must be ten or fifteen years older than either of them. I don't even know why these thoughts are coming to me. Why am I even allowing them to surface? Valery's voice comes back to me. It's a memory that doesn't get played in the normal sequence because I've never allowed it to, never wanted it.

But now I hear him loud and clear.

Don't sit and mourn for me, Con. Don't waste your best years being alone. You have a big heart, find someone to share it with. You deserve love, to be loved.

He's wrong, of course. He was my love and there will never be another. But perhaps sitting alone every night isn't healthy. Have I wasted my best years? I haven't thought of them as wasted, but maybe I can at least spend some time with other people. Tonight, as I drift off to sleep, I feel a tingle of anticipation at the prospect of seeing them again tomorrow.

Chapter 6

Florencio

The warmth of the sun kissing the skin on my back wakes me. I'm sprawled face down on the bed, the sheet barely covering my nakedness. I'm surprised I even managed to undress myself. I was so weary last night when I returned, having walked back up the hill to my aunt's house. I wasn't in any state to work out the public transport system, and my phone battery had died, so I couldn't call for an Uber.

I lie still for a while, enjoying the gentle warmth seeping into me before opening my eyes. When I blink them open, I can see it's late. I haven't fully adjusted to European times yet, so I feel groggy. It's definitely that and *not* the amount of wine I consumed last night. Surprisingly good wine, though between the bar owner and the writer, I feel like I was the one who knew the least. I've been brought up to know and appreciate wine—enough to be able to pick the best wines at a restaurant rather than the most expensive, which is the trap those wishing to show they have money fall into—but it doesn't hold a specific interest for me. In my family, it's used to denote status. Find the hidden gems on a wine list, and you attract the notice of the sommelier. Get his respect and you get the respect of the waiters too. My father always asserts that it helps you get good tables at short notice in the best restaurants. Personally, I think they're just scared of him and what he could do if they didn't accommodate him. But none of that matters to me as I haven't the money to eat at that class of restaurant. My father sending me here because I'm expendable is not far from the truth, though I hate to admit it. Being a tango dancer doesn't make much money, not even enough to live on. I might not have joined the family business, but I am still a part of them and must abide by their rules. I'm allowed to indulge in my passion for dancing, and in return, my father pays for my apartment and gives me an allowance. In short, my father owns my ass.

I'd like to say, not in a literal sense, but in a way that's not true either.

I remember the day I told my father I was gay. I don't think it came as a big surprise to him, but he just gave me one of his long sighs, as if it was just another way I'd deliberately disappointed him, and told me I was not to bring scandal to the family. I understood the threat behind his words. Do anything that affects the business, and I'd be cut off from the family. I like my apartment and I like my life, so I make sure I don't. So yeah, my father owns my ass. But here in Barcelona, I have more freedom. I'm not so easily recognisable and I could have some fun. Nothing serious, though, that's not an option for me. Imagine some poor guy having to meet my father? I can just picture his sneer of disapproval, since whoever I chose would never meet his expectations. If they did, then they wouldn't be with me. Urgh, that's fine. I'm used to it, but I *am* going to have a good time.

The need for coffee is what finally prompts me to leave the

comfort of my bed and get washed and dressed. I find Juana busy preparing lunch in the huge kitchen. She cheerily waves me away from the coffee machine and insists on making me a cup. I'd soon discovered it was better to let her have her own way, though it's an amazing kitchen and I'd love to indulge my other passion—for cooking— in it.

She hands me a steaming cup with a smile and a simple statement. "She's on the terrace."

That my aunt is well enough to be out of bed explains Juana's good mood, and I make my way through the vast house and out to the sunny terrace. I stand on the threshold between the cool interior of what could be described as a ballroom—though that seems like an antiquated term—and the large, sunny, white-stone terrace. It's late spring and warm enough not to need a sweater. My aunt is on a lounger, half under a linden tree, its broad leaves supplying shade. At first, I think she's asleep. Her eyes are closed and shaded by a wide-brimmed sun hat, but when I approach, they flicker open, and she gives me a thin smile.

"There you are, my dear." She reaches a hand out to me. It's instinctive. As a dancer and a singer, she's used to being a star—the centre of attention. She behaves the same even if her audience is only her great nephew. I take it and give it a gentle squeeze before lightly touching it to my lips. Her smile widens as if she's just received her due.

I warmed to her almost immediately when I arrived. I'd anticipated that it would be awkward having a stranger, albeit a family member, drop in on her at short notice, but it's been nothing like that. When I arrived quite late in the evening, she was reclining on a chaise longue in a richly decorated room lined with dark wood panels and velvet drapes.

"Come here, my dear," she'd said as if we hadn't just met for the first time, but were old acquaintances. "Let me see who my nephew has sent." I was a little surprised she expected me. She tipped her head back to look up at me before smiling. It was an encouraging smile, though tinged with a little sadness. "You look very much like her, you know."

"Like who?"

"Your grandmother. She was a beautiful woman, and she turned many heads. She was my best friend, and we used to go dancing together. She could have turned professional like me, but she only had eyes for my brother and wanted to settle down instead."

I hadn't known my grandmother had danced. I hadn't known her well at all, as she passed when I was still young, but I'd always wondered why I had no interest in business and only wanted to dance. I've felt most of my life that I was the anomaly in the family, except for my great aunt Estrella who had left Argentina for Spain decades ago.

"I dance too, Great Aunt," I replied.

"Auntie, please. The 'great' makes me feel so old." I didn't point out to her that I was the youngest of my siblings, and my father didn't marry young, so at ninety-one she was probably old enough to be a great-great-aunt.

"Auntie," I repeated, and she smiled.

"Of course you dance. I noticed as soon as you walked into the room. I can always tell a dancer," she said so matter-of-factly that I couldn't help laughing. Suddenly, this visit had started to look like it might not be as much of a chore as I thought it would be.

I release her hand and look down at her. She has more colour than in the previous days when I've seen her; she looks stronger. When I'd asked her what was wrong with her, all I'd received was an enigmatic, "My dear, I'm ninety-one. Life ails me."

"You look well today, Auntie," I say, sitting on an adjacent lounger.

"I take each day as it comes," she says. "But tell me, did you have fun last night? Juana said you went out."

No secrets in this house, then. Or it could be that nothing ever happens, so I am of interest to them. Probably a bit of both.

"I found a tango bar. La Casa de Valery. Do you know it?"

She shakes her head. "I used to know all the places, but it's been a while since I was in society." Her gaze slips past me as if she's revisiting the past, but she doesn't dwell there long. "Did you dance?"

"I did a little." I give a little shrug.

"You miss it, don't you?"

It's only been a few days, barely a week, but she's right. I've danced every day since I discovered the tango as a teenager. I love nothing better than to lose myself in the fluidity of the movements and the music. Not dancing has made me hyper-aware of my body and it feels odd, somehow different, like I'm living in someone else's skin. I could say all that to her, but as I look at my aunt, I realise that she too would've danced every day, and she probably hasn't danced for several years. It would seem cruel to tell her my woes. Her expression tells me she already knows the answer to her question.

"How do you manage?" I whisper, thinking that growing old doesn't have much going for it.

"I got used to it . . . eventually. But it wasn't easy," she sighs. Then she gives a little shake, as if trying to rid herself of the feeling, before turning back to me and fixing me with a gaze. "What else did you do? It's good to have a young person in the house. Now I can't get out anymore, you will have to have fun for me."

What can I tell her? Nothing much else happened.

"I met a couple of guys. We sat, drank wine, and talked." I try to sound nonchalant, but she leans in a little closer.

"Tell me everything." She might look frail, but her eyes shine with sharp intensity and I know she won't be satisfied unless I do.

"I first met a studious-looking guy. He's English and a writer, very clever, and knew a lot about wine for an Englishman. Then we started talking to the bar owner, which is why I was back late. He's a tango singer and musician."

Delight dances across my aunt's face, and I know this is what she wants. I understand it. We are very much alike.

As I tell her about them both, my mind wanders back to the previous evening. Rafe is certainly not my usual type. It's like he has no idea how good looking he is, so it sits naturally on him. But it's those understated good looks that drew me to him and prompted me to ask him to dance in the first place. It's a damn shame he's straight.

I recall the shock that made his cheeks glow a rosy colour when he thought he'd offended me. It heightened his beauty, the pink of his cheeks against the gold of his eyes, the colours like sunrise on a calm morning after a storm. But I'm not the only one drawn to him if I read Constantin correctly. He seemed unable to stay away either. Constantin is several inches taller than me and well built, with broad, strong shoulders. He, too, is handsome, but a total contrast to Rafe.

His dark eyes and hair match his face, which speaks of a craggy sorrow. He looks like he's lived and lost, and I understand as much from the references he made and the pictures on the wall. He smiled a few times throughout the evening, but it was like it was a forgotten action. I wonder what it would take to really make him open up and smile. Yes, yesterday was very interesting, and as I talk, I find I'm less drawn to my initial plan of trying out the gay nightclubs. I can find those in any city. I'd rather spend more time with the intriguing men I met last night.

I finish recounting as much of my evening as I'm willing to share, and my aunt looks animated.

"You must invite them to dinner." She looks around, already calling for Juana.

"Auntie, we only just met last night."

"I'm old. I might die tomorrow, then it would be too late," she answers bluntly, the decision final.

"Are you sure? Would it not be too much for you?" I'd said they should meet her, but I'd meant for a quiet evening, next week perhaps.

"I used to host dinner parties for twenty people or more." Her tone is dismissive. "Four of us is just a friendly supper."

Juana appears on the terrace, concern on her face at being summoned.

"Ah, Juana! Can you call your sister to help? We're having a dinner party. Tonight," she announces, and Juana, to her credit, doesn't betray anything in her face or manner. Maybe she's just used to my aunt's whims.

"Alas, señora, my sister is out of town until late tomorrow."

"The next day, then. We'll have it the next day," she says in a voice that implies she's used to getting her own way but is utterly charming about doing it, and I wonder how many people she's managed to enchant over the years in the same manner.

Juana merely nods, and it's her job now to make it happen. I wonder if I can help her and her sister with cooking, and perhaps learn some Spanish dishes.

I lie back on the lounger to enjoy the sunshine for a while. No, being sent here isn't half bad after all.

Chapter 7

Rafe

My eyes slide over the words on the page, losing focus. The warmth of the afternoon, along with the soft hubbub of the street below my hotel room, are more effective than any lullaby. I put down the book, take off my glasses, and settle back in my chair. Maybe a few minutes' rest wouldn't be a bad idea. The late nights of the last few days, drinking and talking at the bar, add to my torpid state. I drift off into the pleasant haze between sleep and being awake. The unfamiliarity of the city has had a calming effect on my mind. There are no memories or triggers of anything that brought me here. I can simply exist. I can just be.

The shrill ring of the hotel room telephone cuts through the muted air, jolting me out of my reverie. I frown at it, as if the inanimate object is personally responsible for disturbing me. I'm also not sure who could be getting in touch with me. The ringing doesn't subside, so with a grimace, I rise and walk the few steps across the room and pick it up.

"Rafe! Thank god. I thought something had happened to you." I groan inwardly. Helen, my agent.

"I'm fine," I grunt.

"You haven't been answering my calls, my messages, my emails . . ."

No, I haven't. I didn't feel like I could cope with the upbeat, pull yourself together, motivational speech she's bound to deliver to me. And I don't want it now.

"Are you going to tell me it's time I came home and got back on the horse?"

"No, I . . .well, yes. It's true, though. You can't hide out there forever."

Why not? It's been working so far.

"What exactly is there for me to come back to?" I try to keep the bitterness out of my voice, but fail. I no longer have a publishing contract, my family would only be too happy to see me have to take an honest job, and Loretta, well, I don't quite know how I feel about her at the moment. All I know is that a few weeks ago, I had my future all mapped out. By now, I should be a married man with a six-book contract ready to work on. But it all got knocked off its axis and I'm not sure what to do next.

"You won't find the answers in Spain," Helen replies. Maybe I don't want any answers.

"Have you managed to get any interest elsewhere in the Blackwater series?" I deflect her comment and hear her slightly exasperated sigh down the line.

"Not yet. Too many of the big houses are asking why Deatons dropped it. I'm sorry, Rafe. You're not known as a gritty crime writer. It's not going to be easy to sell it and I might need to go to the smaller publishers." My heart sinks. I feared this might happen. Whilst Deatons isn't one of the big six, it's head and shoulders above the small publishing houses and I'd felt so proud when they'd offered me a contract eight years ago. It hasn't all been easy, and I'm in no way a household name, but I make a decent living. The new contract for the six-book Blackwater series—and the possibility of film or TV rights—had made me feel like I might make it to the big time. Those had been the rumblings. I was an ascending star a few weeks ago. Now, if no one else wants the series, it feels like I'll be starting all over again. The problem is that I spent a year creating the series, outlining it, pitching it—everything short of actually writing it. But now the motivation has gone and I can't find the words. The muse has left me.

"I still can't see any reason to return yet, then," I sigh.

"Being present and over here will show people you're serious about your career. I might be able to get you some interviews."

"TV? Radio?" I ask.

"Probably not." I thought so. "You know they only happen for new releases. Maybe some magazines or newspapers."

Maybe not. I could tell by her voice she wasn't convincing herself any more than me. What was the real reason she wanted me back? True, if I didn't make money, neither did she, but I wasn't the only author she was an agent for. She probably made more than me anyway, with the authors on her roster.

"Tell them to email me the questions, or ask them to call me if you do manage to get an interview." I grit my teeth, feeling petty and irritable.

"Will you answer the phone to them?" she replies archly. I don't always get on with my agent—she can be pushy and I'm naturally resistant to that—and we've had a few arguments in the past. At those times, she often sounds exasperated at best, and at worst, disappointed with me. But she did get me my first break, so I feel I owe her some loyalty.

"Maybe," I answer since I can't shrug down the phone.

"Look, Rafe." Her tone softens and I hear her release a deep breath. "There's something else."

Helen only ever sounds like that if she needs to deliver bad news. So I don't answer, but I brace myself for whatever it is.

"It's Loretta."

Oh. Somehow I hadn't been expecting that. All other thoughts drain out of my head.

"She's been seen with Sloan Thorpe."

"Seen?" I croak out, my voice dry.

"Dinner . . . a club. She was also present at his latest book launch a couple of days ago."

Sloan Thorpe.

Tall. Blond. Chisel-jawed Sloan Thorpe, who also happens to be a bloody good author.

Sloan fucking Thorpe.

Well, shit.

I bet he's not "boring."

I sink onto the hotel bed, my legs no longer able to hold me up.

"Rafe? Are you okay?" Helen's concern sounds far away.

"Yeah." Even my own voice sounds alien to me.

"If you need anything . . ." she begins.

I need to forget it all. Forgetting was what I'd been doing all along, quite successfully, and now it's all vividly brought back to me. I realise she's still talking.

"And so that's why I think you need to come back as soon as possible."

"No." It's the only word I can summon right now. I don't wait for an answer but ring off, slowly placing the receiver down.

Distance, both in space and communication, had been an effective sticking plaster for my problems, one I was happy to continue using. But at some point, the plaster has to come off, it's just a pity it isn't at a time of my choosing.

A myriad of emotions rush through me—hurt, anger, disappointment, defeat, humiliation, and jealousy—all bombarding me at once, their barbs making fresh holes on top of old ones.

Did she leave me for Sloan Thorpe? No, that can't be. She'd called off the wedding, said she didn't want to get tied down, though the wedding had been her idea in the first place. On that last day she'd called me uninteresting, unexciting, and tedious. Well, I bet Sloan Thorpe isn't mundane and boring. I know he isn't, actually. I've met him. He's all charm and charisma. I knew I disliked him.

I'd felt lucky when I met Loretta two years ago, though I'd known of her long before then. She was beautiful, she was rich, and she was way out of my league. As the daughter of Grant Deaton, founder and CEO of Deatons Publishers, I'd seen her both in the office or at functions, but I hadn't spoken to her before. That was until the launch of my fourth book, *On A Turning Tide*. It had got a lot of early reviews, and it was—and remains—my most well-known book to date. After she'd spoken to me at the launch, we'd fallen into chatting whenever I saw her in the office. It took me six months to pluck up the courage to ask her out, and I was amazed when she agreed. One thing I learned early on was that she was used to getting her own way. She decided what she wanted and went for it. I found myself swept up in being her boyfriend, then her fiancé. My book was selling well, so there were signings and functions as well as panels and interviews. I was living my dream, never examining whether I was happy or not. I was happy, wasn't I? It was perfect. Surely, what everyone would want. A beautiful wife and a successful career. I had it all . . . until I had nothing. Until a couple of weeks ago, when Helen had told me the contract that had been set up for the new series had fallen through, hours before I was due to sign it. I'd been crushed. I'd worked so hard on it. I'd turned to Loretta, seeking solace and support, only to find her packing her things, saying she was leaving me and couldn't marry me. She was in tears, and I comforted her, supporting her as she said she wasn't ready for commitment. I believed her until she delivered her final blow and her parting words about how uninteresting I was. I moved through the next few days in a numb haze, dealing with cancelling all the wedding arrangements, the invitations, the wedding list, and the disappointed relatives. My wedding day came and went, and I stayed at home. The next day, I couldn't take any more, and I boarded the flight that should have been taking us on our honeymoon. I've been here ever since.

Now, the distance in space and time, as well as this new information, has given me a fresh perspective. I'd been naïve, and I'd been played.

The hurt still burns through my body, the anger matching it pace for pace. I feel stupid that I was so caught up in the dream I didn't see it for the illusion it was.

But Sloan Thorpe. Damn, that cuts deep. I might have been an ascending star, but he was always going to rise higher and burn brighter than I ever would.

I pour a drink. Anything to numb the pain and humiliation, to make the feelings go away. But haven't I pushed them aside for too long? I've barely existed for the last few weeks, instead just allowing myself to be lulled into thinking everything is all right. The only time I've felt anything like normal has been when I've been in the company of Florencio and Constantin. I glance at my watch. I hadn't noticed it was so late. I don't have much time to get ready. Tonight, we've been invited to dinner with Florencio's aunt, Estrella. I've been looking forward to meeting her and the thought of seeing them again lifts the heaviness in my chest that settled in there when Helen mentioned Loretta. I want to make the most of my remaining time in Spain. I might have told Helen I didn't want to go home, but the truth is I'm due to fly back next week. I leave the drink untouched, not wanting its effects, and take a hot shower instead.

Chapter 8

Constantin

"Are you sure you're going to be okay?" I ask Alena for the tenth time, and she gives me her most withering stare. I deserve it, but I've never left the bar alone for the night before. Accepting dinner invitations, any invitations really, has never been my thing, though there have been precious few invitations, and certainly not in the last few years. When I was setting the bar up, I had an excuse—too busy—but then the invitations dried up as people got the message that I wasn't going to come. So why did I say yes when Florencio came in two nights ago and said his aunt had invited us to dinner? Was it because Rafe was also going? I've enjoyed their company over the last few evenings, more than I care to admit. But saying yes and actually leaving my bar are two very different activities.

"We're going to be fine," Alena reassures me. She's very competent and has been with me as my second in command for the last five years. I've thought of promoting her to bar manager for some time, but it didn't seem necessary as I've always been here. I couldn't leave the bar in more capable hands.

"Perhaps I should stay—"

"What's the real problem?" She stops restocking the fridge and straightens up. I've never confided in her as a friend, but she's seen enough of me to know that I'm not my usual self, and of course, she saw me with Rafe and Florencio over the past week.

"Am I doing the right thing?"

She leans her forearms on the bar and gives me her full attention. "I think you need to get out once in a while. It can't be healthy staying here day after day like a hermit. Everything will be fine. Wednesdays are usually quiet, and I have Anton and the band here if I need them."

"I don't know . . ."

I sense rather than see her exasperated sigh.

"When did you last go out?"

I run a towel over the bar and mumble. "I don't remember."

"Exactly," she replies. "Look, they seem like really nice guys, and to be honest, apart from one of us"—she gestures towards herself, the musicians, and Anton, the other barman —"I've not seen you talk to anyone else for longer. You deserve to have some fun, so go out and enjoy yourself."

"Thank you." I know I'm lucky to have her.

"Estrella Winters?" I immediately recognise the very glamorous, ageing star in front of me, and I receive a wide smile as well as a proffered hand, which I of course take and press my lips to the back of. I turn to Florencio, who looks very smart all in black. His trousers cling to his narrow hips, which sway with a dancer's grace as he moves across the floor to stand next to his aunt, who is elegantly dressed in purple velvet. Her neck is adorned with enough jewels to buy my bar several times over. "Why didn't you tell us your aunt was Estrella Winters?"

"Wait, you're Estrella Winters?" Rafe's voice holds a hushed awe. He enters the room a little behind me. Though we'd arrived at the same time, Rafe's attention had been caught by a large painting in the cavernous lobby of this vast house. He looks very handsome in linen trousers and a loosely fitting linen shirt, both in neutral tones that make his hair seem lighter and accentuate the amber in his eyes. He takes the other proffered hand and repeats the same process.

Estrella looks radiant, basking in the attention.

"You're both so delightful. I think it's been at least a decade since someone has referred to me as Winters. Mostly, I'm asked whether I used to be her." She turns to look up at Florencio. "My dear, you didn't tell me you had such charming friends."

I know of Estrella, of course I do. I own a tango bar in Barcelona, where she's an icon. I've never met her before, though, and if I'm honest, I thought she'd passed away years ago—she must be in her eighties, maybe even nineties. How Rafe knows who she is is a mystery, but then again, the guy has been full of surprises. I'm about to ask him, but Florencio beats me to it.

"How do you know who my aunt is?"

"Well, I wrote a book . . . kind of. I wrote a short story a few years ago based in the French Riviera, mostly Monaco and Saint-Tropez. Set during the sixties and seventies. I know most of the stars who used to go there during the summer and also to the Cannes Film Festival. You were one of the set, weren't you, Miss Winters?" he says, sitting down on the couch next to her.

"Ah, those were the days." Estrella sighs, confirming she was. "There is nothing like lying on Prince Rainier's yacht with a cocktail, watching the sun setting over the ocean."

"But I did a lot of research. I love the stars and old movie icons. You know, like Rita Hayworth, Sophia Loren, Sean Connery, and Steve McQueen."

"Judy Garland?" Florencio's question sounds innocent enough, but I catch his smirk.

"Why, yes, of course, Judy Garland." Rafe answers, smiling briefly up at Florencio before turning back to Estrella. "Do you know Joan Collins?"

"Ah, Joan is three weeks older than me, and would she ever let me forget it?"

Florencio tilts his head and raises an eyebrow at me. I understand him perfectly—this guy is supposed to be straight. I shrug at him and see his silent chuckle.

Florencio offers pre-dinner drinks and I sit across from where Rafe is talking animatedly with Estrella, watching them and wondering who exactly Rafe is.

Dinner is delicious. Estrella tells us that the chef, Sofia, is the sister of her housekeeper, Juana, and caters specifically for customers holding dinner parties in their homes. Juana hovers in the background, trying to be unobtrusive, but is clearly concerned about her charge.

We've been entertained with stories of Estrella's past and some of the stars she met on a couple of brief trips she took to Hollywood nearly fifty years ago. Now, there's a lull while the dessert plates are being cleared. Rafe sits back, looking round the table.

"Do you know, if you'd told me a month ago that I'd be eating dinner with Estrella Winters in her own house, I'd think you were mad."

"What did you think you'd be doing instead?" I ask. I've always been intrigued by him. I know he's a writer and smart, but I also know there's a story to why he's here and why, the first night I met him, he looked like he'd lost everything.

"I would have said that I'd be happily married, having a great honeymoon, and looking forward to returning home and getting sucked into writing my new series," he replies and drops his eyes briefly before looking back up, his mouth a thin line. "But none of that happened."

It's not what I was expecting. I can't quite imagine him with a wife, maybe because I don't want to. Don't I? I'm not sure where that thought came from. I glance over at Florencio and he's giving Rafe a curious look.

"Would you have been happy? Being married?" It's Estrella who voices what we're all thinking.

"I thought I would, but now I'm not sure. Everything happened so fast, and every time I think about it, all I get is a lot of confusion. I don't even know whether I was really in love.

"You'd know if you were in love." I didn't mean to blurt it out. Estrella gives me a shrewd look.

"What's it like? Being in love?" Florencio asks.

I think for a minute before answering. How can I possibly condense it to answer the question properly? How can I put the vastness of love into words? But Florencio is looking at me like he genuinely wants an answer.

"Have you ever felt like you would do anything to put a smile on someone else's face?

"Like every time you wake you discover a fresh new world where the colours are brighter, your senses sharper?

"Felt your heart so full that your chest cannot contain it and it must be shining so brightly that everyone must be able to see it?

"Like you would do anything, even cut off your own arm, rather than let any harm come to the one you love?"

I stop speaking and look round at them.

Estrella is smiling knowingly. Florencio has a hand pressed to his chest, a dreamy expression on his face. Rafe, though, is frowning, his eyes lowered as if he's going through some internal process. He lifts his head and gives a wistful smile.

"I said you were a romantic."

"It isn't about romance," I say sharply. "Romance is the fluff, the small things in the gestures we do. Love is more than that, much more. It's something that weaves its way into every fibre of your being. It becomes symbiotic in your soul, like you can't exist without that part of you anymore."

"Then no, I've never felt that." Rafe's eyes shimmer as if he's trying to discover something past his grasp.

"It must be wonderful," Florencio sighs.

"It's also a curse," I bite out. The whole exchange has brought up the memory of despair along with the euphoria.

"I'm not sure I'm capable of that depth of emotion. It feels too big for someone to bear. I don't think I'm strong enough." Rafe's voice is despondent.

"Strength has nothing to do with it," Estrella says. "We are never given more than we can bear. It's just a matter of being open to love."

"Auntie, have you been in love?" Florencio asks.

"Only once, though I've had many lovers." She smiles serenely.

"Tell us all, Auntie, what was his name?"

"His name was Salvatore. He was very handsome and so charming. He was a dancer as well, that's how I met him. I would have done anything for him and he's one of the reasons I didn't settle in the States. I could never be away from him for too long."

"Do you regret that?" Florencio is hanging on every word.

"I regret nothing. I'm happy with how my life turned out. I never regretted the chance of love."

"Did you want to marry him?" Rafe asks.

"In a heartbeat. But that's the thing about love. You don't get to choose who you fall in love with."

"Then why didn't you?" This is from Florencio.

Estrella pauses slightly and her voice takes on a brittle tone.

"I don't think his wife would've approved."

Chapter 9

Florencio

I stand on the terrace, leaning on the barrier wall. The city is spread out down below, a mesh of lights I can follow all the way down to the harbour. The air is still warm even at this late hour.

I hear a sound behind me but don't turn around, simply sensing the presence next to me. I catch a hint of citrus and vanilla—it's Rafe.

"Constantin painted a vivid picture, didn't he? Do you think you're missing out, not having experienced love?"

"I haven't really thought about it much before. I've always considered it a lofty notion."

"Don't you think everyone deserves love?" he says, his expression almost pitiful. I think of my father.

"No, not everyone. I can think of plenty of people who don't deserve such happiness," I scoff, but he doesn't smile.

"Is love happiness?" he muses, as if asking himself the

question. "It seems much more visceral than the lightness of merely being happy."

"Exactly, an emotion for the thinkers, those who take life seriously. I've never allowed myself to get close enough to anyone to believe love could be a possibility."

"Don't you think you deserve love?" He turns his gaze on me.

I shrug. "I don't get that luxury."

His brows furrow like I've just said the saddest thing he's ever heard.

"Why not? What if Estrella's right and you don't get to choose?"

"I'll just make sure that never happens," I say blithely, and look away until I can no longer feel his gaze on me.

I steal a look at him instead as he stares out over the city. There's something about the set of his jaw that's different. It's harder, like he's grappling with an inner demon.

"What about you? You said you've never been in love, are you missing out?" I throw his own question back at him.

He doesn't answer for so long that I think he hasn't heard me, so it's a surprise when he does speak.

"Just before I came here tonight, I received some news that made me rethink the last two years of my life. Along with Constantin's portrayal of an emotion I thought I knew, but now realise I have no concept of. I feel adrift right now, not sure what's real or not, and I don't know where I'm going. I feel like I'm travelling, but I have no destination and no map to guide me."

"You know the greatest adventures can be found that way."

His smile is wistful as he looks at me.

"You don't need to decide what your future is, just what you want to happen next," I add, surprising myself with a rather insightful remark. Maybe keeping the company of Rafe and Constantin is having an effect on me.

He looks at me for a second before turning his head back to gaze over the city lights. I watch him. There's a lightness to his face that wasn't there before, like he's cast off a heavy weight. The small amount of light shows the shape of his jaw and picks up some highlights in his hair, making it appear golden. He looks timeless, like the surroundings. He's also one of the most beautiful men I've ever seen. I want to kiss those cupid's-bow lips. I want to know if they're as soft as they look. I wonder what they taste like.

Instead, I force myself to remember that he's just been through a breakup. There's also the small detail that he's straight, of course, but that doesn't make me want to kiss him less. I don't even know what I'm looking for. Usually, my hookups are brief and for fun. An unspoken agreement that it's fleeting.

But I'm a long way from home and Rafe isn't like anyone I've ever met before. I don't want a hookup, I don't want to treat him that way. I push the desire down deep inside because it's never going to happen. I've just confessed as much.

The sound of a piano drifts through the air from the room behind us. It must be Constantin playing the grand in the ballroom. Rafe's face brightens at the sound of it, and he turns towards me, his eyes alight.

I swallow down the increased need to cup a hand to his cheek and touch my lips to his. Wow, that sounds a lot like romance. The thought that I could feel that way nearly bubbles up, but allowing it to erupt would spoil the moment. I can't kiss him, so instead I ask.

"Would you like to dance?"

His mouth twitches slightly, no doubt remembering the previous time I asked him the same question.

"I don't know how." His voice is a husky whisper that sends shivers down my spine.

"I can teach you."

Chapter 10

Rafe

I follow Florencio into the ballroom. I'd thought it a lofty name for a room, but now I see why. It's a large rectangular room with high ceilings. Several doors open out onto the terrace that runs the length of the house. The wooden floor is beautiful, inlaid with different types of wood to form patterns, and the upkeep of that alone must be a full-time job. Couches from another era, a more decadent one, sit at intervals along the wall opposite the terrace. At one end, Constantin is seated at a grand piano playing a beautiful tune. Estrella is on a nearby couch while Juana is placing coffee cups on a table.

Just for a moment, I can imagine another time when this room might have been filled with people, the high society of Barcelona, all in their finest clothes. Estrella moving among them as the glamorous host, encouraging them to dance, to drink and have fun. Couples breaking out to take a rest on the terrace, standing under the moonlight, gazing at the city or each other.

The vision fades and I become all too aware of Florencio as he steps closer to me. A nervous flush creeps up my skin, making me feel both hot and cold at the same time. I wipe my hands down my thighs in a vain effort to dispel the clammy feeling. My heart beats a staccato rhythm on my ribs. *It's just a dance*. I push the thought through my head. Except I can't dance. I have no clue what to do. Florencio is going to despair at how bad I'm going to be. It shouldn't matter what Florencio thinks, but for some inexplicable reason, it does. I catch a trace of a scent. It's both floral and darkly indulgent, like a forbidden flower drifting on a hot desert wind. I breathe it in, using it to anchor myself to the now and not let myself catastrophise about what will happen next.

"Are you all right?" Florencio's close whisper brings me sharply out of my head.

"Err, yes. Sorry." I'm not all right, but I don't want to admit it. "I just want to warn you that I have no idea what I'm doing, so I might step on your toes."

"Just relax." His smile is soft. "This is my job. I've seen it all. But everyone can dance, trust me."

He moves so he's standing next to me.

"Shouldn't we be, um, facing each other or something?" I mumble, confused. I've seen people dance the tango, they definitely aren't side by side. They're close, very close, and it's this part that has me jittery. I've never really been that close to another guy. I don't come from a family of huggers either. Constantin's hands on my arms while we were outside was the most physical contact I've had with a guy for, well, as long as I can remember. But that didn't make me feel like my skin was charged with electricity. It was soothing and calming, and I didn't even think about it, it just was. Huh, even that acceptance makes me wonder.

"I want to teach you the basic steps by your side first." Again, Florencio breaks my train of spiralling thoughts, and I breathe deeply, reaching for that heady, warm scent. I focus on what he's saying. "Then, once you've mastered the basic steps, we can try it together." I risk a glance at him, and I can see that he looks relaxed, easy with himself, a professional. Of course he is. I know he's a dance teacher. I'm reading far too much into this and acting like a real jerk. If he can put the effort into teaching me, the least I can do is listen and learn.

"Okay, I'm ready," I say, because this time I am.

"Step forward with your left foot, then step to the right. Step backwards with your left foot, backwards with your right." He pauses. "With me so far?"

"I think so." I nod. It seems easy so far, but many more steps, and I might not remember.

"Good, now cross your left foot over your right and shift the weight to your left. Step back with your right foot and then step to the left. And that's it."

"That's it?" That surely can't be it.

"Well, those are the basic eight steps. Once you can do that without thinking, we can add more. Shall we try again?"

He takes me through the pattern a few more times, at least until I no longer have to look at my feet. Then he turns to face me.

"We'll do it again, but I'm going to be here this time," he says, but doesn't make any move to come closer.

"Aren't we supposed to be touching?" I blurt out and the corners of his mouth twitch.

"All in good time. This way, you can get an idea of where I'll be, but I'm less likely to get my toes trodden on." He delivers the last with a grin. That's fair, I suppose. So we run through it again, this time with him mirroring my movements, or rather, me mirroring his as he's leading. After going through it a few more times, I start to relax, a bit more confident in where my feet are going.

"You're doing well," Florencio says as we come to the end

of the steps and he calls for a halt. "I find that the longer you take to really learn the basics, so they become second nature, the quicker you'll progress with some of the other steps. There is no point learning the fancy parts if you're still thinking through counting to eight in your head."

"I think I've got the idea," I reply, but I don't think there was any need. He'd known when I was ready. It's then that I appreciate how good a teacher Florencio really is, because up until the last couple of times, I had been counting the steps in my mind.

"Are you ready to try together?" he asks and I nod. I think that after seeing the state I was in, he'd given me time to not only learn the steps but also to get comfortable being close to him, so this time when he steps close, I don't jump out of my skin at his touch.

He instructs me on where to put my hands, and with a quick check that I'm comfortable we're moving together. I do count for the first couple of times as I don't want to mess it up, but then I drop my shoulders and let out a deep breath. Florencio mutters a low *"bien"* and warmth spreads through my chest from the praise. But I'm not given time to enjoy it. Up until now, we've been fairly static in the centre of the large room, dancing the steps in a square. Florencio turns slightly, opening up his shoulder, and I find myself following. Suddenly, we're doing the same steps but moving round the dance floor. It feels like I'm gliding around, and it's like nothing like I've ever experienced before. It feels effortless and I feel graceful, which is not a word I've ever attributed to myself. I can't help a wide smile from breaking free, and when I look at Florencio he's grinning back at me. I tip my head back and laugh, euphoria making me feel giddy. A couple of times I glance over to Constantin, who keeps up an accompaniment on the piano. Every time I do, he's looking at us with an intense expression on his face. For some reason, it makes me want to try harder.

I'm exhausted when I finally hit the sheets. It's been a roller coaster of a day. It seems crazy that it was only earlier today I learned about Loretta and Sloan. I peer at my watch. Well, yesterday, but if I haven't gone to sleep yet, it's still the same day. Now, though, I don't feel the same stabbing pain of hurt and betrayal that I did earlier. In fact, I find I don't care so much at all, and that worries me more. Am I as shallow as Loretta? Can I forget about her as quickly as she has about me? Did I really love her? I thought so, but then listening to Constantin talk about love, I realised I don't know anything about it, really.

My thoughts meander back to what was a strange but rather magical evening. I can't believe I met one of the mainstays of the European society set of the sixties and seventies and she's invited us to dinner again in a couple of days. I realise I don't want to go back to England next week.

Did I just think "England" and not "home?" Huh, that is curious. I think it's just because I need to get some sleep . . . that's definitely it. I'm obviously too tired to think straight. I close my eyes and allow sleep to overtake me. I drift off to the feeling of gliding round the dance floor with Florencio's hand at my back and Constantin's eyes boring into me.

Chapter 11

Constantin

For the second morning in a row, I wake up with my hand wrapped round my hard cock, and I'm not happy about it.

I've managed just fine for ten years. Fuck! It's been ten years, and it hasn't been a problem . . . until now. And it's a problem all right. It's fucked up. There's not a damn thing I can do about it. Except ignore it, of course.

I can pinpoint the exact moment it happened. Two nights ago, at the dinner with Estrella, Florencio, and Rafe. I'd asked if I could play the piano. It's a beautiful grand piano, a Steinway, a world apart from the old upright at my bar. Estrella agreed, if I played one of her favourite songs. Then I looked up and saw Florencio and Rafe dancing together. Florencio is graceful in the way only a dancer can be, and Rafe was just being his natural self and enjoying the moment. They were perfection, and I couldn't tear my eyes away from them. How they looked together.

But of course, nothing can come of it. One, Rafe is

straight, though I admit he is full of surprises, and two, Florencio is so damn pretty. So what would they want with me? An old, washed-up widower who will never fall in love again. So yeah, it's pretty fucked up. And now I have a raging hard-on again, which just heightens my bad mood about it all.

Today, we've been invited to dinner again. Knowing I missed seeing them yesterday and that I'm looking forward to seeing them again does nothing to alleviate my foul mood. Neither does the niggling feeling in the back of my head . . . how perverse it is that after ten years of being celibate and not caring one bit, two guys have managed to get past that and knocked me sideways.

No, they haven't. They can't have. It's just the effects of ten years' celibacy, now my cock is acting like it's sensed a dog in heat. There's only one thing to do: take a hot shower and alleviate the pressure that aches so much I can barely walk straight. I run the taps and step under the scorching water, as if almost burning my skin is somehow going to purge all thoughts of them from my system.

As soon as I touch my cock, I know it's going to be frenzied. Images assault me: Rafe's amber eyes, and how they sparkle with delight as he talks about something he's passionate about; Florencio's pretty mouth curving with witty remarks, and those damn hips of his. I gather more soap, my hand flashing up and down my dick, grunting as I let my imagination take me places where they're together . . . and I'm watching. Seeing their limbs tangled, their mouths connecting. It might be a fantasy that can't happen, but fuck, it's hot, and I want to watch and be a part of it at the same time. That pushes me over the edge, and all too soon, I'm spilling into my hand. I stand there panting, letting the water wash away the cum and soap, knowing that whilst it might have relieved the immediate problem, it's done absolutely nothing to diminish the cause. If anything, it's made it worse.

The universe is also definitely against me when my shower turns cold and the water pressure drops. With a roar, I jump out of the cool dribble that my shower has become and vigorously towel myself dry to warm up. I look at the person scowling at me in the mirror. I grimace. There's nothing I can do but get over myself.

Once dressed, my first job of the day is to call a plumber. I can cope with grumbling pipes but not a cold shower. They can't come out until next week, which certainly doesn't help my temper.

"Is everything all right boss?" Alena asks when I snap at her for no reason.

"I'm sorry. I'm just out of sorts." I fill her in on the plumbing problem. She doesn't know about the rest, and I am *not* about to enlighten her.

I thought I'd dressed casually for dinner, but when I appear in the bar, Alena gives a low whistle, and I see Anton smirk. When I glare at him, he turns away, busying himself with putting glasses away.

"That colour looks good on you," Alena says as I reach past her to select a wine—one from my cousin's vineyard. I look down at my midnight-blue shirt.

"Do you think so?" I ask, suddenly self-conscious of what I'm wearing.

"It's perfect." Her smile is encouraging and despite telling myself my appearance doesn't matter, I feel pleased.

When I'm ready to leave, I turn to Alena. "Do you know what to do if there's trouble?"

It's Friday night, and although it's not usually a problem, I can't help but worry. To give her credit, she doesn't roll her eyes or make some smart remark, she just recites my instructions back to me, word for word. Maybe I will make her bar manager, especially if I spend any more time away from the bar. I suppress a chuckle at that thought. This is all fine, but both Rafe and Florencio have homes to go to—homes in other countries, in fact. Whatever this is will be over soon, which is just another reason why nothing is going to happen. Then why am I going at all? For a brief second, I consider cancelling. After all, what is the point if it will end soon? But even as I think it, I know there's no way I'm going to cancel. I don't understand it, but I have to go.

"Hola." Florencio greets me at the door with his wide smile. He moves in for a quick kiss on my right cheek and then steps back. "Oh, you brought wine. Wonderful," he says as I thrust it towards him.

"My cousin's," I say as an explanation as he reads the label.

"It will be perfect." He whisks it away to the kitchen and I can do nothing except follow him.

Rafe is already there with a beer in hand.

"Hi," I greet him.

"I'm told it's *'hola,'* and I have to do this whole kissing thing now as well," he says. "In England, we just shake hands for formal greetings and hug close friends and family."

"Well, we shake hands here, too, if you'd rather," I explain, and I see him wrinkle his nose slightly.

"That seems a bit awkward now we've met a few times, don't you think?"

"I agree. So you want to try a more informal greeting?"

"That also seems a bit weird now that we've been talking about it for several minutes."

I feel a slight ripple of disappointment that I won't be that close to him, even for those few seconds. "Maybe next time then, though I have to tell you that here in Spain, we use both cheeks, not just the one," I can't help adding, and see Rafe nod slightly as if he's filing that away in his brain.

"Something smells delicious." I change the subject before it gets more awkward and because it truly does smell good.

"Well, it's nearly ready." Florencio turns from where he's been stirring something on the stove. "So shoo, off to the dining room."

"Have you done the cooking?" I look around at the pans and dishes adorning the kitchen counters.

"I have and we are having a little taste of Argentina tonight."

"Is there anything I can do to help?" I ask.

He thrusts the wine I brought back into my hands. "Open this, now go." He makes a shooing motion with his hands.

"We've been dismissed," I whisper to Rafe as we walk along the passage to the dining room, enjoying the sound of his laughter.

Estrella enters, aided by Juana, and I greet her in the Spanish way. Rafe, with a little smile, follows my lead. Juana helps her into a chair.

"Lovely to see you again, Miss Winters, and thank you for the invite."

"Do you know, I think I'd like you to call me Auntie too. Both of you." She fixes both of us with her sharp eyes as we sit. "I've never had my family close, and I find I'm rather liking it. It sounds much better than calling me Miss Winters, doesn't it?"

"We could call you Estrella," Rafe offers as Florencio bustles in carrying a large dish that he sets down on the table.

"You could, but I prefer Auntie." She gives a mischievous grin that settles the matter.

The dinner is excellent. We start with provoleta, a grilled cheese, followed by steak with salad and chimichurri. The tarta de ricota with dulce de leche, a sweet, reduced-milk spread, finishes the meal perfectly.

"That was delicious, Florencio. Thank you," I praise him as I chase the last of my ricotta tart round my bowl.

"You're welcome. I enjoy cooking. It's my favourite thing next to dancing."

"That's my first taste of Argentina," Rafe says as Florencio holds his hands out to take his dish for clearing away.

"I'll make sure it's not your last," I hear him reply with a smile. If Rafe understood him, he doesn't show it. Florencio catches my eye as he asks for my dish. "What about you? Would you like to sample some more of Argentina?" He gives me a flash of his teeth.

"Of course, given the chance," I reply, and I get a sassy wink as he rises.

"Can we help clean up?" Rafe asks, jumping up. "I can wash the dishes."

"There's a dishwasher, so no, it's fine. I'll be back in a minute."

He disappears towards the kitchen.

"I'd like some air if you could help me to the terrace," Estrella says, and I go to her aid while Juana helps clear the table. As I escort her through the house, I wonder if Florencio had meant what he said or if he was just harmlessly flirting. Right at this moment, I can't decide which I hope for the most.

Chapter 12

Florencio

When I reach the terrace, the sky is just starting to turn indigo, the inky colour fading to the east where the last of the sun washes into the horizon.

My aunt is in a chair, while Constantin and Rafe are standing by the balustrade, one of my favourite places to look out over the city.

"Are you all right, Auntie?" I ask as I stop by her chair to check on her.

"I'm fine, my dear."

Constantin turns, concern etched on his face.

"I'm sorry if we tired you out the other night," he says.

She waves his apology away. "I'd rather have a night of company and then a couple of days in bed than sit alone to eat. I enjoy having you here. It's been too long with just Juana and myself."

Juana appears at that moment with a tray of coffee cups and a cafetière. If she has a problem with the extra work one more person being in the house brings, she hasn't said so and I do try to help.

Juana pours the coffee, and I help by handing round the cups.

I ask Constantin if everything is all right with his bar. He pulls a face when he answers that this is only the second time he's not been there while it's been open. Does he never have a break? He's looking very sexy in his dark blue shirt and black trousers, and I was only half joking when I flirted with him earlier. I assume he was just joining in the fun when he replied.

Rafe, who is still looking out over the city, gives a big sigh.

"This view is beautiful. I'm going to miss it when I leave."

We all fix our eyes on him. I haven't really given much thought to how long he will be here, my own stay being indefinite. Surely, he can't be leaving soon.

"Oh, when is that?" It's Constantin who asks what we're all wondering.

"I'm due to fly home in two days." Rafe sighs again.

"It sounds like that doesn't appeal to you." Constantin's voice is low.

"No, it doesn't." Rafe becomes animated. Fissures appear in his voice. "I don't have a publishing contract for my books. No one wants to buy them. I don't want to see my ex-fiancé with Sloan bloody Thorpe, who writes better books than me, who's better looking than me . . ."

He flails his arms as he speaks, and Constantin catches hold of his shoulders, rubbing his hands up and down his upper arms until Rafe calms. His shoulders slump. "I have nothing to go back to . . ."

"Then stay." I fight against the hollow nausea that washes over me at the thought of him leaving.

"It's not that easy," Rafe addresses me. Constantin's hands are still gently moving on his arms. The gesture is soft, and I like that Rafe seems to be getting comfort from it. "The hotel was only booked for two weeks, and they have no more rooms available. I've looked and there's nothing else around, not anything I can afford, anyway. With no advance on the next books, I only have my savings and any royalties to live on. I can't stay."

"Then you'll stay here." Estrella's voice cuts through, and as a unit, we all turn to look at her. She gives a warm smile. "I have plenty of room. You can stay here."

I like this idea very much.

"I couldn't—"

"Why not?" Estrella cuts off Rafe's protestations and he sputters.

"It would be imposing."

"I've invited you. Are you going to insult me by refusing?" Even in her advanced years, she's used to commanding attention. "It is not imposing. I shall enjoy having you here, along with my great nephew. There was a time when this house was full of people."

Rafe blinks at her before replying, "Thank you."

"Good, that's settled then." Auntie looks happy that she's got her own way. "I'm getting cold. Constantin, would you be a dear and help me up?"

"You okay?" Constantin gives Rafe's shoulders a squeeze and I see him nod in return. Constantin offers my aunt his hand to help her up before they walk back into the house. The care he's shown towards both Rafe and my aunt makes me feel warm inside . . . well, that and the relief Rafe won't be leaving soon.

Rafe turns to me. "Does she mean it? About staying?"

"Oh, yes. I haven't known her very long, but I think she wouldn't do something like this to be polite. She genuinely likes you."

"She's only just met me."

"I think she is a good judge of character."

He laughs a little, sounding amused. "I could be an axe-wielding murderer."

"Are you?" I ask.

"No, I'm not. I'm just saying I could be anybody."

"You mean you haven't researched it for a book?" The words are out before I know it. I've acted instinctively, not giving a thought to whether he likes being teased. He looks straight at me, and for a beat I wish I could take it back. Then he tips his head back and laughs. I can't help but join in, relieved that I haven't upset him.

"No, not axe murdering." His laughter subsides. "Poisons, though, those are a whole different story."

The laughter dies in my throat. Is he telling the truth? Is he serious? Then I see the smirk on his face.

"Oh, you." I tap his chest playfully. "You had me there."

He's still smiling. "Well, I do know all the effects of belladonna and other substances, but not everything I research for my books becomes a hobby. I'm just saying that perhaps she ought to have known a little more about me before inviting me to stay."

"Well, I'm glad she invited you." Another phrase I blurt out without thinking.

"Are you?" He tilts his head and regards me.

"Yes, of course." I nudge his shoulder with mine. "I haven't finished teaching you to dance yet."

A smile breaks out on his face. I want to tell him how much I want to kiss him, feel his lips on mine. How much I want to taste him and watch his amber eyes shine as he comes undone by my touch. But I don't, not yet. Now he'll be staying here, so I can take my time.

"Then, shall we dance?" He holds out his hand with a smirk, well aware that this time, he's the one who's asked me to dance.

"I'd love to." I bite back any smart remark I might be tempted to make and take his hand, leading him into the ballroom just as Constantin sits down at the piano and starts playing.

Chapter 13

Rafe

It's my first morning in the mansion and I wake feeling refreshed. Maybe because I've slept better than I have done for weeks. There's something about a hotel that makes it feel temporary, which means I find it hard to settle. That, and it was close to the city centre where bars don't close until the early hours of the morning—I have had a few late nights at Constantin's bar too. But without the noises of the traffic outside my window at all hours, I've slept deeply.

Of course, being here is also temporary, and I'm a guest in someone else's house, but still, it feels different. Although Estrella is very generous and gracious and said her invitation is open-ended, I don't want to overstay any welcome. So, after some negotiation—and, boy, she may be old, but she is *stubborn* —we agreed I would stay for a month. I have to remember that she's dying, but if I ask her about it, she says we're all dying and dismisses my question. When I said I was worried about overtaxing her, she said if she needed to rest, she would and that we, myself and Florencio, could entertain ourselves. Once I had satisfied myself that I wasn't going to be a burden—and being told I was just as stubborn as she was—I allowed myself to relax.

A month is a good period. I feel it gives me some breathing space, some more distance from my life back in England. I can decide what I really want to do now, and I will, but first I need coffee. I pull on a T-shirt and some shorts as it looks like it's going to be a warm day. It'll be summer soon, so I might have to get a few more pairs of shorts while I'm here.

I wander through the cool corridors towards the kitchen, where I'm greeted by an amazing smell and Florencio wearing nothing but a pair of loose linen trousers. I would only take the expression "make yourself at home" so far, not as an invitation to wander around half-naked. I stop on the threshold, unwilling to enter just yet. I watch him stir something in a pan, the source of the delicious aromas, and then head to the coffee machine. He's not bulky, but he's more muscled than I thought he would be, not that I've thought about that at all. No, not until now, when I have a view of him topless in front of me.

He catches sight of me, while I'm still leaning against the doorframe, gawking.

"*Buenos dias,*" he calls and I answer the same.

"Do you want some breakfast? There are croissants, toast, or I'm cooking tortillas," he asks, reaching for a bowl, which he starts cracking eggs into.

"Um, just coffee for now." I move towards the coffee machine.

"Did you sleep well?" he asks brightly, and I pop a pod into the coffee machine before turning and replying.

"I did, thank you. It was very peaceful."

"Bien." He starts whisking the eggs.

"Um, is it okay to wander around topless? What would Juana say?" I look around, expecting her to appear at any moment. Whilst I might not understand what she says, I can imagine her frown and a flow of Spanish admonishing him. She might even banish him from the kitchen.

He erupts into laughter, bringing my attention back to him.

"You're so British." He grins. "I didn't realise breakfast had a dress code. Anyway, Juana likes me. Just be thankful I'm not dressed in my usual silk shorts."

He takes the egg mixture over to the stove, giving a little wiggle on the way. Hold on, did he just wiggle his arse at me? Did he also say silk? I really don't need those images in my head. I clearly need some coffee. I grab my cup and take a long gulp before walking over to sit at the table.

Florencio finishes making the tortilla, plates it up, and puts a portion down in front of me.

"You were going to ask for some as soon as you saw mine," he says simply and sits next to me. He's not wrong, it looks appetising.

I take a forkful.

"Wow, that's really good!" I say.

"Told you." He smirks and I eat in silence for the next few minutes, satisfying the hunger that had appeared after I had the first mouthful. When I'm done, I sit back and drink more of my coffee.

"So how come you're so good at cooking?" I'm intrigued by him.

"We always had cooks at home, and I spent a lot of my

time making sure I kept out of my father's way. He rarely entered the kitchen, so I was pretty safe there."

"Was it that bad?" I ask. My parents might not agree with my career choice, but I am loved nonetheless. The thought reminds me that I need to call them today and let them know I'd cancelled my flight home, And I ought to call my agent as well. I put off the dreary thought of that and turn back to Florencio.

"He was never cruel. Well, not physically, but psychologically . . . it hurt. I could never do anything right. I never lived up to his expectations. A constant source of disappointment. At school I was interested in the arts, not maths and business. I have an older brother and sister who love that sort of stuff and they're both top executives in the family business. One of them, and my money is on my sister, will take over from him one day. I'm five years younger than my sister, an afterthought, possibly even a mistake. I'm so unlike my father that I'm pretty sure he might have even questioned my parentage."

"Is there a question about it?" I blurt, then grimace as I realise I've been insensitive. I was so wrapped up in his story, I didn't think.

He laughs. "No, my parents are good together, and I'm more like him than he cares to notice—or admit. I'm stubborn and pretty relentless when I want my own way. Asking for dancing lessons was a battle of wills."

"Did you win?"

"No. I didn't actually take any proper lessons until I was eighteen and decided I wanted to teach it myself. But I loved to dance and asked the cook and the maids to teach me that as well. Another activity that could be done in the safety of the kitchen and away from my father. So before I was ten, I could dance the tango and make a very credible dulce de leche."

It's an amazing story and I'm stunned at how dedicated he is to following the path he wants to, even given the obstacles in his way.

He stretches slightly. "So now you're here, what would you like to do?" he asks with a smile, resting his head on his hand. His brown eyes are soft as he looks at me. I feel like he's genuinely interested in what I might say. It catches me off guard for a minute.

"I have to tell my parents I'm staying here for a while, and my agent too, but then I thought I'd like to read for a while."

"I'm going to spend some time this morning with my aunt, let Juana have some time to herself, but we're going to the bar later. Yes?"

"Of course." We'd agreed that we were going to see Constantin later.

"*Bien*. I think you're ready to dance in public," he says. "That is, if you want to be seen dancing with me in public, of course." His mouth is smiling, but his eyes darken, throwing down a challenge. I wonder if this is one of the times he's like his father. I know what he meant, though, referencing when I refused him the first time. But I'm no bigot, and I have no problem being seen dancing with him,

"I'll gladly dance with you," I reply, and this time, his smile reaches the corners of his eyes, making them crinkle slightly.

"A month!" The shriek pulses down the phone, and I hold it away from my ear slightly. I knew Helen would not be happy, but I didn't expect it at that volume. She launches into a tirade about me not taking my job seriously when she's

working hard to get me a contract. Right now, I couldn't really care. I know I have to face it at some point, but I need this month to consider my options, not a reminder of what they aren't. I only half listen, letting her run her course. But a name snags on my consciousness, and I become fully alert. Sloan Thorpe. By the time she mentioned him the third time, this time asking why I'm not more like him, I've had enough. I thought Sloan had an agent, but something about her words puts my hackles up.

"Did you take Sloan on? Are you his agent now?"

Silence greets me at the other end of the line. Then, after what feels like a full minute, she replies.

"Well, you're not doing much at the moment. I have bills too . . ." It's bullshit. I know she has lots of successful authors she agents for. She just wants to ride on his coattails as he becomes the darling of Deatons.

"Don't call me again," I grind out and cut the call. I throw the phone down on my bed and follow it a second later, lying face down and groaning.

"Am I going to be plagued by that guy all my life?"

I allow myself exactly two minutes of time wallowing in despair before calling my parents. I don't know if I can trust Helen not to, and I don't want them to hear from her that I've extended my stay in Spain.

Luckily, she hasn't, but that fact does nothing to redeem her right now. They take it very well, better than expected, actually. I might have bent the truth a little and said I was working on some new ideas. It might be true by the end of the month, so I don't feel too bad about that. They even surprise me by saying that they might come to Barcelona for a visit. Maybe take in some European cities. That they deserved a holiday and hadn't been away for a while. I'm not sure what they'd think of my current living arrangements. I've been economical with that information as well. But that they can still surprise me after twenty-eight years puts me in a better humour.

I find my way downstairs and find a spot in the shade to read. But first I download a phrasebook and an app. If I'm going to be here for a month, I really want to learn some of the language.

Chapter 14

Constantin

I look at the table filled with dirty glasses and empty bottles and sigh. I really should've cleaned them away last night instead of leaving them for this morning. But it was late, and I was exhausted. Maybe I'm just getting old—too old for entertaining. I laugh at myself, knowing exactly what Estrella would say to that notion. Last night was the second night in a row that Florencio and Rafe have come to the bar since Rafe started staying with Florencio and Estrella. They don't have to. They can stay up at the mansion, but I appreciate their company. Perhaps it's just to give Estrella a break, so she doesn't get too tired.

For whatever reason they come, I like them being here. But it's also difficult, seeing them laughing and dancing together. I join them as much as I can, but I also have a bar to run, and I don't feel I'm doing very well at that right now, not with them there to distract me. They stayed late last night; it must have been three when they left this morning, hence why

I didn't clean up. I grab a few glasses and take them to the sink, then I clear away the bottles. I might have drunk a bit too much rum, which would account for my fuzzy head this morning. I should definitely cut down a bit.

"Hi, boss." Alena comes in just as I'm finishing wiping the table.

"Is it that time already?" We open at noon for most of the year, but when the summer comes we won't open until four in the afternoon, after siesta. I continue to clean the other tables, setting the chairs out ready to open.

"Almost," Alena laughs at me. It's unusual for me to be so out of it, but I do feel sluggish this morning. Luckily, Alena is efficient, and she makes a quick inventory of the fridges, ready to restock them.

"We have thirty minutes if you want to have a lie down. I'll be fine opening up. Anton's coming in soon, so take your time."

I start to protest, but I see the look on her face.

"Do I look that bad?"

She pulls a face, like she doesn't want to offend but she can't be tactful and tell the truth. "Perhaps you just need more sleep," is what she finally settles on, which tells me everything I need to know.

"I'm too old for this," I mutter as I stumble up the stairs. Maybe I shouldn't be trying to keep up with the younger guys. I pull my T-shirt off and sit on the edge of the bed. I fall backwards and lie staring up at the ceiling. The problem is, I know what's causing this mood, what kept me up until dawn, and why I couldn't sleep until the light was seeping in through the blinds. Rafe and Florencio are planning a trip up to Park Güell today. They invited me but I just made an excuse. They did look upset at my refusal and pressed me to join them, but I held fast. There's no way I can go. Park Güell was mine and Valery's place. We spent hours wandering around it. The Hypostyle Room with the columns and domed ceiling was my favourite part and the dragon stairway was Valery's. I close my eyes, refusing to let the memories overtake me. This is stupid. I have no business having thoughts about a pretty guy and a straight one, both at least a decade younger than me. I should give in and let them go, but I can't. I'm unable to shake the image of them from my mind and I'm addicted to it. I must have drifted off as I awake to a low rumble . . . something's not right. I sit bolt upright as the sound intensifies, and a vibration comes through the floor.

I'm on my feet and out the door just as there's a huge crashing sound, and the air becomes thick with dust.

I jump back as the floor gives way. As the noise stops, I cough, trying to see through the gloom. When the dust clears, I just stare, my heart sinking. I look through the hole in my floor to my bathroom, which is now located in the bar.

I hear coughing below, and my immediate thought is Alena. I holler through the gap my bathroom once occupied, my heart hammering in my chest.

"I'm all right, boss," she calls back up and my heart begins to slow down. Thank god, she's all right. "Helluva mess, though." Understatement of the year.

A quick glance at my watch reassures me we hadn't been open, thankfully. But ten more minutes . . . well, it doesn't bear thinking about.

I slowly make my way round the hole, going carefully in case any more of the floor is going to give way. I make it down the stairs and check on Alena. Luckily, she'd been in the storeroom at the time. She's a bit shaken but not hurt, made of stern stuff.

"Anyone else here?" I ask, looking round.

"No, I was just going to finish the last of the restock and then open up. Anton's not here yet either." Well, now we won't be opening today, not for a long while. Maybe never. I push that thought away. First things first, I eye the water now running from the ruptured pipe that used to lead to my washbasin and wonder if the dodgy plumbing had been the cause. It could have been leaking for a long time without me noticing the damage. I locate the stopcock and turn the water off. It subsides to a dribble and then a drip.

"Jeez." Anton lets out a low whistle as he appears in the doorway.

"Don't come in," I warn. "I'm not sure it's safe." He ignores me, edging round the debris and into an unaffected area. I pick up my phone. I need to call the insurance company first. They probably can't send an assessor out that quickly, but I need to know who they want me to contact to make sure the building is safe and if I can begin cleaning up. Right now, I can't even think what this means for my business.

Apart from making a sign for the door that we're closed until further notice, I don't do anything for the next hour until the builder arrives, except look at the carnage that is my house and bar.

Alena and Anton stayed with me, although I told them to go home. They refuse and I'm grateful for their presence. Alena dispatched Anton to a local café to get coffee, because without water, I can't even make that.

As I sit there, I can't help thinking it's a sign. Just when I started to think about someone else, that maybe there was life outside the bar, it made sure my attention was on it. Perhaps it's punishment for me having a fixation on an inappropriate situation. It seems a cruel joke that it's the bathroom that's affected. The shower where just this morning I was jacking off—again, I stop those thoughts immediately. Fine, I curse the universe. If that's how you want to play it. I'll be so busy sorting this mess out I won't have time for anyone else now, anyway.

Chapter 15

Florencio

"Are you ready to play tourist?" I ask, grinning at Rafe as we enter through the gates to Park Güell.

"We *are* tourists," Rafe replies. "We don't need to play."

"Oh, but I like to play." I can't resist and sashay my way to the foot of the dragon stairway, his laughter like a bubbling brook following me.

"Just look at this." He stares in wonder up the dragon stairway, and its impressive statue dominating the centre section. "It's beautiful."

His awestruck voice is a breathy whisper. It's a word he repeats often as we wander around the vast city park. From the coolness of the domes in the ceiling under the doric columns, each dome hosts an intricate mosaic from serpents to the seasons.

We walk for a couple of hours, taking the paths under palm trees that follow the contours of the mountain it's built on.

I'm enjoying the park, but I'm also watching Rafe enjoy it. How his expression changes as he comes across each new feature, and every time he turns to me his face is alive and full of joy at each new discovery. I begin pointing them out for him, just so I can watch his reaction.

The whole park, as with much of Gaudi's work, has an organic feel. Like it's grown out of the landscape, some of it in a psychedelic way, but is still fitting in nature. Rafe in his light linen trousers and his honey-coloured shirt blends in too. After a couple of days reading on the terrace back at my aunt's house, he is beginning to tan, and the sun has lightened the natural highlights in his hair, which just adds to his beauty. I take a few pictures of him when he's not looking, but then he catches me. I ask him to pose, and he shakes his head but gives in with a shy smile.

"If I had known you would take pictures, I'd have worn something more suitable." He peers down at his shirt.

"Why? What's wrong with what you have on?" He looks delicious to me.

"I, um," he stumbles. "Loretta, my um, ex-fiancé, never liked this colour on me. I could never wear it around her."

Clearly the woman has no taste, but then that's obvious as she left this gorgeous, funny, and *very* sexy man. But the way he says it gets my back up and a flash of anger rises.

"Well, first, you wear whatever makes you happy." His small smile at my words causes the anger to fizzle out, and it's replaced by something much deeper. I can't explain why, but I take a step towards him. "I like the colour. It suits you. It brings out the amber in your eyes." I stop speaking, now close enough to touch him.

I watch his throat bob as he swallows. His soft lips part slightly as he takes a breath. The overwhelming urge to kiss him returns. I could kiss him. I'm close enough. It isn't like me to stall, but like last time, I don't make a move. I want him to be happy, more than I want to take my pleasure from him. The realisation hits me full force in the solar plexus, and I take a step back with the weight of it. Stumbling slightly.

"Are you all right?" Rafe's concern is clear as he rushes to my side. My skin tingles as he grabs my elbow to steady me. I'm a dancer, I'm surefooted as a cat. Why the hell does he have me stumbling around like a clown?

"I'm fine," I mutter, hardly able to concentrate now that he's so close and touching me. "Maybe it's the heat."

He gives me a curious look. Yeah, I'm not buying it either. It's not even hot here yet. Not the heat I'm used to, anyway.

"Shall we sit down for a while?" He indicates a bench under the inclined columns of the promenade in front of us.

"Okay." Yes, not being on my feet for a minute would be very welcome. I feel like I'm moving through treacle, hyper-aware of my body, or more specifically the body next to me. When we sit down he releases my elbow, which is a pity, but at least I can now breathe properly again. He turns to me.

"Are you sure you're all right?"

No, I'm not. I can't think straight right now. All I want to do is to lose myself in your eyes, your lips, your arms. But I can't do that. So I have to sit here with my heart racing and hope you don't notice.

"I'm finc," I say brightly. "I just need a minute."

He nods and turns to look out at the view across the city. I try not to watch him, but I can't help it.

A thought begins to gnaw at me, and once it's there, I can't let it go. Does he still have feelings for his ex-fiancé? It opens up a hole in me, a dark one. I have to ask, not directly of course, then I'd sound as crazy as I obviously am.

"Tell me about Loretta."

He turns sharply to look at me, a deep crease in his brow. His nostrils flare slightly. Yes, it's really bad that I'm noticing these details. Then his eyes dim slightly, and he slumps back against the bench.

"No. She's my past now," is all he says.

I don't get the answer I'm looking for, which really is my own stupid fault for asking a dumb question. I don't know whether he won't reply because he still harbours deep hurt, or because what he says is true and he's moved on. I hope it's the last one.

I've broken all my rules. I allowed myself to fall for someone. And what's worse is, he's straight.

Shit.

After I feel like I can move again, I suggest we carry on. But thinking clearly? That might be messed up for some time. We follow the path through rhododendrons and magnolias. It appears the same as when we walked down this path earlier. The trees are the same and other people still pass us and greet us politely, allowing Rafe to practise his *"buenos dias"* at every chance he can. But nothing is the same, and never will be again. Not for me, anyway. I steal glances at Rafe. He's a bit quieter than before and I'm not sure if I've caused it. I feel like I have somehow. Perhaps I shouldn't have brought up his ex. It was a pretty arsehole thing to do, really. I want to lighten his mood somehow.

We reach the serpentine seat, the curving bench forming a balustrade for the roof of the Hypostyle Room. Its brightly coloured, fabulous patterns and motifs are depicted in a mosaic of thousands of ceramic tiles. Rafe's face brightens when he sees it, his expression once more one of joy. I can't blame him. I'm not sure anyone could feel down while surrounded by so much beauty. I watch, transfixed, as he reaches out to touch it, running his fingers over the surface, the tiles—some smooth, some with relief work. I watch his long fingers trace the cracks between the mosaics. I imagine what it would feel like to have those fingers tracing over me, following my contours, looking at me with the same reverence in his eyes. I crave it, the effects making me feel slightly dizzy. I need to get a grip and stop this nonsense. Maybe it is the heat after all. I pull out a couple of bottles of water from the bag I'm carrying. I hand one to Rafe, partly to get close to him again and partly to give his hands something else to do before I lie down on the bench in front of him and offer myself to him. But that's not going to happen because I wouldn't be able to stand his look of revulsion. Straight guys don't go around touching gay ones.

I stand and look over the park, the warden's cottage at the entrance catching my eye.

"Why did Gaudi shape that roof like a penis?"

I hear a sputtering and coughing beside me as Rafe spits out his drink. Shit, I nearly killed him.

"Sorry," I say as he recovers. I offer to help, but he waves me away.

"It's okay," he reassures me, then pulls out his guidebook and finds the right page.

"It says here that it's supposed to be a mushroom. Yes, look, it's red with white spots. Like fly agaric, it's poisonous but also hallucinogenic."

"That explains a lot," I chuckle, looking round at the colours and shapes that make up the park, a common theme of Gaudi's work.

"It says here that he had an interest in mycology. That's the study of mushrooms."

"Well, he was well ahead of his time, then. I didn't think it was a thing people did over a hundred years ago."

"Maybe." He shrugs, looking thoughtful.

"I still say it looks phallic though, and that red bulbous top, surely there must be another meaning."

"Given that, as far as we know, he was never in a relationship with anyone, and there is no recurring theme that points to any more phallic symbols, I'd say probably not." Rafe closes the guidebook and takes another drink, still gazing at the huge rounded tip of the tower of the building. "But you know I'll never unsee it now." He gives me a huge grin. "I shall forever refer to it as the penis house."

"That's odd." Rafe stares at the sign outside Constantin's very closed bar. We'd arranged to come round after our trip. I was hoping we could encourage him to come out to eat with us. He might know of a good restaurant in the area. But the closed door and the sign bring a knot of worry. Rafe knocks on the door, but it's a few moments before someone answers.

A very dusty and grim-faced Constantin stands in front of us. His shoulders deflate when he sees us.

"Oh, I'm sorry. I completely forgot you were coming." He allows us in through the door and I stare at the carnage that was once his bar, my senses assaulted by the smell of wet plaster. "I've been a bit busy," he explains.

"Jesus Christ, what happened?" Rafe exclaims. Quickly followed by, "Are you all right?"

"No one was hurt. But yes, it appears the plumbing problem was a bit larger than I thought."

"You don't say," I retort, and his lips form an even grimmer line. Sometimes, I really put my foot in it. "Can we do anything to help?"

"No." He sighs resignedly. "The builder has been and had a quick assessment. He's coming back tomorrow to go over it more thoroughly. At the moment, we're not even allowed to clean up in case anything else is likely to fall." He looks weary as he drags a hand through his dusty hair.

Alena comes over. "What about if we move the bottles out of the bar and into the storeroom? It's clean in there, and will stop them getting dirty when we do get a chance to clear up."

"Good idea," he says. And then a belated, "Thank you, Alena. Not sure what I'd do without you." He sinks into a chair and it doesn't look like he has the energy to move anything right now.

"We can help with moving stuff. Can't we?" Rafe says, looking to me for confirmation.

"Absolutely. Just put us to work," I reply.

Two hours later, we're all seated round a table, eating the pizza Constantin ordered. We're all pretty tired. After moving the bottles, we also moved any more stock that could be put in the back room, as well as all the glasses, mixers, and anything clsc not nailcd down. It's full in there, but at least it will stay clean.

"What now?" Alena asks, taking a bite of pizza.

"You go home," Constantin replies. "All of you. I've called the band. I've called all my suppliers and cancelled all the orders for the foreseeable future. The building is secure, so there's nothing more we can do until tomorrow."

When we've finished eating, Anton rises, looking quite pleased he's got the afternoon off.

Alena is slower to follow him.

"Are you sure there's nothing else I can do?"

"You've done enough, thank you," Constantin says.

"Okay. Well, call me when you're ready to start cleaning up."

"You don't have to—"

"I want to." She gives his shoulder a squeeze before saying goodbye and leaving.

Constantin watches her go.

"You know, I was just thinking of making her the bar manager a few days ago. It's long overdue. Now, I don't have a bar left for her to manage." He gives a little huff, one that's meant to be humorous even though the situation definitely isn't funny.

"How bad is it?" I ask and watch as he drops his head, taking a deep breath before raising it again.

"It's bad. I have insurance, but I don't think it will cover all of it. This is a big rebuild. Then there's the loss of earnings while it's shut, staff wages, or letting them go, which I don't want to do. I have some savings, but it's going to be tough for sure."

He looks around as if he's seeing the devastation for the first time.

"There's a part of me that wants to just walk away. I don't have the energy to start again."

"Are you really considering that?" Rafe says quietly.

"Not really. This bar is the only thing I have, so without it, I'm nothing. I don't know what else to do."

"Well, the first thing you're doing is coming with us," I state, and see a frown cross his face. "You weren't really thinking of staying here, were you?"

He mumbles something and doesn't meet my eyes. I grab his arm so I have his full attention.

"You cannot stay here. You have no water, and half your house has no floor."

"I'll find somewhere," he says, as if it's the last thing he wants to do.

"No. You'll stay with us," I say firmly.

"But your aunt," he protests.

"Will want you to come to the house. I'm only saying you're coming with us now so I don't have to trail down here later and haul your arse back up that hill when she sends me to fetch you."

That does get a small laugh from him. He knows he's beat.

"Now, if you can get back up those stairs, go grab what you need, otherwise we'll have to make do," I continue, not sure how that would work exactly as none of Rafe's or my clothes are going to fit his broad frame.

"Has anyone told you that you're stubborn?" he says, rising to obey.

"Frequently, and you're welcome," I call after his retreating back.

Chapter 16

Rafe

I notice movement in my peripheral vision and lazily turn my head to see Constantin sink onto the sun lounger next to me.

It's been a few days since his ceiling collapsed and he's starting to lose the lost look he'd had at the beginning. I think he now feels like he has some control, and it's not quite as bad as he feared. Once the building was made safe, we spent two days clearing up the mess. Now, it's been handed over to the builders. He says it will take a month to rebuild and get it passed for inspection so he can reopen. Much sooner than he hoped for, *and* he won't lose the whole of the tourist season. He's come to some arrangement with Alena, so she'll come back when it's ready. That he's able to relax is a good sign, as he's been edgy for days.

"*¿Cómo te sientes hoy?*" I try out the Spanish I've been learning by asking how he's feeling today.

"*Muy bien,*" he answers and I give him a look because I wasn't expecting that answer. He laughs.

"Are you sure?" My Spanish doesn't extend to asking that.

"No, I'm feeling so-so today," he replies. "But your Spanish is very good. *Muy bien,* Rafe."

I stretch languidly; the way he says very good in Spanish makes me do that. He says it like a soft caress and I'm like a cat being stroked. I want to learn more and use my words to push against his hand so his words can caress me again. I've never felt this way before. I don't understand it. It's similar to when Florencio praises my dancing, but that's less a slow caress and more of a tingling on my skin. Maybe I never received enough praise as a child, but I'm loving it now.

There's something about hearing Spanish that I can't get enough of, especially if Florencio and Constantin are talking. More than once, I've feigned sleep whilst I've lain out in the sun, just so I can lie and listen to them. Their voices and intonation send my bones to jelly and my organs to mush. Of course, I can't understand what they're talking about—not more than an odd word here or there, and not enough to even derive context—but I don't care what they say, just the cadence of the language makes me feel untethered to my corporeal self. It's almost sensual.

"*¿Quieres un café?*" Constantin asks, rising from his lounger, and I smile up at him. This one I *do* know, and there's no way I'm not going to want a coffee, but I answer anyway.

"*Sí, por favor.*" Partly to practise and also just to get him to say "very good" again—which he does with a slow smile that reaches his eyes. My breath hitches a little as he says it, the anticipation becoming part of the experience.

He returns a short time later, with the coffee and Florencio in tow. Florencio throws himself down on another lounger with a grunt. He looks very pissed.

"What's up?" I ask.

"Families are the worst." He flings an arm over his face as if blotting out the sun will help.

"My father isn't happy with my *progress reports*." He spits out the last two words.

"What are you supposed to be reporting on?" I ask.

"My aunt." He sighs. "I'm supposed to give him daily updates on her health. I refused. I said I wasn't going to do that. It's not my business, and truthfully, I don't know. She wouldn't tell me even if I asked her. Do you know what he told me to do?"

We both watch him, knowing that we're not required to answer the question.

"Snoop, that's what. I'm not going to do that. And then he said that I should go home for a while, back to Argentina." The last comes out with a cry. "Like he has any use for me back there!"

"Can he force you to go back?" Constantin asks.

"He can't physically force me, but he could stop my allowance, so I'd be homeless and without enough money to live on. I don't make enough to live in Buenos Aires just teaching." He sits up and turns to look at us. He looks genuinely distraught, and I'm thankful that my family isn't complicated.

"Has he threatened to do that?" I ask.

"No," Florencio sighs. "Not yet, but he has hinted at other measures. He's a callous bastard who just has his eyes on what he'll be getting. Knowing him, he already has plans for it. Well, I hope Auntie lives forever." He throws himself back on the lounger and lapses into silence.

Suddenly, Constantin starts chuckling. I haven't heard

him laugh since he got here . . . well, not much at all, really. We both turn and look at him.

"What's so funny?" Florencio demands, his face darkening.

"Well, aren't we a pathetic trio?" He's still laughing.

"How so?" Florencio looks like thunder, and I wonder what he's like when he's really angry. Is it another trait he's inherited?

"Well, here we are, all of us homeless, or potentially so, with no money or little income. And yet we sit here on the terrace of what must be one of the most expensive houses in Barcelona."

"Yes, it is pathetic." Florencio's face loses its fury, but he doesn't look like he sees any humour in the situation, unlike Constantin, which is a strange sight as it's usually the other way around.

I'm not sure I find it funny either. I find it damn scary, if I'm honest. We're here by the grace of a lady who is, by her own admission, dying. It seems a perilous situation to me.

"Well, what are we going to do about it?" I ask, though I have no clue. I guess if it comes to it, I can go home. But the thought of that feels like a bitter blow just when I think everything is going well.

"I don't know." Constantin lies back down. "But right now, I'm going to do nothing but enjoy lying here in the sun." He doesn't even react when Florencio throws a cushion at him, but that he does is a sign Florencio's getting back to his normal self.

I rise and leave them to it. I've had enough rest today, and it's getting a little too hot for me. I'm not sure I'm well equipped for a summer in Barcelona. I'm not used to high temperatures. Instead, I walk through the house, which is wonderfully cool. I look at the art on the wall, wondering if Estrella collects it personally or even knew some of the artists. I spy a door I've not seen before, standing slightly open. I don't like to pry, but we haven't been told that anywhere is off limits, just which part of the house Estrella's suite of rooms is so we don't disturb her if she needs to rest. I look round the door, but the room is empty. It's not a large room, just a small lounge. It's lavishly furnished with velvet drapes and gilded furniture, but what attracts my attention are the pictures. Hundreds of photographs hang on the walls, all of them of Estrella and every star imaginable. I see her with Lawrence Olivier and Richard Burton, Joan Crawford and Rita Hayworth. I can only stand and stare in awe at her incredible life and career. I think back to the stories she's told us and realise we'd only been scratching at the surface. As every new picture catches my eye, an idea starts to form, and I feel an excitement that has eluded me for months. I know what my next project will be.

Chapter 17

Constantin

"How's it going, Con?" Luis's voice down the phone is bright and enquiring. I've called my cousin to fill him in on what happened at the bar before he heard it from elsewhere. His voice changes to concern.

"If there's anything I can do, let me know, okay?"

"Well, maybe don't penalise me for not paying your invoice yet?" I'm only half joking, but Luis immediately responds.

"Take as long as you want. You know you can do that."

"Thank you, Wis." He laughs at the childhood nickname I call him, from back when I wasn't old enough to pronounce Luis. I knew he probably wouldn't have a problem. He might be family, but business is business, and I don't want to take advantage of him. He has a vineyard to maintain, which is expensive and a gamble; one bad harvest can wipe out your whole production for that year. I know he's had his share of difficulties, especially in the early days.

"And if there's anything else I can do, just let me know," he says, and although there isn't, it feels nice to know he's there if I need him. My parents have been similarly supportive, not that they can help either, but the moral support is welcome. I did have to listen to a five-minute talk —short by their standards—about how I never come to visit. I gave them my usual promises of soon and rang off before heading down to the bar to check on work for the day.

It's amazing how easily we can adapt to a new routine, a new normal. It's only been a few days since I was dragged up here to stay in the mansion. Perhaps dragged isn't the right word . . . harassed, press-ganged, bullied . . . Well, whichever it was, I was reluctant not only to leave my bar but also to be so far away from it.

Being here with Rafe and Florencio is both a blessing and a curse. I enjoy their company, of course. Florencio is hilarious and you know exactly what you're getting with him. Most of it is his witty, sharp self, but we've seen an occasional bout of anger and frustration, mostly directed at his family. Rafe is more reserved, and I can't always tell what's ticking inside that head of his, except to know that if he's decided to do something, he puts his all into it. He's learning Spanish at an incredible rate, and we can now hold short conversations.

But being in close proximity is doing nothing for the images of them that taunt me, even chase me into my dreams, and every day it becomes more difficult. I force the images away, becoming haunted by them every time I close my eyes. They mock me, reminding me it's unattainable and the dreadful consequences of giving in. I have my bar to show for that.

We tend to meet over breakfast, then I go to visit the repairs to the bar while Florencio and Rafe go to a gallery or museum, as Rafe seems determined to make up for not visiting them before. Then, the afternoon may be for siesta, reading, or talking. One thing we always do is get together for dinner. Florencio has taken on most of the cooking, though Rafe has been assisting him. I can help a little with some prep work, but I'm no cook. I'm able to fend for myself, and I've managed for ten years without starving to death, but I'm not good enough to allow other people to eat my creations. I've subsisted on the few dishes we serve at the bar, usually too busy to make time for a proper meal. So the gathering together seems strange and yet now, here, the most natural thing in the world.

Sometimes Estrella joins us if she feels up to it. She hasn't for a couple of days, so it's a nice surprise when Juana escorts her into the dining room. Juana no longer hovers in the background. Florencio made it clear that if he was cooking, we were all eating it, so she sits at the table with us now.

Dinner tonight is lasagna. Rafe said he wanted to contribute to the cooking, and it was the only dish he could be certain would turn out edible. It's delicious and I compliment him. Watching the way he responds to praise is certainly not helping my carnal thoughts, but I can't stop doing it. I'm becoming addicted to seeing him soften in response to my words.

I help to clear the plates away and stack the dishwasher

and then we linger at the table with coffee, no one wanting to move too soon. Eventually, Rafe asks Florencio to practise dancing with him. I stay for a while with Estrella. Juana has gone off to tend to some other duties.

Estrella reaches for a packet of cigarettes, I hadn't seen her smoke before and didn't know that she did. She lights up a black Sobranie. Russian and decadent, so she must have them imported.

"Do you mind if I join you?" I ask, pulling out my Marlboros.

"If you want." She shrugs her permission, so I light one up. She takes a long drag, blowing the smoke out slowly and watching me. "Smoking is bad for you."

"You're smoking," I point out uselessly.

"I'm old. It's only luck and stubbornness that have kept me going. But you're still young."

"I don't feel young."

"Believe me, when you're my age, you'll give anything to be your age again. At your age, I was in my prime. Don't waste it by being old before your time."

I shrug and take a drag. Her words don't help that much.

"You should give it up. It'll kill you," she continues.

"And you?"

"I'm already dying. What's your excuse?"

"Maybe I wish I was." My voice is flat.

"Do you?" She narrows her eyes at me.

"I did, for a long time."

"Pah." She sits back, unimpressed by my melancholy. "It takes courage to find something to live for."

Her words bounce off me.

"It's too late for that. My fate has already been decided."

"Fate be damned. Life's what you make it," she scoffs.

"I can't ignore the signs."

"What signs?"

She already knows about my bar, and of course reinforced her nephew's assertion that I was to stay at the house as long as I needed to. So I told her my other fears, that this had happened just as I thought there might be a brightness in my future—not love of course because lightning never strikes twice—but I didn't expand on what that brightness was.

"I can't help feeling that this is the universe's way of reminding me where my focus should be. Back on the bar, back with Valery."

I finish speaking, and she does nothing for a minute but slowly smoke, looking at me intently.

"Your ceiling collapsed because of poor building maintenance as you well know, not for any divine purposes. You smoke and I'll wager you drink too much as well."

I wince at her words and her look shows she saw me.

"Is that for divine purposes too? Don't let your own ceiling fall down, Constantin."

She's obviously done with me as she rises and refuses my offer of help. I sit there for a long time, finishing my cigarette, not sure what to make of her words. As I come to the end, I instinctively reach for another. I stop and stare at the packet for a minute. Laughter reaches me from the ballroom. Florencio and Rafe. The noise sparks an ember deep in my core. I place the cigarette packet down on the table and rise. I make my way to the ballroom. I feel like playing the piano.

Chapter 18

Florencio

"Let's do the basic to the cross," I say, and we move, Rafe stepping perfectly in time. "Now, pivot and step-pivot and step." I guide him through the *ocho*.

"Okay, this is where the fun begins," I say, wiggling my eyebrows at him and making him laugh. "I'm going to *pasada* to block your movement by placing my foot here." I put my foot against the one he's standing on.

"Now you will *pasada*, step over it with your free leg, touch, and then in this sequence you're going to step back. Then we'll step to the side and back to finish. Have you got that?"

"I think so," he replies.

"Right, let's go through it a few times slowly."

We practise the short sequence a few times for Rafe to get the hang of it.

"Is this where we see all the twiddly bits dancers do with their legs? Can I do that?"

"It's one of the times, yes. But let's work on not getting our legs in a tangle by just doing this first."

Constantin appears and sits down at the piano. I shoot him a glance, but his brow is drawn, his face closed, as he looks down at the keys. It's as if he's searching for inspiration there. When he starts playing, it's "Balada para un Loco"— Ballad of a Madman. A curious choice, but he just plays and doesn't look over at us.

"Shall we go again?" I ask Rafe, who's been slowly moving in place; something I've come to learn is his method of committing the steps to memory.

This time, when we run through the short routine, I don't let us stop and reset. Instead, we continue round the ballroom a few times. Constantin changes to a different song and we dance it through again.

Juana brings us coffee, so we take a short break, discussing our plans to visit Montjuïc Castle in a couple of days. We even persuaded Constantin to come with us. The coffee seems to have dispelled whatever was on his mind when he came in.

"I smell coffee," Rafe says when we come together in the middle of the dance floor in the *abrazo*, the embrace.

"We've just had coffee," I state the obvious.

"This isn't a dance for having bad breath, is it, being this close?" He chuckles.

"It's a good job we're dancing and not kissing then," I say. He tilts his head to one side slightly, something I've seen him do when he's thinking. It's cute, and feeling in the moment, I lean a bit closer and whisper, "When I kiss you, I'll make sure I've cleaned my teeth first."

I don't give him time to react. I start dancing, leading, so he has to follow. Which he does, foot perfect.

When we stop again, he doesn't mention it and relief floods through me. I thought I'd blown it then, mentioning kissing. I don't want to scare him off, though he doesn't look scared. If anything, he looks curious. I take it as a positive sign.

"Would you like to learn a couple of, as you say, 'twiddly bits?'" I ask, and his face lights up.

"What are they really called?"

"Well, there is the *boleo*, which is a flick either behind or round your leg. These are improvised, but you could try this in the *pasada*." I take him through the sequence until we get to the block.

"There. Now flick the free leg back before stepping over."

He tries it out.

"*Bien,*" I say for his good first attempt, and he makes a little humming sound that travels straight to my core. Being this close to him is hard enough without him making adorable noises as well.

I was going to teach him the *enganche*, for him to hook a leg with mine, but I think I'll pass. I won't be able to cope with him wrapping his leg round my anything right now. Not if I still want to be able to dance and not launch myself at him and kiss him senseless. Instead, I offer him a variation.

"Then, as you bring your leg back from the *pasada*, hook it round your own and then step. Remember, these have to be quick so we don't lose the beat."

I place my foot in the block again and show him—flick, step over, hook, step back.

"Do you want to try it while dancing?"

"Yes," he breathes, his eyes so close I can see the golden flecks.

"Constantin, can you play something slow, please?" I call out. A few seconds later, he starts up the "Pequeña." I love this song; it's very sensual. Perfect, in fact.

"Are you ready?" I whisper, wanting to make this the

perfect dance for Rafe. If I can't kiss or undress him, this has to be the next best thing.

We move and it's different this time, less like a lesson and more of the way the tango should be danced. He moves well and adds his flicks in. When we've been through the sequence a couple of times, on the third go, I add a couple of my own in, and hear him under his breath speaking so quietly I nearly don't catch it.

"Wow, that's really hot."

Fuck!

"Do you want to improvise a little?" I ask, still whispering, hoping he doesn't make the little humming sound that resonates in my soul again. I'm already finding it intoxicating being this close to him and dancing so beautifully. Thankfully, he just whispers *yes* right back.

We start again, and I whisper each movement to him, just before we dance it. Nothing we haven't done, just stringing them together in a different pattern. He soon loosens up, getting into it, adjusting to being able to pick each movement up from wherever we are. I add in some *boleos*, and when he feels more confident, he does too.

The music stops abruptly, and I halt mid-step. Rafe nearly bumps into me, but I hold him steady. When I look at him, his gaze is directed at the piano. Constantin is staring at us, his expression intense, dark eyes glittering lustfully. It only lasts a couple of seconds and then Constantin closes his eyes and starts playing again. This time, he starts singing, and I can't help but let out a small, huffed laugh, partly in relief.

"What is it?" Rafe whispers.

"You were right, Constantin is a romantic," I say quietly.

"Why?"

"This song is a tango classic. It's called "Todo es Amor." Everything is love."

"Oh, it's beautiful," Rafe says, and I don't disagree. I just want to add, *so are you.*

"Shall we dance for him?" I ask.

Chapter 19

Rafe

I could have danced all night. I laugh as the words from *My Fair Lady* involuntarily erupt from me while I'm getting ready for bed. It's true, though. I enjoy dancing, which I didn't expect, certainly not as much as I do. The lessons have been great, but tonight was something else, and I can see why, regardless of country or culture, dancing is a worldwide language. There's something about moving your body to a rhythm that speaks at a soul level. I pull my T-shirt over my head.

I sing the second line, the words dying on my lips as I come to a halt in front of the mirror. Am I spreading my wings? Doing things I've never done before? Since coming to Spain, I've stood up to my agent, I'm learning Spanish, and how to dance—with a guy.

With. A. Guy.

The words spring to the front of my mind. I don't mind it at all. In fact, I like it . . . a lot. Is that weird? It doesn't feel weird to me. Florencio made a joke about kissing tonight. It has to be a joke, right? Like the joke he made the first time I met him about fucking him. I know Florencio is flirty and likes his fun, and doesn't take life too seriously, so it was most certainly a joke.

But . . . would I kiss him?

I wonder what it would feel like to have his lips on mine. Would they be soft? Would they be warm and wet, or cold and dry? I've certainly not thought about kissing anyone in as much detail before.

I laugh at the thought of it. I know it's not likely to happen. A small voice pipes up in my head. *I wish it would.*

A warmth spreads through me, along with a tingling sensation.

Yes, I would kiss him!

It certainly fits in with the things I've never done before.

I look at myself in the mirror, wondering whether I look any different now I've had this realisation. I can't see anything different. Good. Then maybe he won't notice tomorrow when I see him. Hopefully I'll be able to keep my cool, at least on the outside. Inside I might be a wreck, as my stomach is already starting to churn.

I keep to myself for most of the morning, primarily working on my Spanish.

I definitely wasn't working out how to say, "I know you were joking, but yes, I would like to kiss you." Well, maybe I was, but there's actually no way I'd say it, in English *or* Spanish.

I've also been working on my idea. After checking my

notes on my laptop, it's time to put my plan to Estrella. I'm really excited at the prospect of doing this—okay, a large part of the excitement is the research, but I think it would be really popular. I just hope she agrees. I get my opportunity on the terrace after lunch. Florencio and Constantin are there. I haven't told them of my plans either, as I want it to be a surprise.

"Estrella, has anyone ever written your biography?"

She turns her head and regards me.

"Why would anyone want to do that?"

"You've led an interesting life, have so many stories to tell, and met every star imaginable. People would love to know more about that."

"My dear, you are sweet, but no one cares enough anymore. Who would care about me? In this modern world, no one cares enough about anyone anymore, do they? No one cares enough to come to see me now I'm dying."

"But—" Florencio starts to speak but Estrella cuts in.

"Hush, child. Did you come because you wanted to? No, you came because you were sent. Your father didn't care enough to come himself. He only sent you to make sure I haven't spent his inheritance or left it to a dogs' home."

She pauses and Florencio frowns.

"Don't look so glum, child. I'm not blaming you. I pity you. You're young and who cares enough about you? After all, you were the one they could spare."

Florencio drops his eyes as she turns her attention to me.

"What about you? Who cares enough about you?"

I stutter under her scrutiny. "My agent?" Though, after our last few conversations, I'm not sure about that.

"Pfft, someone who makes money from you. Who else?"

"My family, I guess." That sounds lame, even to my ears.

"That tells me everything. Where is your passion, your drive? It is passion and love that make us care enough."

I wither under her gaze. She turns to Constantin.

"Only Constantin had the right idea, yet that, too, is an illusion. Valery was the lucky one. He had you who cared enough about him. Sadly, you don't care enough about yourself."

"What do you mean?" His face darkens.

"You've been working every day for the last ten years, living someone else's dream. Was it worth it? Was it worth giving up your own dream for someone else's?"

Constantin looks hurt, almost like he'd been punched. "How can you say that?"

"Oh, it's noble. You get full marks for being noble, but that in itself is tragic. By living someone else's dream, you're forgetting to live your own. It's a waste."

He looks like he's about to say something.

"Don't look so angry. You only feel that way because you know it's true. You're just afraid to do anything about it. You've forgotten what living is."

We all sit in stunned silence. I was not expecting that outburst, and of course, it's all my fault.

"I'm sorry, I didn't mean to—"

"Why are you apologising?"

I don't really know. Probably for causing her reaction, which has affected the others. Of course I don't say all that. My natural shyness springs forward to take over, and I stumble over my words.

"I . . . I'm sorry—"

"Do you apologise just for existing?" she says, her voice softer than it had been during her tirade.

I close my mouth, lost for words. She has a point, a very big one.

I need to say something to defend myself. Though for a moment I can't think how. I begin to speak but she starts again.

"If the next words out of your mouth are 'I'm sorry,' then I'm seriously going to reconsider allowing you to stay here anymore."

What? My stomach plummets. Does she really mean it? I think everyone could hear my jaw hit the floor. But when I look at her again, she's smiling. She said it precisely to stop me from apologising, which I absolutely was going to do. I don't even notice it. It's like a verbal tic. Relief washes through me that I'm not going to be thrown out . . . Well, not today, anyway.

I take a deep breath and try to manifest some inner Estrella. "You haven't answered my question? Has anyone written your biography?"

She nods an acknowledgement that feels like approval and answers.

"No, they haven't. At least, not that I'm aware of or have authorised."

I knew this. Or, well, from my research, I was pretty certain that one hadn't been published so far. But I don't know whether there was a project that had been started, or if rights had already been given.

"Can I write one please?"

"Why?" Her answer is simple, but for some reason, I don't think she means it as a simple question.

"Biographies are hugely popular. Everyone likes to snoop into someone else's life. Not only will people get to hear about your incredible life, but they'll get an insight into the lives of all the stars you've met as well."

"Yes, you've told me that. Now tell me why you want to write it."

I blink at her. I feel excited about writing it, but she wants to know why. Can I put it into words? I chuckle inwardly, that I'll probably be all right as long as I don't apologise. I get off the lounger, finding it easier if I'm moving.

"Since I started listening to the stories you tell us, I've been fascinated by the life you've led. Your career has spanned many decades and you've met so many people. I've always had an interest in the stars, and to hear about them from your perspective would be really special for me. When I discovered your room of photographs . . ." I pause, catching myself about to apologise for being in a room I might not have been allowed to be in. Then I remembered that this was all an assumption, and I hadn't been told that. I swallow and start again, remembering how it made me feel instead.

"When I was in the room surrounded by all those pictures, I was transported to another time, another age. I could almost hear them talking, their conversations, a whispered snippet of gossip, the laughter, the good times as well as the bad. I wanted to stay in there for a while . . . with those stars, with you. I'd like to bring that to the readers." I stop, panting slightly with the need to draw breath. My heart beats fast as I await her verdict.

"I knew there was some passion in there somewhere," she says, and I relax a little, still unsure what she thinks. But then she smiles.

"If you can create that, then I say yes, you can."

"Thank you so much." My knees go weak with relief, and I lean against the balustrade for support.

"Good. I'll have my lawyer draw up a contract," she says, and I remember the legal side needs to be dealt with. Heaven knows what Helen will think, but I don't care.

"It will be amazing!" Florencio jumps off his lounger and I'm drawn into a big hug, which takes me by surprise. I enjoy being enveloped in his arms after the emotions of the last few minutes and lean into it, hugging him back.

# Chapter 20

Constantin

I can hear Florencio's raised voice from my room. We all have bedrooms next to each other—Florencio in the middle with myself and Rafe on either side—occupying a different part of the house from Estrella and Juana. I step out into the hall, meeting Rafe coming out of his own room, no doubt disturbed by the same noise as me. Florencio's door is open and we can see him sitting on the bed, almost shouting down the phone.

"I don't care what you said. I'm not doing it."

I glance at Rafe, and he shrugs. Clearly, he doesn't know either. We're due to leave for our trip to Castle Montjuïc in a few minutes.

"Yes, señor." Florencio forces the words out and rings off. He flops back on the bed, his arms outstretched.

Rafe is first through the door and I follow closely behind.

"Is everything okay?" he asks and Florencio finally notices we're there.

"No, it's not! I hate my family," he says vehemently.

Rafe sits on one side of him and I sit on the other; he ping-pongs his head between us.

He stops his head and looks straight up at the ceiling. "My father is still threatening to cut my allowance."

"That sucks," Rafe says.

Florencio sighs loudly. "I need to find a way to live without him. I'm twenty-six. It's ridiculous at this point. I'm pathetic."

"I don't think you're pathetic," Rafe says quietly.

Florencio twists to look at him. "You're so sweet, but I need to do something. I can't let him keep controlling my life. *Urgh*!" He grimaces and resumes staring at the ceiling.

"We'll help you come up with something," I say, though I'm not sure what right now.

"Yes, of course we will," Rafe chimes in.

"Thanks." Florencio gives a crooked smile.

"Do you still want to go to Castle Montjuïc?" I ask.

Florencio sighs again, closing his eyes. "My father wants a video call in an hour, and I can already feel a migraine coming on. I'll just stay here. You guys go and enjoy yourselves."

"Ah, you sure? Will you be all right?" Rafe asks.

"Oh, I'm sure I'll get over it, given enough time," he says dramatically, which I know means he really will be fine.

We stand on the terrace above the parade ground. From here, we can walk around all four sides and look out over the whole of Barcelona. It's an impressive view. The Castle is a military fortress, built in the seventeenth century. Being involved in both the defence and the subjugation of the city, it's seen several wars and skirmishes over the centuries.

I've not seen Barcelona from this vantage point before. Why is it we can live somewhere and never visit some of its heritage and museums? We don't become tourists in our own cities.

"Do you think Florencio will be ok?" Rafe asks, his gaze focussed on something in the distance.

"Today or long term?"

"Both, I guess."

"Yes, he will, on both counts. He's strong and resilient. He'll think of a way. We will do what we can to help him."

Rafe gives me one of his brilliant smiles. The way his face lights up when he's happy makes him one of the most beautiful men I've ever met.

Just like yesterday when Estrella said he could write her biography, which is a brilliant idea. I didn't know he'd been planning it. We walk around the walls, then down past the stone bastions and sentinels across the harbour. We walk in silence, but it's not uncomfortable, more that we're caught up in our internal thoughts.

Since yesterday I've been reflecting on Estrella's words. I was angry with her for a while, but I don't think she's correct. I haven't wasted my life, I can't have, because the alternative doesn't bear thinking about.

We walk along the moats, now excavated and landscaped, until we reach a dead end. There's a walkway several metres above us on one side and the fortress walls on the other. I stop as we can't go any further, but Rafe walks round the perimeter, lost in thought.

When he reaches where I've been waiting for him, he looks up. There's a crease in his brow.

"Is everything okay with you?" I ask. I don't like to think that he's worried about something.

"I don't know. Well, I think so." He gives a half smile, but he doesn't sound convincing.

"Do you want to talk about it?" I offer. He leans back against the fortress wall, tipping his head back and exposing the long white column of his throat. It's distracting and I struggle to tear my eyes away from it so I can listen to him.

"Since I've been in Spain, I've felt different. Not at first, but I was mostly ignoring everything—including my feelings—at the time. But since I met you and Florencio, I've felt something changing, especially since we've all been at Estrella's house.

"I feel free. I'm no longer afraid of my future, though there is still so much that's uncertain. I'm also not dwelling on the past because I'm beginning to understand what it feels like to live in the now. Does that make sense?"

He turns his head, his amber eyes searching mine for some confirmation.

"I think so," I say, his face captivating me. I know I can answer better than that, but I have no practical advice. After all, am I not guilty of living in the past? "It makes sense to me."

"I thought at first, it was just being in a different country, but whilst that is a part of it, I think there's a catalyst. Like you and Florencio. And Estrella, well, she's a force of nature, isn't she?"

He laughs and I join in. "She certainly is."

"She has a way of making me think outside of myself," he says. I join him, leaning against the wall, looking across the old moat.

"I'd say it's her speciality," I reply in solidarity. "She has me questioning my whole life."

"Does it need questioning?" he asks quietly.

"This is the very question I'm asking myself." I sigh and

we lapse into silence for a few minutes before Rafe speaks again.

"Do you think she was the same with all those stars she met? I can just imagine her down in Cannes telling Audrey Hepburn what she thought of her many affairs and marriages. I wonder what impact she had on them all and the long-term consequences of that. It might have changed the course of many people's lives."

"She's like a pebble thrown into a pond, the ripples reach the shore."

"That's very poetic, but then we know you're the romantic one."

I turn to look at him, and he's smiling at me. I can't help but return it. "I would never consider myself romantic."

This time I don't look away, watching his soft golden-brown hair being moved by the gentle breeze blowing across this high ground. His smile fades, and he starts chewing on his bottom lip. My eyes are drawn to it.

"Something else is changing," he says hesitantly. I give him my best "I'm listening" look, allowing him space to talk if he wants to.

"Is it changing, or just a curiosity? I don't know, as I'm trying to navigate uncharted territory here. Well, for me, at least."

"What is it? If you want to tell me, that is," I say softly. He looks so vulnerable and I don't want to pressure him.

He gives a little sigh. "Maybe I'm just imagining it. After all, Florencio jokes most of the time and he flirts a lot. But I think in his way, that said, he'd like to kiss me."

My breath stops in my throat. I couldn't speak even if I wanted to. I try to focus on what he's saying and not on the images that have plagued me for the past week.

"I think I'd like him to." It's barely a whisper and I

understand Rafe has confessed something to me. The uncertainty in his voice pulls on my heart, and I want to reassure him it's okay to feel whatever he's going through right now. But my brain can't process it, especially not in English.

"No me sorprende. Yo también quiero besarte."

He draws back slightly, and inwardly I curse myself. Instead of being supportive, I just messed it all up. His face creases slightly in concentration.

"I know only a couple of words there, not enough to get a context."

I swallow. This is going to get really messy and I'm conscious it might break the trust Rafe put in me with his confession. I've shot my mouth off, or rather I was thinking with my dick because that wasn't rational behaviour. But I will not lie to him.

"I said, 'It doesn't surprise me. I want to kiss you, too.'"

I try not to wince at how it sounds to me. Instead I wait, hardly daring to breathe and ready to offer a thousand apologies.

All my focus goes to his lips as he presses them together for a few seconds, then he parts them and licks them. I've already spent hours thinking sinful thoughts about those lips. This isn't making it any easier.

I almost miss his next words.

"Okay then."

"What?" Confusion clouds my thoughts.

"Okay then. You can kiss me."

"Oh." I'm really messing this up, big time. "I hadn't expected that."

He frowns slightly, as if he's done something wrong.

"I'm lost here. Did I read this wrong? You said you wanted to. But you weren't actually asking? I'm feeling a lot of things lately, and it's all a jumble. So yeah, I could have got confused, but I'm trying to decide what I like as I sure as hell don't know anymore." He pauses to take a breath and I see him about to launch into another speech. His face has closed down and taken on a nervous look. It's all my fault. I'm such an arsehole.

I push off from the wall and stand in front of him, bracketing him with my arms where he's still standing.

"Will you let me explain?" I keep my voice soft.

His face is still drawn, his jaw clamped shut, but he nods.

"I'm sorry. I'm making a huge mess of this. I definitely want to kiss you. I wasn't lying to you there, which is why I said it. But I also wasn't expecting you to agree, and it caught me off guard. I'm rather out of practice at this." I offer up a half smile and he relaxes slightly.

"What I don't want to do is put any pressure on you. I get that you're going through some feelings, and I'm sorry that I messed up for you there too. Say the word and I'll back off, give you time to think everything through, and I'll listen and be here for you."

He lets out a long breath through his nose, his shoulders loosen, and he tips his head back to look me in the eye.

"Will you stop apologising and kiss me?"

I lean forward and gently capture his lips, poised in case he changes his mind. He doesn't, and I press harder. He opens his mouth and my tongue tangles with his. He opens further, deepening the kiss, and my knees almost buckle. He puts his arms round my back and pulls me closer until we're touching knee to shoulder. My brain nearly short-circuits at having him pressed so close to me. My cock is as hard as a rock and he can probably feel it digging into his thigh. It takes every ounce of self-control not to grind against him. I catch his bottom lip in my teeth, and he lets out a little whimper. Friction be damned. I nearly come there and then. I draw back slightly, not wanting to end it, but if I don't, I might not be able to control myself. I don't want to scare him off.

He looks so delicious with his bruised lips and shining eyes that I nearly attack his mouth again. I push myself back slightly, trying to put a little distance between us.

"I'm glad I said yes," he says with a smile that reaches deep down into the dormant part of my heart and rips the door right off.

Chapter 21

Florencio

"If you can't do the job I asked you to do, I'll send someone else. Martina has just finished a contract, so she has a week free. She can do it."

Not my fucking sister. She's always been used as an example of how things should be done whenever I didn't live up to his expectations.

"No, there's no need for Martina to come."

My father's face on the screen goes still.

"Prove it to me. I need that information, Florencio. You have one more week to get it. If I don't have it by then, Martina will be coming over for it and bringing you home."

He ends the call without waiting for me to respond, but then he doesn't want my response. He never wants to hear what I have to say. He didn't even ask how Auntie was, though I'm not sure why that should surprise me.

I slam my laptop shut. I'm fed up with being treated like a child. He's never done any differently and he never will. I can't live like this any longer. I want my own life. I want to live without the threat of losing it all constantly hanging over my head.

The migraine that has been hovering all morning descends, and I manage to stagger to get some meds before collapsing back into bed.

When I wake a few hours later, the migraine is just a shadow, but I don't feel any better about my life. I go in search of Auntie and find her in her rooms. She's resting on a couch, Juana reading to her.

"My father has threatened to send Martina over and drag me home if I don't give him what he wants," I announce.

Juana gets up to leave, but I doubt there are many secrets between her and my aunt, so perhaps she doesn't want to listen to me complaining. I can't blame her.

"You know I'm not going to give you that information, and neither is Señor Bernat."

I flop down in the chair that Juana vacated. I knew Auntie wasn't going to disclose what was in her will. She told me that the day I arrived. She would welcome my company, but she knew what my father was up to and would not be indulging him. She didn't refute my assertions that he thought she might have left everything to a cat shelter. She'd just laughed. I don't care what she does with her money. I just care about my life, and I do not want to go back to Buenos Aires. At least, not yet anyway.

"Have you considered why your father is being so insistent? Why does he need to resort to threats?"

I haven't, not really. I thought he might have had the

money planned for a big investment opportunity that was coming up. My father has always been assertive when it comes to business, but he is becoming more aggressive, far more than I have ever seen him before. There has to be more to it than simply wanting to know his inheritance. There's only one person I trust to find out that sort of information, so leaving my aunt resting, I go make a call.

Cooking always calms me, so I throw myself into making dinner for when Rafe and Constantin return. I try not to think about how much I've missed them today. I need the comfort of a familiar recipe, so I'm making pizzas. I stir the sauce while the dough is proving, letting my mind slip into the rhythm of what I need to do at each stage. I haven't heard back from Julio yet, but then he said it would take a few days. I'm surprised he agreed to help me, but then he always did have a soft spot for me. He works in analysis management for Delgado Media. He's amazing with data, and if anyone can find something amiss, it will be him. Still, it leaves my nerves stretched and I take a few deep breaths while I prepare the pizza bases. I make a variety, and if there are any leftovers, we can have them for lunch tomorrow.

I hear voices in the lobby of them returning, so I place the pizzas in the oven and set the timer.

"I'm in the kitchen," I call out to them.

"Something smells good. Did you cook dinner?" Rafe asks, entering the kitchen.

"I did. Pizza. They'll be ready in twenty minutes." My breath catches like it always does when I see him now. I'm not used to the bubble of excitement that threatens to burst through every pore. Normally, I relish the feeling, but today it just makes me more highly strung than a violin. Does he look slightly nervous? No, maybe not. It is definitely my nerves.

"Thank you, I'm starving." He fetches a beer from the fridge. "How are you feeling?" He comes over to me and I'm hyper-aware of his presence. "Was it awful with your father?"

"As bad as could be expected. He threatened to send my sister over to drag me home."

"That seems harsh." Concern creases his brow, and I wonder what it would be like to be in his arms. I could do with a hug right now. I could ask, but I don't. Instead, I apply myself to setting out plates.

"I think there might be something else going on, so I called in a favour."

"Oh?"

"I'll tell you as soon as I can, I promise," I say with a sly smile, receiving a little laugh in return.

"Wow, what is that delicious smell?" Constantin appears in the doorway. Rafe stiffens next to me. He doesn't move or look around at Constantin, who is also taking a beer from the fridge. Constantin doesn't look at Rafe either, and barely even looks at me. The hairs on the back of my neck rise. Something is off here; I can sense it. Did they argue? I thought I heard them talking in the lobby, so it can't be that. But something is definitely different. I look between them, but neither of them says a word, and Rafe still hasn't moved.

"Okay, what's going on?" I ask.

"Nothing," Constantin says. Taking a swig of his beer, he momentarily meets my eyes. I know that look. I've seen it plenty of times before. *Guilt.*

I back off a couple of paces so I can keep them both in my eyeline.

"What happened?"

"I said nothing," Constantin almost growls.

"You know you're a lousy liar, don't you?" I say peevishly.

I flick my eyes to Rafe, who is worrying his bottom lip, refusing to speak. My stomach drops to the pit of my core and nausea takes its place. Whatever this is, I know I'm not going to like it.

"Tell. Me. What. Happened." I spit out, folding my arms and waiting for an answer.

Rafe turns to look at Constantin. A flash of anguish crosses his face and a silent question passes between them.

Constantin shrugs and Rafe deflates slightly.

He turns back to me and takes a deep breath.

"Um, we kissed."

I feel like I've been punched straight in the stomach. My legs can no longer hold me up and I sag onto a stool.

"*Noooooooooooo!*" I wail loudly.

It wasn't supposed to happen this way. I thought Rafe was growing to like me. Me! I've wanted to kiss him for so long, but I've held back, waiting, finding a level of patience I never knew I had. And then Constantin just swoops in and takes him from under my nose. I don't stop to think that Rafe might have something to do with it. No, it's all Constantin's fault.

I try to blink back tears, but they fall anyway.

"Are you all right?" Constantin moves to my side and places a hand on my shoulder. I shrug it off violently and he backs off slightly from my glare.

I can hardly breathe with the crushing in my ribcage. How could he do this to me? The final wire holding me together snaps and my heart falls, shattering at my feet. Anger pours through the hole in my chest.

"No, I am not all right," I grind out. "I'm very far from all right. Everything is ruined. You've destroyed everything. Rafe. Was. Mine. He was mine."

"I kind of thought you were joking," Rafe says quietly.

"No, I was definitely not joking." I round on Rafe this

time. "Who wouldn't want to kiss you? Have you looked at yourself recently? With your British accent, your golden eyes, and soft hair. Your sexy-as-fuck tan—"

My outburst is cut off as he takes the two steps that separate us and cups each side of my face in his warm hands, fusing his lips to mine.

It isn't soft either; it's hard and grasping and primal. I can hardly breathe, but I don't want it to stop. He takes from me, his tongue searching and exploring, and I give to him. There's no way I can resist. Whatever I was expecting kissing Rafe to be like, it wasn't this, and I'm very glad I was wrong about that. He deepens the kiss, his teeth grazing my tongue and making my head swim with pleasure. He's taken my anger, and as he eventually slows, the soft tenderness kindles a new hope inside me.

I vaguely hear Constantin mutter. "Christ, that is *so* fucking hot."

Rafe pulls back and rests his forehead against mine, his eyes locked onto me and his hands at the back of my neck. His chest heaves as his breath comes in short pants and his face glows with a rosy flush.

For a full minute, there's no sound except our breathing.

The oven timer beeps, breaking the silence, and Rafe releases his hold on me, stepping back slightly.

I stop the noise of the timer and turn back round to face them.

"Sit. Eat. I think you have some explaining to do."

Chapter 22

Rafe

I look at the remains of Florencio's pizzas on the table in front of us. They were as delicious as their aroma promised, and we demolished the lot. We did what Florencio told us to do—we sat and ate. We even managed to talk. Just small talk, though. No one wanted to disturb the essential task of devouring the pizzas. But it was good that we didn't lapse into an uncomfortable silence.

We discussed toppings, and I received various reactions from incredulity to disgust at the English predilection for putting pineapple on pizza.

But now the plates have been cleared away, and Constantin is making coffee, I know I have to say something. I need to try to make sense of it all, but I'm not sure that I can, let alone put it into words.

Constantin places a coffee in front of me and slides back into his seat. Florencio brings his and sits too. I look at them both. Constantin is sullen and withdrawn, and Florencio seems fragile, which is not a look I've seen on him before. It's all my fault, but I have no idea what to say except that I *need* to make it right again.

I'm confused by what's happening to me, while exhilarated and terrified at the same time.

I take a deep breath and decide to just tell the truth.

"I'm going to start with an apology. I created a mess, and I don't know what to do. The last week has been incredible for me, being here with both of you, and Estrella has been like nothing I've experienced before. It's made me question a lot of what I thought I knew and where my life has been heading.

"It feels like I'm in a different world; it looks the same but is also so incredibly different. Here, the colours are brighter, the senses are sharper, and there are so many things I want to experience. Florencio, you opened the door for me and invited me through it. When I'm with you, I feel exhilarated. I'm alive, and I want to explore how that makes me feel. Constantin, you make me feel so safe that exploration won't be like jumping off a cliff and free-falling.

"When I woke up this morning, I'd never kissed a guy. And now, I've kissed two. I never meant to hurt anyone, so Flo, I'm so incredibly sorry. I honestly thought you were just flirting with me."

"I *was* flirting with you," he says with a quiver in his voice that breaks something inside me. "I've wanted you since I first saw you. It has taken epic self-control to be patient. I didn't want to rush you because I wanted it to be special. I was flirting to see if you would ever be interested in me." His eyes are glistening on the edge of tears.

Shit, this was much worse than I thought.

"It worked, Flo, it really did." I reach for his hand, relieved when he doesn't snatch it away.

"Then why Constantin?" he says, his eyes flicking over to where Constantin just watches.

"He asked."

Hurt flashes in Florencio's eyes. I'm being clumsy with my words. "What, so it would have been that easy all along?" His voice is dull, without his normal beautiful tones.

"No, it wouldn't. If anyone had asked me even a week ago, I would have thought the notion ridiculous. But you've both changed my outlook and expanded my universe. I'm like a butterfly emerging from a chrysalis, and I'm curious about the world you're showing me. For too long, I've lived a small life, always saying no. I want to say yes, to see where that takes me. Constantin asked, and I said yes."

"So what happens now?"

I take another deep breath. This is the part that has been on my mind throughout dinner and I could easily break this whole situation.

"I still have much I want to experience and a lot to learn, and I'd like you both to teach me."

Florencio frowns. "So you're experimenting, and then what? One day, you get to choose one of us? No thank you!" This time he does pull his hand away, and I curse inwardly.

"No, that's not what I'm saying. I'm trying to tell you I don't want to choose."

I pause. I'm out of words.

Constantin leans closer to Florencio.

"Two weeks ago, a guy walked into my bar. He was funny, so damn pretty, and sexy as hell. Then he struck up a conversation with a guy I'd just met the previous day, one that was beautiful and smart and intense."

Florencio raises his head slightly, and a spark of something indecipherable crosses his face. "Go on."

"Well, before long, I couldn't get these guys out of my

head. Not *one* of them, *both* of them together. They plagued my thoughts.”

“I knew it! I knew you’d been watching us,” Florencio says with a note of triumph in his voice.

“Yeah, I’m not proud of some of those thoughts.” Constantin gives a half smile. “But what happened today was spontaneous. It was an opportunity I took because the moment was right.” He reaches a hand out to the back of Florencio’s neck, his thumb caressing his cheek. “Given the opportunity, I’d kiss the pretty guy too.”

“But of course,” Florencio says, drawing a huff of a laugh from Constantin, as if it’s natural that everyone would want to kiss him. Then he takes a deep breath. “I need to think about this.”

Constantin moves back out of his space, and I get up to make more coffee. No one speaks for a while, and I try not to look at him so he doesn’t think I’m staring, but when I take a peek, his face is edged with anxiety.

“What’s wrong?” I ask.

He sighs loudly. “All I can think about is that if I leave the room, you two will kiss again.” He swings his gaze between us.

Oh, I wasn’t expecting that.

“We won’t,” I say, but it’s Constantin that gets up.

“I have some paperwork to do for the insurance, so I’m going to leave you two to talk.” He doesn’t wait for a response before going out the door.

Florencio stands. “I want to be alone for a while,” he says and leaves too.

Left alone, the silence is deafening, and the walls seem to crowd around me. Needing some air, I walk through the house and out onto the terrace. This morning, I felt free and full of possibilities, a life to live anew. Now I just feel like I’ve created a tangled mess.

Chapter 23

Florencio

"How could they? How could they?"

The words have been reverberating round my head for the last hour, and I can't seem to make them stop. Every time a rational thought tries to push through, "How could they?" shines like a neon sign across my mind. Can't they see that Rafe is mine? That I'm the one who's in love with him?

In love.

The words brand themselves across my heart.

I knew I'd fallen way too deep, but is it love? I think back to our first dinner when Constantin explained what it was to be in love. I thought it was a wonderful notion, one for other people, and I was immune to it. But now the words are there, and I can't take them back. I can't push them back into the depths of my heart.

When Constantin gave his grandiose speech, he didn't give the whole picture. He didn't say how much it hurts.

I curl up in a ball on my bed, trying to make sense of it all.

I feel drained. Maybe I should go back to Buenos Aires. Perhaps it would be better to go back home. Forget about Rafe and everything here. Go back to being the dutiful son to my family, finding pleasure in casual hookups for the rest of my life. But even as I think it, the thoughts turn bitter and I know I don't want to go back to that same existence as before. I, too, have felt a shift being here, not just with Rafe, but with life.

A knock on my door startles me.

"Who is it?"

"Constantin."

I let out a deep breath, waiting three seconds before replying. "Come in."

He enters. The room is mostly dark, just a lamp on the dresser is lit. He sits down on the bed behind me.

"I came to see if you're still mad at Rafe."

"No, I'm not mad at him." I sigh, uncurling and turning over to look at him.

"But you blame me, don't you?"

"Yes," I say bluntly, but even when the word leaves my mouth, I know it's not true. "No, I don't. Not really. It just feels unfair. I feel like a kid who's spent ages saving up for a toy only to see it sold to someone else just as he reaches the toy shop."

"Are you calling Rafe a toy?" He snorts.

"Your attempt at humour is terrible."

"So was your analogy." It's a fair point, but his saying it doesn't help.

"Can't I just wallow in misery in peace?" It comes out as a whine.

"You have it that bad, huh?"

"*Urgh*, is it that obvious?" I curl up again as if that offers me any protection from my feelings, but I don't turn away from him.

"Why don't you tell him how you feel?" he asks.

"I can't. You saw him. He's trying to process a lot of changes in his life, trying to work out who he is. I don't want to weigh him down with my feelings."

"And I thought I was supposed to be the romantic one." His mouth lifts at the corners.

"That sounds tragic, not romantic to me."

"Giving someone space to figure everything out, to let them become who they're meant to be? I'd say that's romantic."

"I just thought it would feel different." I shrug.

"I understand. This is all pretty new for me too. Do you know today is the first time I've kissed someone in ten years?"

"Um, no. Wow."

"I had thought it would never happen again. I didn't even want it to. Being a widower at thirty-two, I accepted it was just my lot in life. I run a bar. I've seen a lot of guys over the last ten years. But not a single one of them caught my attention."

"Surely you've been propositioned?"

"I have, but none of them ever sparked enough interest for me to take them up on their offers."

"Not even a hookup?"

"No."

"So, you've not—"

"My sex life, or lack of it, is not up for discussion right now," he growls, which I admit is very attractive. I laugh at the thought that before I came to Spain, if anyone had growled at me like that, I'd have been on my hands and knees offering up my arse for them to do whatever they wanted with it. But not now. Have I changed so much?

"My sex life isn't funny," he protests.

"I wasn't laughing at you. It was just a memory," I say, and he seems to accept my explanation.

"What I'm trying to say is that after a very long dry spell, you two have awakened something in me I thought was lost forever. It came as a shock to me that I'm attracted to you both . . . a lot."

I sigh. "I just don't know what to do. I don't want to feel left out. I don't want to be unchosen."

"No one says you have to be," he says softly, raising his hand and brushing my hair away from my eyes. It feels comforting, but then he pauses as if he's just realised what he's doing.

"Don't stop," I whisper and he resumes.

"There are no guarantees in this world. We never know what life is going to throw at us. Maybe we have to take chances as they come along, or we might never experience the joy this world has to offer."

"Or we could not take any chances and just protect ourselves from the heartache."

"That seems a sad and lonely way to live to me. Joy and sadness are two sides of the same coin, but until we toss it, we don't know which side it's going to land on."

I raise myself up and scoot closer to him. He put his arms round me, and I lean into his broad chest. The steady beat of his heart feels solid as he envelops me in a safe warmth. His lips graze across my forehead.

"What do you want to do now?" he whispers into my hair.

"I want to see Rafe," I say against his chest. I feel him nod and release his hold slightly.

I look up at him. "You won't tell him, will you? About what I said?"

He frowns at the thought of it. "It's not mine to tell." Then he gently kisses my forehead before letting his arms fall and allowing me to get up.

"Thank you," I say as he also stands.

"You're welcome. I hope I've helped."

"I think so."

"What about me?" he says as I close the bedroom door.

"I still haven't made my mind up," I say. It's the truth, as I want to talk to Rafe first.

"Take all the time you need," he answers before turning back to his own room. The implication of what he said only reaches me as I'm halfway down the stairs.

I find Rafe on the terrace looking out over the city. I stop in the doorway, just watching him for a minute. I don't think I'll ever tire of watching him, but I can't put this off forever.

"Hey," I say as I stand next to him, catching his citrus and vanilla scent on the slight breeze.

"*Hola,*" he replies. That he's still practising his Spanish makes my stomach flip.

"I'm sorry," I say. "I overacted. You're free to kiss whomever you want. It's none of my business. It's just that I wanted it to be me."

He turns to face me. "I'm sorry too. I never planned any of this. I just have these huge feelings inside me and I needed to let them out."

"I . . . I like you a lot, Rafe, but I don't know where I stand. I don't know how to make any sense of this. I'm normally a one-and-done kind of guy, but I don't want that with you."

"I like you too. A lot. And I also like Constantin." He closes his eyes for a second before continuing. "I'm not playing the field, trying to decide between you. What I'm asking is that we explore this together, all of us. To be honest, it scares the hell out of me, but in here—" He thumps his chest with his fist. "It feels right, and nothing has ever felt this right in my life. I want to trust that and see where it goes."

I can't help but admire his sincerity and I want more than anything to be with him. That's not even an option for me.

He lets out a small, mirthless chuckle. "And as for where anything actually goes, well, I can't get my head round that right now either. But I'd like you to guide me and teach me—both of you." He looks so earnest, and I smile because there couldn't be a more Rafe-like expression for asking for help on how to figure out sex. I definitely want to help him with those lessons. I catch a fleeting thought that Constantin would be part of it, and I think back to how it felt when he held me a few minutes ago. I understand what Rafe says when he says he feels safe with him. He exudes that in bucketfuls. I could do with more of that in my life . . . and maybe I can get him to growl again. The thought of it sends a shiver down my spine.

Rafe has turned back to stare out across the skyline and a memory comes back to me.

"Do you know it is on this spot, the first time you came for dinner, that I decided I wanted to kiss you?"

He faces me, his eyes widen, and he smiles. "Back then?"

"Yes, and every time I've seen you since."

I move closer to him. So close that I can feel his breath on my cheek.

"Can we have a do-over on that first kiss?" I whisper. "I want to try again."

"Yes." His breath hitches slightly.

I push him back against the balustrade and he puts his hands on my hips, pulling me closer. His lips are soft, and I take my time tasting each in turn. As I press my lips to his, he opens for me, and I slowly explore him with my tongue. He moans against my mouth, and I thrust in deeper.

I reach up and tangle my fingers in his hair, gently pulling his head back and moving to kiss down his neck to find that sweet spot in the hollow of his neck. As he moans again, I utter "*bien*" against his skin, enjoying the way his body melts into me and he hums with pleasure. I work my way back up his throat and devour his beautiful lips again.

"That was perfect," he says breathlessly as we part, and I give him a grin. It was pretty perfect for me too.

His attention moves and he looks over my shoulder. I twist and see Constantin framed by the doorway. I wave him over.

"How long have you been there?"

"Long enough." His voice is low and husky and I feel a thrill that he's been watching us.

Rafe doesn't say anything and I get the feeling he's waiting for me. I open up an arm.

"Come and join us for a hug." I invite Constantin into a three-way hug. He steps forward and puts his arms round both of us. I lean into his warmth and Rafe leans his head on his shoulder, all the while looking at me. I see him mouth the words "thank you" to me. I still don't know if I'm doing the right thing, but it doesn't feel wrong, so I will trust in that and see what happens.

After a minute, I look up at Constantin. "Do you feel like playing? Because I feel like dancing."

Chapter 24

Constantin

The night air is cool on my skin, a welcome sensation after the heat of the day. I couldn't sleep and needed some air so I've come outside, only wearing my boxer shorts. I didn't bother putting more clothes on, since I don't expect to meet anyone else at this hour of the night. The only light comes from the glowing end of my cigarette. I've tried to give up, but it doesn't matter what Estrella says, it's not that easy. Over the last week, I've worked on cutting down, but it's been a roller coaster of a day and I need something to help me relax so I can get some sleep. I finish it and contemplate another when I hear a noise behind me. I twist my head to look over my shoulder, but I can't see who it is silhouetted against the faint light now showing behind him inside.

"You couldn't sleep either?" he says in Spanish. It's Florencio.

"No, I thought some air would help," I say, and he walks

over to where I'm standing. He turns and hoists himself up to sit on the flat stone wall I'm leaning against.

He draws a leg up, wrapping an arm round it, and rests his cheek on his knee. "Is it helping?"

I give a derisive snort. "Not really."

He, too, is just wearing shorts. In the light now spilling out of the house and across the terrace, I catch sight of his lean, smooth body. He gives a sly smile; he's caught me looking. It's no bad thing, and after earlier today, I'm glad he doesn't mind that I find him deeply attractive. But it just reminds me of the reason I came out here in the first place.

I look away, unsure of myself.

"What is it?" he asks.

"For half the day I've been elated, but the rest of the time I've just been thinking, 'Con, what are you doing? Do these gorgeous young guys really want a washed-up old dude in their life?' I feel like an old fool."

"How old are you?"

"Forty-two."

"That's not old," he says. I look for amusement or judgement in his warm brown eyes and find none.

"I'm sixteen years older than you, fourteen more than Rafe."

He shrugs as if it means nothing to him.

"Think about it, Florencio. It's a big gap."

"It's not to me, and I'm sure it's not to Rafe, so it's you who has to get their head out of their arse about it," he says.

I sigh. It's true. I really want this to work, so it's something I need to get over. Half of it was worrying what they thought, but if it doesn't bother Florencio and Rafe, then I can't let it bother me either.

I'm startled by a poke in the ribs. "You look good for it as well."

I look down at my body. I guess it's not bad. Lifting crates and moving barrels for the bar keeps me fit enough.

"I like this." He runs his fingers across the smattering of dark hair on my chest. I shiver at his touch. It's been a while since anyone touched me like that. His expression changes to one of compassion, as if he understands why my body reacted that way.

He moves his bent leg and hooks it round me, drawing me over to stand between his thighs.

"I've seen you not hesitate to reach out and comfort Rafe and myself. Who's there to take care of you?"

He plays his fingers up my rib cage and across my chest. It sends little bolts of electricity across my body, making it difficult to concentrate as his touch awakens a long-forgotten pleasure.

I swallow. "That's not actually comforting Florencio."

He gives a little laugh because he knows exactly what he's doing.

"I'm guessing you're a very tactile person and it's sad you haven't had the opportunity for so long." His fingers keep up their soft stroking on my skin, moving them round to my back. I'm struggling hard to keep control. I drop my forehead onto his shoulder and my hands onto his thighs, not thinking too much, just letting my hands drift in a slow rhythm.

I lift my head slightly and press my lips to his shoulder. He tilts his head to give me access. It's an invitation, and I answer. I plant kisses up his neck and across his jaw, and a moment later I find his lips with my own. At first, it's like a soft caress as he gently teases at my lips, leaving me wanting more, then runs his hands up behind my neck and pulls me in deeper. He opens his mouth; another invitation. I push my tongue in, letting it dance with his. I wonder if I can devour him whole when my hands brush fabric. It's soft and silky.

I draw back and look into his glittering eyes.

"Fuck! Florencio, are you wearing silk?"

"Fuck? No, not yet. Silk? Yes, absolutely." I almost whimper. "And Florencio, it's rather a mouthful, don't you think? Rafe's already claimed Flo, so you can think up your own name for me."

"*Are* you a mouthful?" I raise an eyebrow at him and receive an almost feral grin.

"You'll have to find out."

"You're going to be trouble, aren't you?" I laugh, relieved that whatever barriers he had up against me seem to have come down.

"Maybe," he says, giving me a sly smile. "But it'll definitely be fun."

"I'm up for that." I chuckle as I attack his mouth for another kiss.

Chapter 25

Florencio

I wake up feeling like I haven't slept at all, my eyes are gritty, and my mouth feels like I've been sucking on sandpaper.

But worst of all, my head feels like it's full of knotted yarn. I can't seem to unravel it.

Going outside to try to clear my mind last night didn't work, either. I just ended up kissing Constantin. Urgh, no, that's not fair to him. I made the decision to do it. But that's when it got more complicated. For me, at least. Rafe seems to think this is easy, that somehow the three of us are going to work out. But it's not that simple, life never is. It's messy and complex. Actually, he didn't say that. He said he'd like to try, which comes down to the feeling that I don't know what's going to happen, and *that's* the real problem here. The not knowing, it's twisting my insides like they're on a spin cycle.

I've always flirted around anything more serious than one night. Two would be a rarity. But I hadn't even kissed Rafe and I knew he was special, someone I wanted a chance with. And then there's Constantin. I loved how my body responded to him, so that's confusing the hell out of me. Perhaps it's just pent-up frustration. I haven't had sex for a while, after all, much longer than I'm used to. But no, I'm not sure I can use that excuse. Even kissing Constantin feels different, I can't define it, but it's like he needs us too. Messy and complex.

So, who am I doing this for? For Rafe, for Constantin, or myself?

I'm not sure I have the answer, or that it is straightforward, but not having a clear picture of what's going on is eating me up.

I think we all need to have a talk.

I feel better that I've at least made one decision and go in search of the others.

I find Rafe in the kitchen, making pancakes. Or rather, making a mess. He appears to have got flour and batter all over the counter. He spins around when I enter and looks so happy to see me that my heart starts a cadenza in my chest. The effect settles my stomach a little as I walk over to him.

"*Hola*," he says and steps close, so close I can smell his citrus and vanilla scent. He places a hand on my hip and it's all the encouragement I need to kiss him gently.

"Good morning," I say as he releases me and turns back to the stove.

"I'm making breakfast," he says, flipping a pancake in the pan.

"I think we need to talk. All of us." I start helping clean up. He glances at me with a slightly painful expression.

"Oh." He deflates a little. "Why does 'we need to talk' always herald bad news?"

"It's not bad, but it is important," I say and he nods, the happy look gone from his face. I feel bad, of course I do, but we need to do this, or I think I'm going to turn myself inside out.

"Hey," Constantin calls as he walks in. He looks at me with a question on his face. I shake my head slightly, confirming that I haven't told Rafe we kissed last night. He makes for the coffee machine instead of coming over, and I breathe a small sigh of relief.

"Breakfast is nearly ready," Rafe says over his shoulder at Constantin, who grunts a "good" in return.

Rafe places a stack of pancakes on the table. There is fruit, syrup, and honey to add to them. Constantin brings us coffee and we sit and eat.

"These are good," Constantin says as he swallows a forkful of his first pancake. He's not wrong, they are delicious. Rafe's smile is halfway to returning.

"I was thinking we need to talk about how we're going to make this work," I say, mostly directing my speech to Constantin this time.

"I agree," he replies, but his voice is hopeful.

Rafe looks up from chasing the last bit of pancake round his plate and looks between us. "Did I miss something?"

"I've thought long and hard about what you're asking of us, and I'd like to try too," I say, trying for casual.

"The three of us?" His face lights up once again and I feel it's the right time to own up.

"I couldn't sleep last night, so I went outside to get some air. Constantin had the same idea. We talked and we kissed." I pause and watch him closely, trying to gauge his reaction. Because if, when it comes down to it, he can't cope with the thought of us kissing, then this could all be over before it even starts. I hold my breath as his face changes into a big smile.

"This is good, isn't it?"

"I don't know," I say, and he frowns at me slightly.

"Rafe, you've drawn us into your orbit, but I need to know what trajectory we're on."

I take a deep breath, preparing myself for the next part. Considering that I'm usually very blasé about sex, this is not a conversation I've tried to have before, but then, this is new territory for all of us.

"We just kissed, but what if we'd wanted to do more? What then? Would that be okay or not okay? I feel like we need to know what our . . . your expectations are here, so we can explore this together without hurting each other."

His face creases slightly and he worries his bottom lip as he thinks about what I've said.

"Oh, yes. I see what you mean. I hadn't thought of that, had I?"

I don't want to point out the understatement of the century, so instead I reply.

"This is why it's important we discuss it now."

His gaze bounces between us before he runs a hand through his hair. "Okay, how do we do this?"

I stall. Now I've got this far, I don't know how to proceed. I'm used to a culture where you kiss whomever you want, you have sex with whomever takes your fancy. Hurt doesn't factor into it, because nothing ever reaches below the surface. My reaction yesterday surprised me, and I don't want that to happen again.

Constantin reaches across the table for Rafe's hand, and then he takes mine. His hand is large and warm. It's comforting. He gives mine a squeeze and I hope it means that he understands me a little.

"When Florencio told you we'd kissed yesterday, how did that make you feel? What was your immediate thought?"

He doesn't even hesitate with his reply.

"I felt a burst of happiness. I was worried you two wouldn't like each other. I'm glad it happened."

I try not to snort at how his reaction was the polar opposite of mine but fail, receiving a small frown from Rafe and another squeeze from Constantin. He continues. "So, let's stick with kissing for a minute. Are you saying you don't mind if any one of us kisses the other?"

"I'm okay with it," he says.

"Good. I'm fine with it, though I'd rather watch." Constantin gives a little chuckle. "Florencio?"

I swallow round the knot in my throat. It would be hypocritical for me to say I'm not happy about it, considering what I did last night. But that isn't the problem here.

"Kissing isn't an issue for me. What I'm more worried about is exclusion. One pair of us drawing away from the other one." Or rather Rafe and Constantin becoming something more and me not being a part of it. That's at the root of my turmoil. "That's where we have the capacity to hurt each other, and it's what scares me." I know as I say it, I can't predict what might happen, nor can I be the keeper of anyone's heart but my own, but at least I've voiced my fears.

Rafe's fingers find mine, and he interlaces them, giving me a tentative smile.

"Can we agree that if any of us feel excluded, we can voice it and talk about it?" I'm not so naïve as to think this is the perfect solution. Life doesn't work like that, but I need to believe that it can. I need to believe this will work, or the anxiety will never cease.

"Yes, I can agree with that," Constantin says.

"I agree," Rafe adds. "Is it like a pact?"

"Of sorts, I suppose, as long as I don't have to sign in blood," Constantin says with a grimace. My mouth twitches, and my nerves are still frayed, but the roiling in my stomach is easing.

"There are other bodily fluids," I can't help quip and Constantin laughs, relieving some of the tension. We release hands and I reach for my coffee, pulling a face at how cold it is.

"That's the other question here. What about when we want to take things further?" Constantin asks. "What do we want to agree on here?"

This time Rafe chimes in. "I think for now we only go there when we're all present?"

"Is that practical?" I ask, trying to think up all the scenarios I can and giving up almost immediately as there are too many.

"Or as a pair, but checking in with the other first and gaining consent?" he queries and Constantin nods. That seems about as fair and workable as we can make it. Even though I wanted this discussion, it's starting to feel a bit clinical to me.

"Well, I hope I haven't killed any spontaneity now." I grimace.

"I don't think so," says Constantin. "I think it helps. At least we won't be second-guessing ourselves."

"Oh, look at the time!" Rafe jumps up. "I'm due to meet Estrella and I'm five minutes late." He leaves the room in a whirlwind.

"Have I done the right thing?" I muse when Constantin and I are left alone.

"There's nothing wrong with stating your feelings and wanting to make sure they're protected," he says, getting up. "I need to get down to the bar. I'll see you later." He stops as he passes behind my chair and places one of his large, warm hands on my shoulder. I look up into his dark eyes.

"It will be all right." I know he can't promise that, but I appreciate him recognising the need to say it.

"Thanks," I say, and then because I need to move past this. "You stole his first kiss, so I call dibs on the first blow job."

His eyes swirl darker, and he leans down close to my ear, his voice husky. "That's all right, because I'll be watching."

Chapter 26

Rafe

I read through the document on the desk in front of me and then look up at Estrella.

"Are you sure about this?"

She's sitting behind the large wooden desk, which belongs to another era just like the rest of the room and the lady who owns it. I've not been in this room before, but it seems to be an office of sorts. Along with the desk that sits in the centre of the room, there are several chairs, a couch, and four tall wooden cabinets. One of them is glass-fronted and contains a number of trophies. There are only a few photos on the walls here, but there are several framed awards.

Señor Bernat, her lawyer, a small but efficient-looking gentleman, is sitting next to me, but he hasn't said much apart from being introduced.

"Would it be in the contract if I wasn't serious?" I wilt a little under her gaze, just a little, as I've learned her bark is much worse than her bite and she is actually a very generous person. Letting me stay here in the house is one example of that, and this contract is another.

I'm allowed free access to all her personal diaries and photograph albums. I thought I would have to interview her to get my information, or have some limited access to documents, not to read her innermost thoughts. That is surprising enough in itself. But also that she wants no share of any royalties. There is a requirement that a small percentage go to a charity here in Barcelona, but I don't recognise the name.

"Is there anything you don't want me to write about?" I ask. I would respect her wishes if there were a subject that she felt was too private, even though those are usually the parts that really sell books.

"No, that's written into the contract, too. I don't have any really interesting skeletons in my closet." She laughs, and I double-check the document to find it.

To me, it looks all in order, but I'm not an expert. I know who can help me, though.

"Do you mind if I get this checked?"

"I would think you were lacking if you didn't," she says in her blunt way.

Señor Bernat also answers.

"Of course, have anyone you want to look it over. Shall I return tomorrow?" This last question he directs to Estrella. "I will bring the other papers for you to sign."

He rises and we shake hands before he takes his leave of Estrella.

"Now that I've got used to the idea of this biography, I think I'm going to enjoy it," she says. Getting out of her chair, she finds her walking stick and goes to one of the cabinets. She beckons me over.

"I wanted to show you these." She pulls a set of keys out of the pocket of her light cardigan and unlocks the door.

Inside are row upon row of notebooks, journals, and diaries. There are hundreds of them, all neatly shelved.

"These are my diaries," she explains and then points to a row of larger tomes. "Those are all my press cuttings."

"I, um." It's incredible and exciting but also a little overwhelming now I'm looking at them. "I thought I'd be interviewing you."

"You can, but I don't have the time or energy to tell you everything, so you can read these and then ask me what you need to. I think it will be quicker this way, don't you?"

A thought strikes me, one I hadn't considered before, but now seems glaringly obvious.

"Are they all in Spanish?"

"Of course." She looks at me with a beaming smile, while a knot forms in the pit of my stomach. I'm not sure about quicker. I'm going to have to really work on improving my Spanish. She's eyeing me as if she's waiting for my reaction and I can't help but wonder if she deliberately set me the challenge.

"Can Florencio and Constantin help me translate?"

"If they want to." I gain another smile from her. I hope they'll be willing to assist me. I'll ask them as soon as I've sent the contract off. I collect it from the desk and head straight to my room.

I carefully scan each page with my phone and then email them off, following it up with a phone call to my father.

"Hello son, this is a nice surprise." I pull a face at his tone, acknowledging my own failings in not getting in touch very often, glad it's not a video call. Also, I'm calling him at work rather than in the evening when I would normally phone for a catch-up.

I fill him in quickly on the project and the email I sent him.

"Are you sure this is wise?" he asks, and I bite back a terse reply. I know he asks out of concern, but I'm tired of always feeling like I have to justify myself to him. Urgh. So I clamp my jaw and count to five.

"It's a great project, Dad. It's what I want to do." Not outright lies, but I'm used to giving them contorted versions of the truth. I hear a little sigh, and I don't think for a minute he believes me, but he agrees to look over the contract for me that evening and call me back. Having a lawyer as a father does have its advantages.

I thank him and ring off. Now for the more difficult conversation.

"You're doing what?" Helen's shrill voice almost pierces my eardrum and I hold the phone away from my face. It's the response I expected, though, so I'm not surprised.

"Yes, as soon as the contract has been checked, I'm making a start."

"Have you gone completely mad?"

"I don't know, have I?" It's perhaps not a question I should ask, but it does take some of the wind out of her sails and she stops yelling.

"I don't know what's got into you," she says more in her normal tone. "It's like you're deliberately trying to be the most unsellable author on my books."

"This isn't about you, Helen," I reply. "It's about doing something that feels right." This is really all I'm trying to do in my life.

"I can't sell this, Rafe," she says, her disappointment clear. I skip the part where I could point out that she couldn't sell my Blackwater series either. I'm not that mean, but I'm also not going to back down on this.

"Maybe the problem isn't me then," I say and ring off, aware I might just have lost my agent. The thought doesn't bother me as much as it would've a few months ago. For now, I'm going to concentrate on writing this book and worry about trying to sell it later.

My stomach rumbles, and I realise how late it's getting. I also haven't seen Florencio and Constantin for most of the morning. I miss them and want to ask for their help with the diaries.

I go in search of them and find Florencio in the kitchen, turning what look like small pasties in a cast iron pan.

I snake my arms round him, and he turns his head for a kiss. It feels easy and I'm happy Flo initiated the talk we all had this morning. I'd got caught up in the expansiveness of my own horizons and was careless about how the others would deal with it. That they haven't told me I'm being ridiculous is a huge relief, and the large feeling in my chest keeps growing even if they have brought me back down to earth.

"They smell delicious," I say, reaching around him to try to sneak one out of the pan.

"Hey!" He hits my hand with the spatula.

"I can't help it. I'm starving, and they look so good."

"Give me five minutes and they'll be ready."

"Hmm, if I have to. What are they?" I grumble.

"Empanadas." They still look like little pasties to me.

"You know I'd pay good money for your cooking, though I'm glad I don't have to. I'm already poor."

He spins round. "Say that again."

"I'm poor."

"No, not that, the other thing."

"I'd pay for your food?" I ask.

"Yes, that. Would you? Do you think people would pay? For my food?"

"Absolutely. I'm not an expert, but it's miles better than most of the food I've had since I've been here. Lucky me."

"Maybe that's it!" he says excitedly. "My way of not having to rely on my father."

"That's great," I reply, and his excitement is infectious. "But how?"

"I don't know yet, but there has to be something I can do."

"Um, what about doing something with those?" I point to the pan, which is smoking slightly, just as a burning smell hits my nostrils.

"*Puta madre!*" he exclaims, rescuing the empanadas, which are only a little burnt around the edges. "Look what you made me do."

"Me?"

"Yes, distracting me with your good ideas."

"I'm pretty sure I didn't do anything."

He eyes the empanadas cooling on the plate with a look of distaste, as if their presence offends him. I pick one up and take a bite, blowing over the filling to cool it enough to eat. It's amazing . . . if I ignore the very slightly burnt bits.

"Noooo. You have to dip them." He almost takes it out of my hand, but I whisk it out of his reach. He's not taking my food from me. "Here in the chimichurri I made."

I dutifully dip it in the herby sauce.

"Mmmmm, okay, that takes it to a whole new level."

"Told you." He looks smug.

"So, what was it you said when you burnt them? Put mad where?"

He laughs. *"Puta madre."*

"Puta madre," I repeat. "What does it mean?"

"Madre is mother, and *puta* basically means whore."

"Oh, I'm definitely using that. I'll remember *madre* and *puta* . . . she puts out for money." I laugh and Florencio giggles.

"What's so funny?" Constantin enters carrying a box of beer, which he sets down near the fridge.

"Flo is teaching me swear words in Spanish."

"Is he?" He comes over and leans down for a quick kiss before turning to Florencio for the same. I like this greeting much more than the traditional cheek kiss.

"Yes, today I've learnt *puta madre.*"

Constantin snorts a laugh then spies the plate of empanadas and makes to grab one. He gets the spatula across the hand treatment as well.

"Get off, these are for lunch."

"But I'm hungry now and it's almost lunchtime," Constantin grumbles.

"You know I'm starving," I say and Florencio sighs.

"All right, give me ten minutes to cook the rest of them and we can have lunch."

Whilst he finishes them off, I help Constantin put the beer in the fridge and ask him how the repairs to the bar are going.

"There's been a delay. The builders have been let down for some of the materials so they are trying to get them from elsewhere. They hope it won't take too long, but it's frustrating and there's nothing I can do about it," he says glumly.

I guess he's not used to having no control over all aspects of his bar. I hope I can take his mind off it with the diaries.

The second batch of empanadas didn't get burnt and are

even tastier than the first—if that's possible—and they all get eaten, even the blackened crispy ones.

Florencio eyes the empty plates with a mixture of pride and dismay.

"I was hoping to save some of those. How do you both eat so much?"

"I can't resist your cooking." Constantin sits back and pats his stomach.

"I seem to recall you had just as many as us," I protest and get a grin from Florencio. He knows it's true. "Perhaps you didn't make enough," I say, but in truth, I'm glad he's happy to cook. We'd soon all get bored with pasta every day if I had to cook.

Over coffee, I tell them about the contract for the biography and the diaries. They both readily agree to help me with the translations. They also offer to read some of them when I explain how many there are. I think they're keen to find any juicy gossip, but I'm just grateful for their assistance. I can't wait to get started.

Chapter 27

Florencio

"I think I've found something," Julio says down the phone, his voice hushed.

"What something?" I ask. "And why are you whispering?"

"I'm at work, in the stationery cupboard." He gives a nervous giggle.

"Don't get caught. Call me from home next time," I tell him, worried that he'll get in trouble. He's already risking his job to help me.

"I will, but I wanted to tell you now," he says, lowering his voice. "I've found an anomaly. It might be nothing, but it's interesting enough to follow. I'll call as soon as I can."

He rings off before I can say thank you, so I text it instead and receive a smiley emoji in return.

I take a deep breath. While I'm hoping for some explanation of my father's behaviour, that there could be something seriously wrong makes me nervous. I try not to think of it for the moment. I won't know any more until Julio calls me back, and I'd rather do something positive about my future, so I go to find Juana. I want to talk to her sister.

I blink my eyes open, stretching, and my hand hits the notebook I'd been writing in before I fell asleep. After Juana gave me her number, I called Sofia, who was very helpful and had some good advice. I still don't know how I can turn my love of cooking into a way of sustaining myself, but she offered to let me join her and see what she does. It could be an option for the future.

"Hey." Constantin pokes his head round my open door, looking as sleep-ridden as I do. My door was ajar, and I said if it was open, they were free to disturb me, but if it was shut, to knock.

"Hey. Come on in," I say, inviting him over. He comes and sits next to me on the bed.

"I was going to suggest we could all siesta together." He gives a small, hopeful smile.

"You don't take siestas," I laugh.

"I do when it's very hot in summer. I even open the bar later." He shrugs a little. "It's starting to get warmer, so I was thinking we could start."

"I'd really like that." We could do with some downtime after the last couple of days. Just spend time relaxing together.

"Rafe isn't in his room. I just checked," he says. "I don't think he knows the concept of siestas."

"I don't think he does," I chuckle. "Shall we go find him and convince him of the benefits?"

"All of them," Constantin says, but before he gets up, he

turns back to me with a twinkle in his eye. "I'm pretty sure he has a praise kink, you know?"

"I'm almost certain he has."

"Does he know? Should we tell him?"

"He has no idea," I reply. "And yes, of course, we'll tell him . . . eventually." I grin as I clamber off the bed and head to the door, Constantin's deep laughter following behind.

We finally track him down in a room I've only been in once before, when I explored the house in my first few days in Barcelona. Then, I was awestruck by the photographs on the walls. Now, most of them are no longer on the walls, but arranged in a semi-circle round Rafe, who is sitting amid them on the floor. Constantin sits on a couch opposite him and I flop onto the floor, leaning back between Constantin's legs.

"Hey guys." He looks up at us distractedly. He's clearly in the middle of something.

"Rafe, what are you doing?" I ask.

"Cataloguing all these photos. I want to know what's available in case I can use any of them. Also, they might provide me with some ideas on how to structure the biography, rather than just as a linear timeline. But aren't they beautiful?"

He holds up a picture of Estrella and Richard Burton. "I wonder what Elizabeth Taylor had to say about that?" he remarks and then brandishes another of Estrella, this time with a good-looking gentleman in ambassadorial attire. "He looks swoony, don't you think?"

"Are you lusting after famous dead guys?" Constantin asks, idly running his fingers through my hair. I like it and lean into his touch.

Rafe looks up. "Appreciating their good looks is not lusting."

"It kind of is," I say with a smirk.

"But I've always liked . . . Oh." Rafe giggles as he processes what he's just said.

"Anyway, what person works through siesta?" Constantin asks.

"You don't have siestas." Rafe grins.

"Not yet, but when it gets warmer I do."

"Really?" Rafe looks like he's waiting for the punchline.

"Siestas are so good. They're a chance to rest, or to spend time together."

"We could make our own version," I suggest.

"Like how?" Rafe tilts his head to one side.

"Come over here and I'll show you."

Rafe moves some of the pictures out of the way and crawls over to me, kneeling between my legs.

"Like this?" he asks.

"Closer," I say, and he leans forward. He puts his hands on my shoulders and looks at me with his beautiful smile before I pull him into a kiss. It's needy, and I open my mouth, inviting him in, loving how he responds. His tongue finds mine and they tangle together. I place a hand on the back of his head, deepening the kiss. I feel Constantin shift position on the couch. His hand is still in my hair, his touch becoming electric the more we kiss.

Rafe pulls back, catching his breath. His eyes are soft and dreamy, his lips wet and glistening. His gaze shifts up to Constantin, and in the next second, he kneels up to kiss him too. His groin is right in front of me and my cock starts to thicken in response. His T-shirt lifts, exposing a strip of creamy skin. It's more than I'm capable of resisting and I press a kiss to it. He stretches a little, and I lay open-mouthed kisses across his stomach. I slip a finger into the waistband of his shorts, running it around the top, and I feel him shiver a little. I tip my head back to look up at them. Constantin is right, it *is* hot to watch them. I'm getting harder by the second, and judging by the bulge in Rafe's shorts, I'm not the only one.

Rafe breaks off and looks down at me. I tug a little at the waistband.

"Can I?"

His nod is all the encouragement I need. I ease his shorts down over his hips, freeing his cock. I quickly glance back up to see Rafe attack Constantin with his mouth again. His cock juts out at me. It's long and slim and pretty much perfect like the rest of him. A bead of precum forms at the tip, and I moisten my lips, gently licking it off with my tongue. I hear a little moan and that spurs me on to swirl my tongue round the head before taking the tip into my mouth. He makes another sound, and the thought of him moaning against Con's mouth in response to what I'm doing to him makes me rock hard. I run my hands along his arse, pushing his shorts down further. I squeeze his cheeks and pull him closer, engulfing the whole of him. My nose hits the golden hair at the base and I catch his citrus and vanilla smell, inhaling deeply. I have a fleeting desire to shower with him so I can wash him all over in it. His hips lurch and he thrusts into me. I suck him deeper, helping him find a rhythm as I play my tongue round the base of his cock until his thrusts become too fast. I let him drive into me, fucking my mouth over and over. I become aware of something pressing on the back of my neck; Constantin is as rigid as I am. I shouldn't find that a turn-on, but I do. Rafe's abs tighten, and his buttocks tense under my hands. I play my fingers over his crease as he arches his back and cries out, cum hitting the back of my throat. I hold him there until he starts to sag, and his softening cock slips out.

He manages to hoist himself up onto the couch, lolling against the back, his face blissed out.

"That was . . . That was . . ." He stops stuttering and just smiles. I climb off the floor, my cock aching and desperate for relief. Constantin smiles and I straddle his lap. I reach down and run my hand over his bulge. I was right, he is hard.

"Do you want me to take care of that?" I ask.

"I want you to." He smiles and pulls his shorts down. His cock is thick and framed by dense black hair. I lick my lips despite myself. He tugs me forward and I lift slightly to take my shorts over my hips. He swipes a thumb through my precum, lifting it to his mouth to taste. His eyes glisten and he smiles, then he draws me closer with a hand on my hip until his cock is lined up against mine. His large hand envelops both of us and he starts stroking up and down. Our combined precum doesn't quite provide enough lube, so I spit on my fingers and smear it over our tips, letting his fingers work it down. I roll my hips, going with the movement, enjoying the friction of him moving against me.

"Holy fuck!" Rafe's eyes are wide as he watches us disappear and reappear in Constantin's hand. I reach for him, and he kisses me before dragging his eyes back to where I'm about to spill all over Constantin's hand.

"Gonna come," I utter, feeling the familiar tingle in my spine. I tense, trying to hold off as long as possible.

"Yeah," Constantin says and comes with the next stroke of his hand. I let myself go and follow his release with my own a few seconds later.

I slip off his lap onto the couch, Rafe shifting a little to allow me to sit between them.

None of us speak for a spell. I'm too spent and need a minute. Constantin's head is thrown back, and he looks relaxed.

Eventually, the silence is broken by Rafe.

"Well, that was fucking hot."

Constantin laughs. "I said siestas were good."

Chapter 28

Constantin

"We found this when we were clearing the last of the rubble." The building foreman hands me an ornate box that I instantly recognise.

"Thank you." I try to sound casual, but I hug it close to myself protectively. I listen to the rest of his progress report with only half an ear, my thumb playing over the corner of the box lid that looks to have been broken.

The work is going well, and they plan to be finished in just under two weeks' time, with a new boiler being fitted next week. Then I can get in and clean everything properly. The entire bar area will need a deep clean and I dread to think what my apartment looks like. The foreman clears me for going up there, now that the building is structurally sound and the staircase and floor have been rebuilt.

I encounter a couple of workmen. One is plastering the new walls in the hallway, whilst the other is working in the bathroom, getting ready for the new bathroom suite that's being installed in a few days. I'm pleased that despite the delays they've had with some materials, the schedule isn't far off the plan. Provided nothing else goes wrong, I'll be able to open in three weeks' time.

I walk through into my bedroom and shut the door behind me. I look around in dismay. Although this room hadn't been affected by the collapse, there's still a layer of dust covering every surface. I can't even strip the bed and wash the bedding until the new boiler is in place. I sit on the bed anyway and place the box on my knee. Now I can look properly, I see that a corner of the lid has broken off, the wood splitting along the grain. If it had been in here, instead of on the small bookcase I had in the hallway, it would never have been damaged. I turn it over, relief washing through me that the rest of it is intact.

I set it back down on my knees, but I don't open it. Instead, I trace the carvings on the lid with my finger. Valery made the box for me, for our first anniversary of being together. He was always practical, wanting to learn new skills. He'd attended a woodworking course for several weeks and returned one day with this small wooden box. I loved it instantly. The sides are sanded perfectly smooth and waxed, so they have a silky finish that shows off the beautiful patterns in the grain of the walnut. The lid is thick and has intricate carvings of Flor de Mayo, May's flower, the national flower of Gran Canaria. The delicate petals are exquisitely carved. I cease my fingers' movement and remember his face when I opened it, his pleasure in my enjoyment. He was like that. He loved giving me things just to watch me open them or unwrap them. Many of the things he gave me are in the box—some more carved pieces, including a small bird, a guitar, and a peach.

There's a large stack of photographs, including lots of Polaroids. Valery loved the instant camera and there are a myriad of pictures of us together here in Barcelona, at the Park Güell, as well as on trips back home to Gran Canaria. I've kept every hand-written note he made. He loved to create little sayings or pictures and leave them in places for me to find. There are postcards of some of our favourite places as well as a few poems. I chuckle at being called romantic. Valery was always far more romantic than me.

Also, there are treasures in the box. The most special are our wedding rings. I took mine off after he died and reunited them on a chain and kept them in a small ring box laid amongst the other keepsakes.

My fingers reach for the brass catch, but I stall. I used to spend hours taking out the contents of the box and sitting amongst the photographs, reliving all our moments together. But it never did anything but keep me locked in the box with the memories. I don't want to get caught up in the melancholy anymore. My thoughts turn to Rafe and Florencio and how much has changed over the last few weeks. How I've felt lighter and no longer wake up feeling like I have nothing to look forward to. I know I can never fall in love again, but with them, I feel on the brink of something good. A sense of belonging that I've not felt in ten years.

I let go of the catch and hold the box for a minute, tapping a tango rhythm with my fingers. Leaving it closed, I rise and walk to the closet. I store it on a shelf out of sight, the safest place I have at the moment. It will never stop being important to me, but right now I want a brighter future.

With a spring in my step, I start the walk back up to the Pedralbes district and Estrella's mansion. I'm looking forward to seeing Rafe and Florencio again.

Florencio

Rafe almost bounces into my room with a sheaf of papers in his hand.

"This is it. I signed. I can now officially start your aunt's biography." He lets out a whoop and falls back on the bed.

He turns his head to look at me. "I'm going to grab some of her diaries and make a start."

"Now?" I ask, crawling over to him.

"It's going to take me a long time to translate them from Spanish." He stops, wrinkling his nose a little and frowning slightly. "Sorry. Did you have other plans?"

"I always have other plans," I say, looking down into his golden eyes, watching his frown turn into a smile.

He reaches for me, letting the papers tumble to the ground as our lips meet. It's a short and sweet kiss and I pull away, wanting to gaze at him some more.

I trail my fingers down his cheek, across his jaw, and down his throat, watching him swallow expectantly, waiting for me to make a move. It would be too easy to start something I can't stop, and I remember the rules we made, the ones I wanted. So instead, I smirk.

"I'll come and help you with the diaries for another kiss."

He agrees, and this time, I start where my fingers are at the hollow of the base of his neck. No one said it had to be a quick kiss. I take my time working my way back up his throat, murmuring along his jaw before finally finding his mouth, revelling in how needy he is as he kisses me back, how he responds to me keeping him waiting. I part us, just for a second to whisper *"muy bien"* against his lips, hearing him moan as I kiss him again. I need to stop now, or I won't be able to, and I *did* promise. Reluctantly, I stop and disentangle myself from his arms. What I want to do to him can wait. For now.

He sits up and wipes a hand across his lips.

"I never knew kissing could be so . . ." He pauses, searching for the right word. "Erotic?"

I glance down and see a definite bulge in his shorts. I tear myself away before I break my promise and my rules.

"You've got a lot to learn." I chuckle and offer him a hand up. I don't know how much sexual experience he's had before, but it's a little sad that he's just discovering this now. I can't wait to teach him.

"So where are we doing this?" I ask, holding a box full of Aunt Estrella's diaries that we've collected from her.

"In the Hollywood room," Rafe says blithely.

"The Hollywood room?" I have no idea what he's talking about.

He opens the door to the room with all the photographs, which are now mostly back on the walls.

"You named it, right?"

He shrugs. "I thought it appropriate."

It is. "I like it." I eye the couch. It's probably an antique, and I hope we didn't leave any stains on it yesterday. It looks all right, though. I don't think my aunt comes into this room anymore, but still, I don't want to ruin her antiques.

I place the box down on a chair.

"Are you thinking of using this as a workroom?"

"I was, but we could do with a table so I can set my laptop up."

"I've got an idea; be right back." I go in search of my aunt and find her resting in her rooms. We have dinner planned for later, so she's conserving her energy. She tells me where I can find a suitable table and I go back to the Hollywood room, meeting Constantin in the lobby.

"I brought lunch," he says, holding up some paper bags.

"Perfect. Drop them in the kitchen and give me a hand."

"With what?" he asks, following me through the kitchen to a storeroom beyond.

"We're turning the Hollywood room into an office for Rafe."

"The Hollywood room?" He frowns. "Is that the room with the photographs?"

"The very same."

"Did Rafe call it that?"

I just give him a look and he laughs as he picks up his end of the table. "Was he ever really straight?"

"The jury's still out on that one." I hoist the table, and we carry it through to the room.

"Oh, that's perfect," Rafe exclaims when we enter. We set the table down and place a few chairs round it.

"Good. Now come and get the lunch I brought."

"What are you looking for?" Constantin takes one of the diaries and throws himself onto the couch.

"Anything interesting," Rafe says. Then follows it up with, "Okay, that wasn't very helpful, was it?" Constantin snorts.

Rafe rips a couple of pieces of paper off his pad and hands one to each of us.

"First, write down which diary you have and the dates it covers. Then, as you read through it, note any significant events that occur and any important details. Also, jot down people she meets. Hopefully, we can build up a picture of her life and I can use these details to decide the structure of the biography. Then I can use what you've written as an index to find the information for the details."

"That's impressive," I say. "It's like you've done this before."

"Well, not quite on this scale." Rafe laughs.

I grab a diary and settle into one of the large, comfortable chairs. Rafe sits at the table with his laptop, a diary, and a notebook.

We work for a few hours, exchanging a few little quotes. The diaries we're going through are of her early life, and I gain a few interesting facts about her life growing up in Argentina and my own grandparents.

I'm roused from my absorption in the diary by Rafe nudging my foot. I look at him and he tilts his head towards Constantin, who's fallen asleep.

"Should we wake him?" he whispers.

"Is he grumpy when he wakes up, do you think?" He seems like he might be the type.

"There's only one way to find out." Rafe is already walking

over to the couch and kneeling down beside Constantin. I join him.

"Constantin," he says quietly, but there's no movement.

"Constantin." This time he gives a little sing-song voice.

"Mmmm, siesta," he mumbles, barely coherently.

"Ah, I put him to work and didn't let him have his siesta." Rafe giggles quietly. "Does he need more rest, do you think?"

"Maybe, just never say it's because he's old," I warn.

"Constantin, wake up," he says again, but Constantin still doesn't stir. I look around the room, my eyes stopping on a tall vase in the corner with several peacock feathers arranged in it.

I grab one, and standing behind the couch and out of reach, I hover it over his nose.

Rafe looks at me, his eyes alight.

"Do it," he whispers and sits back a bit.

I gently tickle Constantin's nose with the feather. His face scrunches, and he moves his face to avoid it. I tickle his nose again and he cracks an eye open. He sees Rafe first, then catches sight of the feather and me holding it beyond.

"*Gilipollas,*" he growls.

"What did he call us?" Rafe asks.

"He said we're arseholes, and he's definitely a grump when waking."

He sits up and glares at us, his face still sleep-mussed. "I wasn't asleep," he protests.

"Oh. So you heard us discussing how handsome you looked then?" Rafe presses his lips together in silent laughter.

"*Gillipollas,*" he utters again, but there's no bite to it, and he gives a chuckle. "Have I mentioned how beneficial a siesta is?"

"Several times." Rafe rolls his eyes.

"Well, I don't have time," I say, looking at my watch. "Sofia will be arriving soon."

I'm excited to try some new recipes and learn how she prepares a dinner party for her clients. It's fortunate that Estrella wanted a small dinner party today so I can learn here in a familiar setting. Estrella has invited Señor Bernat and his wife. She's also insisted that Sofia stay to eat, and with Juana there will be eight of us. I give them both a quick kiss and a promise I'll see them soon and head to the kitchen to start preparing the food.

Chapter 30

Rafe

"Sorry, I didn't mean to fall asleep." Constantin rubs the back of his neck.

"It's fine. You weren't asleep long."

"I know." He yawns and stretches. I yawn too.

"Do you need a break?" His mouth quirks up at one corner. I look back at the pile of diaries. We've barely scratched the surface, and there is so much to do, but I was starting to lose concentration. Flo's comment earlier about starting immediately springs to mind. Am I being boring by working all the time? Loretta's taunt echoes round my head.

"I could do with one." I yawn again. The tiredness has crept up on me.

"C'mon." He stands and pulls me up, too. He leads me out of the room and up the stairs.

He opens the door to his room and I stall on the threshold.

"Are we doing anything we need to ask Flo about?" I ask, and he turns to face me.

"Well, I was planning to have a nap." He steps forward into my space. "What did you have in mind?" His voice is deep.

"Sleep?" My own voice sounds high and squeaky.

He cups my cheek and presses a soft, warm kiss on my lips. My stomach flips. If he's going to do that, I might not be able to sleep. He smiles, his dark eyes crinkling at the corners. He walks backwards to the bed, and I allow myself to be pulled along with him. He kicks off his shoes and climbs onto the bed, lying down. I lie down next to him, facing him. He scoots a little closer and kisses me again.

"Turn over," he instructs. When I do, he puts an arm round me and pulls me in close.

"I've never done this before?" I say.

"Done what?" he mumbles into the back of my neck.

"Been the little spoon."

He chuckles and wraps his arm a little tighter. He's warm, and I feel safe with him curled around me. I'm already starting to drift off.

"Well! Is this what happens when I leave you alone for five minutes?"

I blink awake to the sight of Florencio standing over us, his hands on his hips.

"Hey, Flo." I'm still groggy and can't manage more words right now.

"There I am, working hard on dinner when I think, 'I'll make the guys a coffee as I know they're working hard, too.' But then I find the room empty, and when I eventually track you down, you're asleep!"

His mouth is smiling, and his eyes are dancing, though, so I think he's just teasing.

"You brought coffee?" I feel Constantin's low rumble against my back as he peels himself away and sits up, pushing himself back to lean against the headboard. I do the same.

Florencio sits on the side of the bed and hands Constantin a mug, which he clasps in both hands. He takes a long swig and then sighs, tipping his head back and closing his eyes. "That's perfect. You're like an angel, a coffee-bringing angel." He opens his eyes and takes another gulp. "Thanks, Cio."

I look between them and see the smile on Florencio's face.

"Cio?" I ask.

"He said that as you had taken Flo, I had to come up with another name for him."

I don't remember when I started calling him Flo, or even asking him if it was all right. I can be a blundering klutz sometimes. But if he asked Constantin to choose something else, I guess he's fine with it.

"Cio, I like that. But I remember my words were, 'Florencio is a mouthful.' Though from what I've seen, I don't think I'm the mouthful here." He pointedly looks down at Constantin's groin, deliberately licking his lips. The action and look in his eyes make my own cock twitch in memory of those lips round it yesterday. I want more of that . . . much more.

"You can just call me Con. Both of you," Constantin answers, chuckling.

"Can you stay for a while?" I ask, noticing he'd brought three cups with him.

"Yes, I have about half an hour before I need to get back to the kitchen." He climbs onto the bed and wriggles his way to sit between us. I shift over a little to make room. Then he holds his hands out for his coffee, which I dutifully pass to him and then reach for my own.

The dinner is absolutely incredible. Sofia and Florencio did an amazing job. Everything, from the vine tomato gazpacho to start, followed by roasted sea bass, to the merlot poached pears with cinnamon and vanilla for dessert. Everything was accompanied by the perfect wines. Constantin enquired what the red with the main course was, which started a conversation with Sofia in Spanish that I couldn't follow well, though I managed to understand more than I would've a month ago. I heard Constantin mention his family, and Sofia kept up a volley of questions. I liked that the conversation was in both languages. I didn't want them having to keep to English just for me, it would have made the dinner stilted and awkward. As it was, I was able to sit and enjoy listening to the cadence of the language, picking up words and trying to give them a context. When Florencio and Constantin talk Spanish with me, they take it slowly, which I appreciate. But trying my skills where there are multiple voices, all speaking naturally, is a challenge I enjoy.

I'm still at the stage where I have to take a phrase and translate it back into English in my head, which is what happens when Señora Bernat asks me a question.

"He oído que eres escritor. ¿Qué libros escribes?" I stall for a minute, working out how to describe the types of books I write in Spanish. I must look puzzled as she follows up with, "I'm sorry. Should I have asked in English?"

"I understood the question," I reply. "But I'm not sure I have the words for the answer."

She laughs a little, and I warm to her. Switching to English, which she is very proficient at speaking, we talk about books. I learn her name is Dominica, and she and

Señor Berat have three children all around my age. She's a good dinner companion and I'm pleased to have the opportunity to talk to her. She doesn't mind when I ask if I can try out some more Spanish with her, and is very gracious with my clumsy pronunciations.

I step back, cross, pivot, step, then glance over at where Señor Bernat and his wife are also dancing, and stumble. Florencio's hands tighten and he doesn't let me fall.

"What is it?" he whispers.

"Look at them. They're so good." They are very impressive dancers.

"They're like sixty years old. They've probably been dancing for forty years. Of course they're going to be good."

He has a point. He puts his hand on my cheek, dragging my gaze back to him, and he gently strokes his fingers down my face. He leans closer, his lips almost touching my ear.

"The tango is a dance of passion. You shouldn't have eyes for anyone else."

I shiver and see a smile play across his lips.

"Shall we start again?" he murmurs.

"Please."

We dance another song before taking a break. I sink into one of the comfortable chairs that have been arranged around low tables at one end of the ballroom, near the grand piano. Estrella is already ensconced in one, and Constantin leaves the piano, claiming the other one. Señor and Señora Bernat sit across from us. Florencio has disappeared, saying he'll be right back.

Florencio reappears after a few minutes with Sofia and

Juana. He's carrying a tray of coffee cups and a cafetière. Juana goes to a cupboard in the corner and brings out some bottles of spirits and liqueurs, as well as some glasses, in case people want to try them outside of their coffee. I try a shot of whisky in mine. After the wine at dinner, the hit of alcohol with the caffeine shot makes me a little lightheaded, in a good way, where everything seems to be in slightly sharper focus.

Florencio asks Dominica to dance, and I watch them, becoming mesmerised by their movements. He looks in his element, and I feel a pang of guilt that he's so talented and the only person he's had to dance with for the last few weeks is a slow beginner like me. It's good to see him really enjoying dancing. Señor Berat asks Sophia to dance, and she readily accepts.

Florencio and Dominica stop, and he offers a dance to Juana. She protests at first, but between his persuasion and Estrella's encouragement, she relents, though she is hesitant at first. I watch Florencio put her at ease, and I'm reminded that he's a natural teacher. She's soon enjoying herself.

"Do you want to dance?" My attention is broken away from watching the dancers by Constantin's deep voice. I glance at the piano and Dominica has taken his place.

He offers his hand and I take it, letting him pull me up, out of the chair and onto the dance floor.

"I didn't know you danced," I say when he pulls me into a close hold.

"What kind of person would I be if I ran a tango bar and didn't know how to dance myself? But I rarely get the opportunity, or find someone I want to dance with." He says the last part with a small smile on his lips and a promise in his eyes.

With one large warm hand pressed into my back and the other clasping my hand, we dance. He is larger and more solid than Florencio, and it takes me a few minutes to adjust to that, but I don't stumble as we glide around the room.

I look up at one point and am pleased to see Estrella dancing—slowly—with Señor Bernat. She looks so happy, and I'm pleased we've been able to give her this evening.

Then a hand grips my hip, and another holds my shoulder. Florencio. We don't stop dancing, and he moves with us.

"I think you've stolen my dance partner," he says, his voice low.

"I rather thought he was *ours*," Constantin replies with a deep rumble.

We get to a pivot step, and Florencio catches me, keeping me facing him, so I'm now in his arms and he is taking the lead.

"I thought you just wanted to watch?" he says casually.

"Watching is part of it. Sometimes it's more pleasurable to join in." Constantin runs a hand down the centre of my back, blazing a trail of heat that makes me catch my breath.

Florencio blocks my foot, and I step over his, turning to Constantin, his look of longing making me swallow before I step back into Florencio's arms and we move again. Step, back, back, cross, pivot. Constantin claims me this time, and I hear Florencio chuckle slightly, almost as if he conceded and allowed it. The sequence is the same—step, back, back, pivot—but this time, as I turn between them, I see they have their eyes locked onto each other.

Then I'm in Constantin's arms as we turn as one.

"There is room for all of us, don't you think?" Constantin asks.

"Yes, there is," Florencio says softly, his fingers playing over my hip, leaving a small tingle with each fingertip. The song finishes and I'm caught between them both. The air sizzles between us and I see Constantin swallow before he steps away and goes over to where Dominica is rising from the piano.

"What just happened?" I whisper, as Florencio's arm encircles my waist and I become aware of the heat of him behind me. He murmurs close in my ear in a voice that turns my skin electric.

"You're about to find out."

Chapter 31

Rafe

"Have I told you how beautiful you are?" Constantin says, pushing a stray curl off my forehead.

I rest against my bedroom door as he supports himself against the door frame, leaning in close.

"No one has," I whisper, and he gently touches his lips to my jaw.

"That's a surprise, because you're one of the most beautiful men I've ever seen." He kisses the other side of my face before brushing across my lips. My stomach bottoms out and my blood drains south.

I can't think straight, anticipation and arousal are sending my senses into overdrive. I take a breath, trying not to let my knees give way. This is going to lead somewhere and I still have enough presence of mind to remember our promise to each other.

"Where's Flo?"

"He said he'd just be a couple of minutes," Constantin

replies and kisses me. My legs are not going to hold me up much longer. I reach for the door handle behind me, stumbling a little as the door opens and I lose its support.

I walk backwards and Constantin follows me, leaving the door open.

I put my hands on his chest, feeling his solidness and warmth. He places a hand round my waist, and with the other cupping the back of my neck, we kiss. It's unhurried and deep. He explores my mouth, and I let him. He tastes of coffee and brandy and just a faint hint of smoke, which I don't mind too much.

I'm aware of Florencio coming into the room, closing the door and placing something on the dresser. Then I feel his arm round my waist as well.

"That looks good. Can I get some, too?" His voice is playful. Constantin breaks off, his gaze lingering for a second before he turns to Florencio and kisses him just the same.

I rest against his chest, catching my breath and watching them. It's beautiful to watch and my thickening cock wholeheartedly agrees. I have no idea what will happen next, but excitement overcomes any nervousness. They break off from kissing and Constantin releases us, stepping back.

"What happens now?" I ask, looking between them.

"I watch." Constantin smiles and walks backwards, even further into the shadows of the low-lit room, seating himself on a chair.

Florencio reaches up and traces a line down my throat with his finger, reaching the top button of my shirt.

"Can I?" His politeness is achingly sweet, but I don't think it's usual.

"Yes." He starts to undo my buttons.

"Do you always ask first?" I tease a little and he smiles.

"No, but none of them have been you."

Awareness of my inexperience creeps round the edges of

this moment. Does he think I might change my mind? I don't want to let the thoughts intrude, but doubt is a persistent fellow.

"I'm sorry that I'm new to this, but I'm not going anywhere."

He finishes unbuttoning and pulls my shirt open, exposing my chest.

"Has it occurred to you . . ." He pushes the fabric off my shoulder and lightly kisses me there. "That I might want to savour every second of this moment . . . burn it into my memories? That I want to take it slowly, for myself as much as you?"

Oh.

"No, sorry, I thought . . ." I pause. What did I think? That Florencio was just going to take what he needed. I know he hinted that this was his way when we first met, but that's not the Florencio I've grown to know and develop feelings for. What those feelings are, I haven't yet labelled, but I know they're in danger of running deep.

He stops and looks me in the eye. His eyes are their gorgeous soft brown, but there's a tightness to his expression.

"You're very special, Rafe. I want this to be good for both of us."

His words fill me with a soft glow that builds in my core.

"Can I undress you?" I ask and his smile lights up the room.

"I'm all yours."

I slowly unbutton his shirt, pressing a kiss to his chest as each new section of skin is revealed. I follow the buttons down, kissing his tight abs and sinking to my knees in front of him. I look up and see he's watching me. I keep my eyes on his as I unbutton his trousers and ease them down, revealing deep red silk. Dear gods, he wasn't joking about that. I run my hands down over his butt, the silkiness sensual under my fingers. I trail my fingers back up the front of his thighs, feeling his hardness under the fabric, between his legs.

Taking hold of the waistband of his shorts, I pull them down, releasing his cock with a slight bounce.

I've never been this close to another man's cock, not even my own, as I'm not a contortionist. I wonder what it tastes like. Would it be heavy on my tongue?

"Can I suck you?" I whisper, not taking my eyes off the sight in front of me. I'm entranced by the beauty of it, framed by black hair, precum oozing slightly from the red end.

It twitches, and Florencio chuckles.

"I think it's onboard with that idea."

I lick the tip, tasting the precum—it's not bad. I place my mouth round the end, finding my way by instinct. I swirl my tongue round the head and shaft, exploring every vein and ridge, slowly working my way down, feeling the weight of it and taking him deeper.

His hand grabs the base of his cock, circling it and squeezing while he puts his other on my forehead.

"Rafe, stop, please," he gasps.

I pull back, popping off the end. I'm confused. I was enjoying myself.

"What's wrong? What did I do?" I'm about to apologise.

"Nothing. It's good, rather too good." He gives me a lopsided smile. "I don't want it to be over too soon."

He releases himself and kicks his trousers off, before helping me up and undressing me.

"I have an idea," he says with a sparkle in his eye and pulls me onto the bed.

"Kneel here." He pats the coverlet, and I move into position. He lies down, his head almost between my knees and his body away from me.

"Kiss me."

I glance over my shoulder at Constantin. He's undressed

at some point and is now reclining in the chair, one hand wrapped around his cock. He presses his fingers to his lips and blows us a kiss.

I turn my attention back to Florencio and lean down, capturing his bottom lip in my teeth and tugging gently before devouring him in a hungry kiss.

"Still want to suck me off, *niño de oro*?" I don't know what he called me. My brain can't process anything other than the first part of his question.

"Yes, please."

"Good, because I'm desperate for another taste of you."

I kiss him again before moving down his chest. I lick at one of his nipples, teasing the hard nub with my tongue, feeling him stretch and groan from my touch.

"Muy bien," he whimpers, and I press harder until he arches off the bed. I continue down, pressing licks and kisses onto his skin while uttering phrases in Spanish, too quiet for me to hear.

I suck on his hip, enjoying seeing the red mark bloom there. Only then do I make my way back to his cock. I hover over it for a second, inhaling his exotic floral scent. His fingers, which had been gently stroking my skin, dig into the back of my thighs as he pulls me down, wrapping his tongue round the head of my cock and sucking on the end. I take him into my mouth, and from this angle, I can take him further than I had before. I get lost in the dual sensation of working my tongue on him while his mouth engulfs me in warm heat.

It's exquisite. I don't even know my own name. Almost nothing exists outside our connecting mouths and cocks. A few details seep through, like his hands running across my arse, gently kneading my cheeks. His fingers run down my crease, grazing my hole, and I groan. I bob my head in time to his thrusts, letting the roll of his hips overtake me. A gentle breeze across my arse and a warm breath of an unheard word are the only sign of anything changing and they don't prepare me for the warm wetness against my hole. A tongue licking around the rim and then pushing into me. It's all I can do to stop myself collapsing, between thrusting into Florencio's mouth and pushing back on Constantin's tongue for more. How can anything feel so good? I can't hold on much longer. It's too much. My orgasm builds, a deep warmth in my loins intensifies as my balls draw up. I come in a shuddering rush. Strong hands hold my hips as Florencio gives one final thrust upwards and his release hits the back of my throat. His softening cock slips out of my mouth, and he releases his lips from around mine and crawls out from under me. My forearms are on the bed, and I rest my head in my hands, blissed out. Constantin's hand remains grasping my hip, holding me steady. He smooths a warm hand down my back, crooning softly.

"*Muy bien*, just a few minutes more."

"I thought you were just watching." I chuckle.

"I couldn't resist myself, watching your perfect hole flashing at me from across the room. I had to join in, taste it for myself."

I hold still for him as he drags his cock along my crease and stops by my hole. He doesn't push in, but I feel the knock of his hand against my cheeks as he jerks off against my pucker. He grunts a couple of times and comes with a low moan. His release drips off me onto the bed. He lets go and I collapse face down, not caring about anything, too spent, too happy to do anything more than close my eyes and sleep.

Chapter 32

Constantin

"Ow." A cramp in my leg wakes me up quicker than a dousing with cold water, but it's effective. I rub my calf in the half-light, easing the pain away. There's a stirring next to me and I remember we're all still in Rafe's bed. The evening comes back to me, and I smile. Watching Rafe and Florencio together was hotter than any of my dreams, sleeping or awake, had been. Florencio is curled against me, looking young and vulnerable in sleep, though I know he is anything but. He's feisty and funny. Rafe is on Florencio's other side, facing him, their legs tangled together.

It takes me a few minutes to realise Rafe's eyes are open.

"Hey, *precioso*," I say softly. "Are you awake?"

"Mmmm," is his sleepy response as he smiles lazily.

"How are you doing?"

He rolls onto his back and stretches with a yawn.

"I'm good. How about you?"

"Yeah, I'm good too."

He turns back onto his side towards us and looks at Florencio.

"Am I crazy for wanting this? For hoping it can work?"

His voice is tinged with wistfulness.

"We are built on hopes and dreams. They are what inspire us. If we reach for the stars, we might make it to the moon, but if we aim for the moon, we might not get off the ground."

"Romantic." Florencio's voice is languid as he blinks his eyes open. "Some of us are trying to sleep without all your flowery nonsense."

"Flowery nonsense, huh?" I raise an eyebrow at him.

"Yes, you know I don't believe in all that." He grins up at me.

"That's too bad."

"Why?"

"I guess you'll never know." I kiss his nose and roll over to get up.

"Hey," he calls, raising himself up on one elbow, "Are you going to leave me hanging like that?"

"Yup."

"*¡Que maleducado!*" Florencio flops back on the bed.

I leave the room, hearing Rafe no longer able to control his giggling.

I go to my room, and find a pair of shorts and pull them on before going down to the kitchen.

I meet Juana, preparing breakfast for Estrella.

"How is she?" I ask while I set out a tray and work the coffee machine.

"Last night tired her out, more than she'll admit. I'll make her rest for a few days to get her strength back."

I set out a plate and load it up with croissants.

"So, are you boys getting on well?" Juana asks pertly.

I look at her to see if there's any hint of judgement about us, but I see none.

"Boys? You can't be much older than me." I huff a laugh. Juana is in that indeterminate zone of middle-aged women where she could be fifty or I could be way off.

"I'm old enough to call you boys," she says, looking pleased, anyway.

"Yes, you could say we're getting on well." That's all I'm going to tell her. What else can I say without giving her explicit details—which is never going to happen.

I'm saved any further questions by my phone ringing.

"Hi, Wis." I'm always pleased to hear from my cousin.

"I was just seeing how the repairs are going," he says, and I fill him in on the latest and how I should be able to open in a couple of weeks.

"That's good. I was thinking, we hardly ever get a chance to see each other, and I know when you get back in that bar, I won't be able to prise you out again. Why don't you come up to visit for a couple of days before then? You could do with some time off." I don't mention that I'm getting plenty of relaxation and time off right now, but I'd like to see Luis again.

"Sure, I'd love to. How about next week?"

"That would be perfect."

"Hey, Wis? Can I bring a couple of friends?" After he agrees, I ring off. I don't want to go into lengthy explanations on the phone. My cousin knows me the best, so I think he might be surprised when I bring Rafe and Florencio. It's still pretty surprising to me.

When I take the breakfast tray to the bedroom, Rafe and Florencio are as I left them, still lying in bed, facing each other, talking and laughing. Seeing them together causes a fluttering in my chest that stops my breath. I can't think why. Maybe I'm having a heart attack, yes, that must be it.

I put the tray down a little too sharply.

"Are you okay, Con?" Rafe asks and I take a deep breath

before turning round. My heart returns to normal. It could be an early warning. Perhaps I should get it checked out.

"I brought breakfast." I pass them each coffee as they sit up.

I bring my own coffee and the plate of croissants over and sit on the bed.

"Mmmm, I could get used to this," Rafe says, taking another bite of his croissant while I tell them the plans to visit my cousin and his vineyard next week.

Chapter 33

Florencio

"Damn." My phone rings just as I'm retrieving some polvorones, shortbread biscuits, from the oven. I dance across the kitchen to put the hot tray down as quickly as possible and slide the phone out of my back pocket as quickly as I can.

"Hi, Julio," I say as I cradle the phone to my ear.

"Hi. I can't talk for long. I'm going to send you a file. Look at the profile for Caerus. Gotta go." He rings off before I can ask him anything more.

This is the information I've been waiting for. I start to clear away the pots and utensils I've been using and stack the dishwasher. I clean down all the surfaces in the kitchen, even the ones I haven't used. I look at the time and reason with myself that I might as well make a start on the sauce for dinner. I'm stalling. Now I have something significant enough for Julio to send it, and I'm reluctant to see what it might be.

After finishing the sauce, clearing away, and unloading the dishwasher, I stand for several seconds wondering if I should clean the fridge. Even though I know it's going to be a problem, I just need to bite the bullet and take a look. I don't want to be alone when I do it, though, so grabbing my laptop from my room, I head to the Hollywood room, where I know Rafe and Constantin are working. Rafe, with our help, is over halfway through my aunt's diaries, and we've looked at most of the press cuttings too. Rafe has started to create an outline and fill in most of the references from the diaries. He's also building a huge bank of questions for Estrella. She's kept to her rooms since the dinner a few days ago, and I haven't been to see her. We've been relying on updates from Juana, but I want to check in with her soon.

"Hi." Rafe looks up briefly from where he's bent over his large paper plan across the table. Constantin is in his usual place, sprawled across the couch.

"I received something from Julio," I say, putting my laptop on the table but keeping it closed. "I'm not sure I want to look."

"Will it be bad?" Rafe asks.

"I don't know." I'm starting to get a headache just thinking about it. I lean forward and rest my head on my laptop.

"Hey." Constantin's hands on my shoulders are a comfort and I raise myself up and lean against him. "It will be all right, I'm sure."

Rafe scoots his chair round to sit next to me and takes my hand. "Whatever it is, we're here for you."

With their support, I feel ready to at least take a look. As I wait for the laptop to fire up, I ask if there have been any interesting snippets from my aunt's diaries today. Sharing some insights into her life and some of her wittiest comments has been one of my favourite activities over the last few days.

"Well, there was a time when she told Brigitte Bardot that chasing passion was never going to bring her love," Rafe says.

"She really did that?" I can't believe how she managed to get away with it. But then again, I *have* met my aunt.

My anxiety ramps up as I navigate to my emails and see Julio's at the top of the list. The message is short. Not even a greeting.

This is all I could find. If you have any questions, you can call me after seven tonight.

I click on the file to download it. It's a spreadsheet with several pages. There are a lot of lists of large sums of money, but understanding these is not one of my strong points, which is one of the reasons why I didn't join the family business.

"What does all this mean?" The figures swim in front of my eyes, and the looming headache inches closer.

Constantin releases my shoulders and claims a chair on the other side of me. "May I?" He gestures to the screen, and I swivel it round for him to take a closer look.

"It seems to be some sort of financial forecasting and investment sheet."

"When Julio called, he said to look for Caerus."

Constantin frowns for a minute, as if thinking. "It sounds Greek, but I'm not familiar with it?"

"You know Greek?" Rafe asks.

Constantin shrugs. "A little, as well as French, German, and enough Italian to get by."

"Wow, that's impressive."

"I come from an island which is a tourist destination. I picked up a lot when I was younger."

"It says here Caerus is an old Greek word, and in Greek mythology, he's the personification of opportunity, luck, and favourable moments." I look at the search browser.

"A gambler then?" Rafe says.

"My father would never gamble," I say and look back at the screen, suddenly unsure of my statement.

"Look here, this section is funding. Then this here"—he

points to the screen—"is a future investment, and it says 'secured' next to Caerus. Which means he already has the funds. But what are we trying to find?"

"What is the Caerus project?" Rafe asks, and as he says it, a memory stirs at the back of my mind.

"Hold on." I do a quick search and find the information I'm looking for. "Caerus is a casino complex due to be built next year by a business consortium."

"So your father's investing in a casino?" Constantin asks. "This sheet looks like it, but why were you sent this if he's secured the funds? What's the relevance?"

"But, what if . . ." Rafe rises and starts pacing the room; he's in full thinking mode. "What if he's only said it's secured in order to make sure he's guaranteed his investment slot? I can imagine having a stake in a casino is very lucrative? Is there any other information?"

Constantin turns back to the sheet and searches for a while.

"Oh." He sits back with a grim look on his face. I look at him and then at the screen. Rafe comes to stand behind us.

"I hadn't seen this sheet at first, as it was right at the end of the workbook. It's a breakdown of the Caerus funds. Some of it looks like it's coming from other maturing investments, but the bulk of it says '*legado*.'"

Legado means legacy. I'm stunned, and it takes me a minute to speak.

"Do you think he's promised to invest the money based on knowing he'd get my aunt's inheritance? It would account for him sending me here and his aggressive threats."

"How much is the investment?" Rafe asks.

"Fifty million in total, with at least forty of that down as *legado*," Constantin reads from the screen.

Rafe whistles.

"Does your aunt have that much?"

"Honestly, I don't know," I reply. "I have no idea what she has. It's not my concern, though it clearly is my father's."

"Well, this place must be worth around twenty-five million euros," Constantin says. "The financial information is in US dollars, and the exchange rate isn't much different at the moment, so maybe a few more dollars. There are some antiques and art which could be worth a lot, and if she has any investments . . ."

"Okay, stop please," I say loudly as nausea threatens to bring up my breakfast. "It all sounds so callous to talk about my aunt in this way. I can't stand it." I snap the lid of the laptop down.

"I'm sorry, Cio," Constantin apologises. "I didn't mean to upset you."

I sigh loudly. "It's not you, it's my father. I want to talk to Julio, but he said after seven. I assume he means the time over there, which isn't for hours, so I can't do anything else right now." I stand. "I want to be on my own for a while." I leave them before they can try to stop me, which in their sweet and concerned way, they will. But I want to think this through on my own, decide what questions I need to ask Julio, and work out how to deal with my father's threat. Before I go to my room, I want to check on my aunt. It's only as I near her part of the house that I realise I referred to Buenos Aires as over there and didn't say the time at home.

"Come here, my child." My aunt beckons me closer to her bed. "What's the matter?"

"Is it that obvious?" I ask, wondering if she has a superpower. She's sitting up, supported by a bank of pillows, looking elegant as always in a satin robe.

"You wear your heart on your sleeve. So, what's worrying you?"

I had no intention of telling her about my father, but it all comes tumbling out anyway. She doesn't speak or offer her opinion, she just sits with an infuriatingly enigmatic smile on her face. When I finish, she waits a few seconds and changes the subject.

"I would like to see some of the sights of the city again one last time. Will you organise that for me?"

"But Auntie, you haven't been out of bed since the dinner party a few days ago!" She looks so frail, even if her spirit is strong.

"We can always find the strength in ourselves to do something we really want to, don't you think?"

I know that arguing with her was futile, so I agree. "All right, when . . . and I mean when"—I hold up my hand to emphasise my point—"you're feeling strong enough, we can arrange a day out for you."

"Good, that's settled." She reclines her head back on her pillows and closes her eyes. I know when I've been dismissed. She's the most admirable woman I've ever met. I wish I could summon a fraction of her strength. But right now, I need to work on my own problems.

Chapter 34

Rafe

I look at the unfamiliar email in my inbox. It's not unusual to receive emails from strangers; most of them are spam, or offering marketing services, explaining how much they can help me market my book with emails full of grammatical errors and questionable spelling. But this one catches my attention. It starts off polite enough, overly polite even. Well, more of an archaic style of writing, which I find intriguing. Then it veers into effusive and apologetic but inherently charming. On top of all that, the subject matter is interesting. He's offering his services as a literary agent.

I look at the name again: Noah Ellington. It's vaguely familiar. The email also mentions a connection to my father, so that's the first call I make.

"Dad, do you know a Noah Ellington?" I ask once we've exchanged greetings.

"I've not met Noah, but I do know his father, Henry Ellington; he's a client of mine."

"Did you recommend he contact me?"

"Ah, yes, I might have suggested it. I should have warned you, but I didn't think he would go through with it, or at least not so soon. I only met with Henry a couple of days ago."

"Well, he's keen, I'll give him that. But I wasn't aware I was in need of a new agent." I can't help bristling slightly at the interference by my dad.

"From what you've told me about Helen, I was under the impression it was imminent."

I have been putting off thinking about my agent for the last few days. With her not being able to sell my series, her refusal to try to sell Estrella's biography, along with taking on Sloan Thorpe, I'm not sure I can trust her anymore. But to find a new agent seems a drastic step to take. Still, there can't be any harm in finding out a bit more information about him, just in case. I compose a quick reply and go to find Constantin. I'm walking down into the city with him today.

Although it's early, there are already plenty of people also enjoying the fine weather as I amble down La Rambla. I don't have any particular destination in mind, I just want to soak in the atmosphere. I hardly did any sightseeing when I first arrived in the city, but I walked along the La Rambla almost every day. I look at the shops and cafés I used to pass on my daily walk from my hotel to Constantin's bar. Everything feels different even though it's familiar. Even the gentleman I used to see reading a paper with his espresso is in exactly the same seat. As I walk, I try to fathom the incongruity of it all. The sights, the sounds, the smell, and even the very air is changed somehow. I stop in the middle of the wide pedestrian street and allow humanity to flow round me. The bewildered feeling dissipates as I hear snippets of conversation—parents calling their children, lovers having heated arguments. I don't catch all of them, as they speak fast, and my vocabulary is still fairly limited, but the last time I walked down here, it was just background noise. I tip my head back and stare up at the sky, a grin forming on my face and jubilation bubbling up so I can barely contain it. Barcelona hasn't changed, I have. I already knew change was happening, but I considered that more centred around my sexuality and the expansiveness of feelings I have for Florencio and Constantin. This feels different; it's weightier somehow, more fundamental. I pick a seat at an outdoor table at a café and a waitress approaches. Without hesitation, she addresses me in Spanish. Previously, either the servers would instantly discern I was British and choose English, or they would speak Spanish and wait patiently for me to hesitantly try to tell them I didn't speak it, or try not to wince as I murdered their language. I answer in Spanish and am still rather dazed that she doesn't grimace, but appears back with my coffee very promptly. As I sit and watch the world go by, only one thought comes to mind: I could do this forever.

Chapter 35

Constantin

"Can you teach me some phrases in Spanish?" Rafe asks, putting his coffee mug down and sitting back against the pillows on the bed. Dragging him away from the biography for a rest was hard work, but he was practically falling asleep at his computer. We've finished most of the diary translations and he's planned the structure of the biography. Once he gets into the work zone, we have to remind him to eat. I've been making sure he rests regularly, which is where we all are. Florencio made us coffee after we had a siesta.

"Your Spanish is getting better. What phrases did you have in mind?" I ask, taking a swig of my coffee.

He runs a hand through his hair.

"I want to suck your cock."

I nearly lose my coffee while Florencio tips his head back and laughs.

"Quiero chuparte la polla," I say when I recover.

"Quiero chuparte la polla," Rafe repeats, then utters it a few more times. *"Quiero chuparte la polla."*

"You say it one more time and I might take you up on the offer." I'm only half joking because hearing him say it in Spanish with a tinge of an English accent is goddamn sexy, and I'm getting turned on.

He laughs. "I'd rather you did more of what you did the other night."

"You liked that?" I ask, moving up the bed until I'm kneeling between his legs.

"I did." He licks his lips expectantly.

Florencio leans close to him and whispers.

"The phrase you want here is *fóllame*."

"*Fóllame*? What's that mean?"

"Fuck me."

"Fuck me?"

"No, *Oro*, I won't, but Con will," he says gently.

"What do you mean? And what's *Oro*?"

"*Oro*, gold. *Niño de oro*. Golden boy. Like your eyes," Florencio explains.

"I like that. *Oro. Oro.*" He rolls the word around as if he's finding the shape of it. "But what did you mean about *fóllame*?"

Florencio looks at me, and I tilt my head slightly. *Go ahead*, he nods in understanding.

"I only bottom, topping isn't my thing. And Con here, I guess tops."

I rub the back of my neck.

"Yeah." It's been a long time since I bottomed, only once, when I was experimenting as a teenager. I learnt very quickly what I did and didn't like.

Rafe frowns a little. "So what am I supposed to like?"

"Whatever you want to, *precioso*. That's for you to figure out."

"With our help." Florencio nudges him with his shoulder.

"And the three of us?" Rafe brings his hands up to make an entwining gesture with his fingers. "How does that work?"

Florencio reaches up and cups his cheek with his hand, pressing a soft kiss to his lips. "I'm sure we can use our imaginations."

Rafe turns to me with a glint in his eye.

"*Fóllame?*"

His sweet earnestness pulls at my heartstrings.

"Now?"

His answer is to sit forward, press his lips to mine and whisper. "*Sí, por favor.*"

A tendril of warmth uncurls in my core and wraps round my cock. There's no way I can resist him if he asks in Spanish.

"Let's take it slowly." I kiss him back, then ease his T-shirt over his head and push him back to lie against the pillows.

"There's lube and condoms on the dresser." Florencio points to the wash bag he brought in with him the other night. He turns and kneels next to Rafe, kissing him deeply. As he pulls back, Rafe looks at him with a tender smile.

"Lucky you, you never forget your first time," Florencio whispers before moving out of the way. Rafe turns his head back to me, his beautiful golden eyes full of a trust that takes my breath away. I run my fingers down his chest, licking my thumbs before brushing them across his nipples, pressing the hard pink nubs until he moans softly and stretches languidly.

I grab the waistband of his shorts, and he lifts his hips so I can ease them down his legs. His cock looks delectable, springing out of a cloud of golden curls. I can't resist pressing a kiss to it before placing his legs over my thighs. I reach for the wash bag, cursing that it's too far. Florencio comes to my aid, jumping up to fetch the lube and a condom. As he passes them to me, I pull him close for a kiss.

"You all right with this?" I want to check in with him.

"Wouldn't miss it for the world." He stretches out on the bed next to us, bending an elbow and resting his head on his hand.

I run my hands up Rafe's thighs, gently massaging my thumbs into his soft skin. I brush a finger along his taint, against his pucker, and he whimpers. My already rigid cock twitches at the sound, pushing at my shorts. I coat a finger with lube and gently circle his hole, watching every twitch he gives. He bites his bottom lip, his gaze intense as he watches me like he's trying to commit everything to memory. I breach him with one finger, his breath hitches and he tenses, and I stop, waiting. Have I gone too far?

"*Ohh*." He relaxes and lets out a long breath, his mouth widening to a smile. "How can that be so good?"

I huff a breath of relief and push my finger deeper. I thrust it in and out a few times before trying a second finger. I see him swallow before he starts pushing back onto my fingers. I bend down and lick along his lips, wanting to taste him. He opens his mouth, and I kiss him deeply, leaving him breathless. I twist my fingers slightly to hit his bundle of nerves, making his hips buck, and I chuckle as he dissolves back into the bed. I keep up a steady rhythm, every so often grazing his gland, each time eliciting another delicious moan.

"You're doing so good," I croon, and he reaches for his cock. "That's it, touch yourself. Make yourself feel good." At my encouraging words, he tips his head back and arches his back. His eyes are closed, his lips parted as he pants and groans. Rafe had asked me to fuck him, but I don't want to disrupt the moment. He's exquisite and I just want to watch him lose himself as he thrusts back on my fingers and then into his own hand. I risk a glance at Florencio, his eyes are glassy, his lips wet from running his tongue over them.

"That's good, *precioso*, so good." I add a third finger, and he gives a grunt of satisfaction. I'm transfixed, watching his body writhe as his tight hole grips my fingers.

"Muy bien," I utter, lost in the moment as much as him. My cock aches painfully and I could almost come just watching him. *"Muy bien."*

He fists the sheets with one hand as the other flashes up and down his cock. His hips rock with every thrust of my fingers.

"Muy bien, precioso, muy bien."

His hole clamps round my fingers as he cries out, cum erupting and covering his chest. He shudders and stops his hand. I slide my fingers out and he whimpers as if he feels their loss. Slowly, he opens his eyes, blinking at me. I lean down and capture his lips in a gentle kiss.

"Did you enjoy that?"

He lets out a little chuckle. "I don't know how I can describe that. I . . . I . . ." he pauses. "No, I can't. You've chased all the words out of my brain."

My cock is still rigid, and I adjust myself to make it more comfortable. He glances down at my erection and pulls a little face. "Oh, I'm sorry. I had all the fun and that looks like it needs attention."

"It's all right." I sit back on my heels, hoping to ease the aching.

Florencio draws himself up to sit.

"Maybe I could help with that?" His voice is sultry, and any effort to think I might be able to will my erection away goes straight out the window.

"Yes. Perfect," breathes Rafe. "I want to watch this."

Florencio pulls me towards him and strips off my T-shirt.

"Shorts off and sit," he orders, pointing to the head of the bed, and I don't hesitate to obey, his bossiness sending a thrill through me. He undresses quickly, like he doesn't want to waste any time, and keels in front of me, his cock as hard as mine.

"Watching you take Rafe apart was divine, but I don't have the patience for that now," he says reaching for the abandoned condom packet and ripping it open, "So I hope you're on board with this." He looks up at me, the condom poised over the angry red head of my cock. His assertiveness sets my nerves tingling, and I can't wait any longer. I want whatever he's giving.

"Hell yeah." I thrust up, willing him to go quicker. He laughs as he sheathes me in one move. He coats me liberally in lube and raises himself up.

"Wait, aren't you going to prep?" Rafe asks with awe.

"When you get used to it, you don't have to do so much prep, sometimes not at all. I happen to like the burn, and after so long, I want to feel every bit of it," Florencio says, sinking down onto me.

He lets out a satisfied groan as he bottoms out and then fixes me with a stare that I recognise. Like a starving man in front of a feast. It's the same look I saw reflected in the mirror at me when I first gave in to the thoughts of seeing these incredible men together. If it's been too long for him, it's been ten years for me. Then he starts moving, riding me, bouncing up and down. I can't move to the force of his thrusts, but I'm not required to. He's taking from me, using me. His hands grip my shoulders, digging his fingers in as he levers himself up and down on me. I grab one of his hips, mostly to anchor myself, feeling the need to hold on to something. It's relentless and I love it. He mashes his lips to mine, possessing my mouth and stealing my breath. At some point, Rafe's fingers find my other hand, lacing our fingers together, and I grip them.

I can feel the swell of my orgasm rising. I don't think I could hold back if I wanted to.

"I'm gonna come," I croak.

"Yes, you are." Florencio's voice is laced with a smug satisfaction that pushes me over the edge, and my climax rips through me. Florencio rolls his hips one more time, exploding all over my chest.

As his breathing returns to normal, he grins. "Damn, I needed that."

I laugh and pull him to me. He's not the only one. He hugs me, smearing his own cum over his chest, and I hold him close. Rafe kneels and wraps his arms round us both. We part slightly to let him into a three-way hug. Rafe finds my mouth with his, kissing me gently, before seeking Florencio's lips for the same. It's Florencio who pulls back and looks down with a grimace.

"I think we ought to get cleaned up."

He slides off my softening cock and stands, offering his hand to Rafe to go shower. I stare after them for a minute, joining them as soon as I think I can stand again. My chest feels warm, and it's not just from the orgasm. I know that love can never strike twice, but I feel incredibly lucky to have these two guys in my life.

Chapter 36

Rafe

I close my notebook and go to take my leave. I'm grateful that Estrella's been able to answer my questions over the last few days. The biography is slowly taking shape. I haven't been this excited about a project for a long time. It's partly Estrella's indomitable spirit and her amazing story, but a lot of it is the involvement of Constantin and Florencio. Their help has been invaluable, not only with translating the diaries and press cuttings, but also with making suggestions or listening to my endless talks about it. On top of that, they look after me, and Florencio makes sure we're all fed. To me, it would be a chore, but cooking seems to be his second favourite activity after dancing. And Constantin makes sure I rest, which, when I get focused on a project, can be something I don't do enough of. But they bear my single-mindedness with good humour and so far haven't accused me of being boring, even though I'm sure I am. How much they care settles in me, a warmth that seeps into my bones, laying claim to my soul.

I bid Estrella goodbye, and she promises to come down to dinner later. I knew Florencio was cooking something special when he shooed me out of the kitchen earlier.

Outside her suite, Señor Bernat is waiting to see Estrella. He's accompanied by two gentlemen I've never seen before. I ask after Señora Bernat and receive his thanks for enquiring.

"I hope we can see her again soon," I say, and ask him to pass on my best wishes to her before leaving them to their official business and going back to my work in the Hollywood room.

After dinner, instead of us going to the ballroom as usual, Estrella invites us to her suite.

"I want some help with my collection," was all she would tell us, and we exchanged puzzled looks as we trailed after her. She led us through her sitting room to a slightly smaller room. We all stop and stare in surprise when we realise it's a dressing room. There are rows of hangers lining three of the walls, with the other wall stacked with boxes of all shapes and sizes. Hat boxes and shoe boxes sit amid a range of others. All of them look very expensive.

"Welcome to my collection," Estrella says and arranges herself on a chair in the middle of the room.

Most of the clothes on hangers are encased in protective covers, some of them transparent. A colour catches my eye, it's a dusky rose pink.

"Can I?" I ask with my hand on the covering.

"Of course," Estrella replies. "I want you to look at them."

Florencio needs no more encouragement and starts investigating.

I withdraw it and undo the zip, uncovering the dress I recognise from one of the pictures in the Hollywood room. The bodice is decorated with gems in a floral pattern, and the skirt and sleeves are full, overlaid with chiffon.

"Was this the dress you wore in the picture with Gene Kelly?" I ask.

"Yes, it is." She smiles wistfully, almost as if she's remembering the occasion. "The shoes I wore are here somewhere, too." She gestures to the dozens of shoe boxes stacked up.

Meanwhile Florencio is pulling out garment bags and opening them, exclaiming at each new piece he discovers. I do a full three-sixty trying to take it all in.

"Have you kept everything?" I ask.

"Most of them. The trouble with society is sometimes you can't be seen in the same outfit more than once. These days, designers lend stars their dresses, but back then we were given them, and some I purchased. Some were bought by admirers. But yes, I still have most of them."

I let out a low whistle. "This must be worth a fortune." I don't think I could hazard a guess as to how much, but a lot.

"There are a couple of pieces, along with all my jewellery, at the bank."

"There's jewellery as well?" Florencio squeals and affects a mock faint before spinning off to return to his exploring.

Constantin sinks into a chair next to Estrella.

I start investigating some of the boxes. There are hats of all shapes and sizes. Gorgeous shoes from some of the most famous designers. I pull out a pair and hold them in my hands. The irony of the situation is not lost on me, that Loretta would give her right arm to hold a pair of vintage Manolo Blahniks and it's because of her that I am. An idea starts forming, one I couldn't have conceived if I hadn't seen this collection. Kneeling amid the boxes, I pull out a few more pairs of shoes and hats.

"Delice, if you could see me now," I hear Florencio utter as he uncovers another new treasure. I don't know who he's referring to, someone back in Buenos Aires I guess. He finds a cache of feather boas and winds one round each of us. He wraps one round my neck, but I pay him no heed. Now that the idea has taken hold, I can't let it go. I feel the familiar spark when I know something has potential.

"Can I use these for your biography?" I ask.

"What do you mean?" Estrella fixes me with her sharp gaze.

"I have the basic structure of the biography planned, but nothing to tie it all together. But these have significance." I gesture at the shoes and clothes. "So maybe I could tell your story through them. Pick out those which have the most importance or were worn at the most prodigious events and let them lead us into the period of your life that they represent."

She regards me for a long minute and a sinking feeling takes hold. I thought it was a good idea—I'm sure it is—but now, under her intense stare, I start having doubts. My throat goes dry, and I try to swallow. After what feels like an hour, she nods and smiles.

"I love it. I'm sure you have some ideas about what to use, but I can pick out some that are significant to me if that would help."

"Thank you and yes." I breathe a sigh of relief. Excitement reforms along my veins with the affirmation that it is a good idea.

"But as for actually using them, you'll have to ask Florencio." Her voice silences us. Florencio whirls round from where he's trying on a hat and stares at her. Constantin leans towards her slightly, his voice low.

"I hope you know what you're doing."

"Young man, if I wanted advice from someone less than half my age, I'd ask for it." She quips back. "I might not be able to break the laws of this country, but I can circumvent them the best I can."

Constantin smiles, accepting his reproof with grace.

"What do you mean, *ask me*, Auntie?" Florencio asks, his voice unsteady.

Estrella turns in her chair to address him. "Because I'm giving my collection to you. Everything in this room and at the bank."

Florencio's eyes widen and he clasps a hand to his chest. "Nooo. Nooo. You can't do that."

"I can do whatever I want," Estrella retorts. "And I choose to give it to you."

Florencio looks like he's about to pass out, so I go over to him. As I pass Estrella, I hear her whisper to Constantin. "I think I'll leave telling him about the art until another time."

I put my arms round him, and he hugs me like a lifeline.

"Congratulations," I murmur to him, and he pulls me tighter. He eventually relaxes his hold, and I release him. He turns to his aunt.

"Thank you. But what am I supposed to do with it?"

"Donate it, sell it, keep it, wear it. I don't care," Estrella replies.

"I'm not really into drag," Florencio bites back, which for a guy adorned in a feather boa, a fur coat he's slung over his shoulders, and a large-brimmed hat, seems a funny thing to say and I let out a giggle.

Florencio looks down at himself and starts giggling too.

"I don't know," I say. "I think this would look excellent on you." I brandish the dusky pink dress I'd found first, holding it up against him.

He draws his head back slightly and says with a hint of disgust, "*Cariño*, that is absolutely not my colour."

He divests himself of the coat and hat and goes to kneel before his aunt.

"I can't accept this, Auntie. It's too much."

"It's my choice to make," she says.

"But I've done nothing to deserve it."

She places a frail hand against his cheek.

"You've brought me more entertainment and joy in the last few weeks than I've had in years."

He covers her hand in his. "Thank you."

"I've arranged for the items in the bank to be transferred into storage in your name. You will need to provide identification and sign some paperwork. Señor Bernat will be back in a few days with the documents."

Florencio lets out a deep sigh and sits down, leaning his back against a stack of slim boxes. One of them dislodges and falls on him, the contents spilling out.

"Ow!" It's more of a surprised exclamation than actual hurt. He looks down at a lap full of silk. He delicately holds up a camisole in pink silk.

"Um, Auntie?" he enquires.

"I said I had admirers." She shrugs. "Many of them would send me lingerie."

"Did you ever wear any of it?" His nose wrinkles slightly at the thought and he looks like he's about to throw it away from him.

"Not that I would keep in here," she cackles. "But it would be churlish to send it back, and it was too nice to throw away."

She bids us goodnight and leaves us alone.

Florencio visibly relaxes slightly and starts taking down the boxes, opening them and looking inside.

"What are you going to do with all this?" I ask Florencio,

sitting next to him and having a peek inside some of the boxes too.

"I have no idea. What am I supposed to do with it? Give it to a museum?"

"You could sell some of it," Constantin says, and Florencio's head snaps up.

"Would there be enough to set up on my own? Start my own business?" He laughs at the prospect.

"Easily, I'd say," Constantin agrees.

Florencio holds up a lace bustier. "This is a genuine Dior. My friend Coco would kill for this." With care, he packs it away again.

"What are they?" I ask, pointing to a few boxes he's put aside.

"They're for me," he says with a slow smile.

"To wear?" I can't keep the surprise from my voice and am immediately embarrassed. Of course, Florencio can wear whatever he likes, but women's lingerie causes some sort of snag in my brain. Years of unconscious bias can't be undone in a few short weeks. "Shit, sorry. I shouldn't have said that."

"Not everyone likes jockstraps and tighty-whities, though I appreciate a guy in them as much as anyone. But to wear, I much prefer something like this." He holds up a cami set in the richest dark red silk I've ever seen.

I hear a sharp intake of breath and look to see Constantin lick his lips, his eyes dark and swirling.

"See? Con approves." Florencio flashes me a quick grin. "We should find something for you."

"Me? No, I don't think I—"

"If you were both wearing those, I don't think I'd be able to let you leave the room . . . ever." Constantin's voice is gravelly and my cock twitches, thickening slightly. How is him being turned on at the thought of me in silk so arousing to me? Surely that's not possible. But a turned-on Constantin is a delicious thought.

"We'd better take these back to our rooms, then," Florencio announces, standing, picking up the boxes, and adding another one to the pile. "I have something perfect for you," he whispers in my ear, but looks at Constantin as he says it.

"Is that drool?" he says playfully to Constantin as he walks past him, causing Constantin to chuckle and roll his eyes.

We're passing through the lobby back to our rooms on the other side of the house when there's a knock at the door. Florencio frowns and hands me the boxes he's carrying while he goes to answer it.

"Who can it be at this hour?"

With the feather boa still draped round his neck, he opens the door to an elegantly dressed but tired-looking woman with straight black hair.

"Hello, Florrie. Are you going to invite me in, then?"

Chapter 37

Florencio

"I didn't think he'd actually send her," I grind out for the umpteenth time as I pace the kitchen where Rafe is making pancakes for breakfast. My sister arriving on the doorstep late last night was a shock I still haven't recovered from.

Last night's conversation didn't go well, and after I showed her to a room—because even though this isn't my house and I don't want her here I'm not going to leave my sister on the doorstep—I crawled into bed with a headache. I even slept in my own room, not seeking out the others, which I now regret because I'm jittery. Rafe catches me as I walk past and presses me against the countertop, bracketing me with his arms.

"Stop and breathe for a minute," he says. "I know this isn't ideal, but what can she actually do?"

"I don't know," I whine, and Rafe gives me a little smile. My heart jumps because he never seems to mind if I'm being dramatic or, as I am right now, pathetic. I wish I could tell him how much I love him. I would if I thought he might even half love me back. But I can't think of that right now. I take a few deep breaths, and he patiently waits for me to recover.

"Okay, probably nothing," I concede. It's true she's not going to discover any more than I did about our aunt's will, but that isn't the point. He sent her and that's enough to send me spiralling. Every step of my life, it's been "Martina can do this," and "look how well Martina can do that." She's the chosen one. In the end, I gave up trying. I was never going to come close to her in achievement or his affection, so why bother? So the fact she's here speaks volumes.

"Good, that's better," Rafe says, and I take another deep breath, inhaling the citrus and vanilla of him, using it to ground me. It almost works.

"Except drag me home," I wail piteously.

"Really?" Rafe asks, his mouth twisting with incredulity. "Your sister, who let's face it is the same height and weight as you, can physically make you board a plane you don't want to get on?"

"Well, when you say it like that." I give in disgracefully and peevishly.

"What's this really about?" His tone is gentle.

"My sister has always been the shining example, the heights I could never attain. I thought she used to be shown as a way to make me try harder, but I think it was just a way of showing me how much of a failure I am." I hang my head.

"Hey." He lifts my chin up and looks into my eyes. "You're not a failure, you're anything but." He kisses me softly. "You're smart and funny and sexy as hell. You're generous, a brilliant dancer and teacher, and an amazing cook." He kisses me again and my stomach flips. "You're really special to me and I—"

"Well, isn't this sweet?" Martina's voice cuts through whatever Rafe was about to say, and right now I want to slice her head off as I'm sure he was going to say he loved me, or something close to it. Close enough for me.

"I come all this way and find my brother canoodling with the . . . Who are you?" She directs this at Rafe. I don't know if he understands her, as she's speaking Spanish *very* quickly.

He doesn't turn round, and he hasn't taken his eyes off me, nor has he let me go. Which is probably a good thing, as I seriously might swing out at my sister.

"He's a guest in this house. Which is more than you are," I say through gritted teeth.

"I'm family." She heads straight to the coffee machine as if she owns it. I don't know what's got into us because, despite my father's games, I used to have a better relationship with my sister. I don't remember her being such a bitch.

"Did you get what you came for?" I ask, knowing she'd planned to visit Estrella early.

"She's tighter than a saint's arse, that one," she sneers. "I'm going to see her lawyer, so I'll get the information I need." I can't believe how she referred to Aunt Estrella, but bite it back for now.

"When are you leaving?"

She sits down at the table with her coffee. "Our flight leaves tonight at seven."

"I'm not going anywhere," I state with some force. Rafe, possibly thinking I'm not going to do anything I might regret, though that's too early to call, steps back and continues with making breakfast.

Martina swings her head between us, her eyes narrowing.

"What exactly is going on here?"

"None of your business." I cross my arms, partly as a defence mechanism but also to keep myself from wanting to lash out at her.

"So all this time you've been here telling our father you can't find anything out, you've found yourself a fuck buddy."

"Martina." I growl a warning at her.

"Where's the hunky but grumpy looking one I saw last night? Is he a fuck buddy too?"

I don't even bother to answer her.

"You're not seriously imagining you're playing happy family here, are you Florrie?"

"No." I scowl, not wanting to admit how close she is to the mark.

"Florrie." Her voice changes, which instantly puts me on alert. She's even more deadly when her voice is sweet instead of sharp. "You know this can't last, don't you? Our aunt is dying. I'm surprised she's still alive, to be honest. But then what happens? You'll have to come back home, and this will all be over. You've had your fun, but you might as well come home now. It'll be easier, don't you think?"

Rafe puts the plate of pancakes on the table, adding honey and fruit.

"Flo, you should eat." The first words he's said since my sister entered the kitchen. I see the moment when she realises he's English and her smile turns sickly.

"This is a dream, Florrie, an illusion. Your place is back with your family."

I sit at the table despite having lost my appetite. Rafe offers a plate to my sister.

"Hello, I don't think we've been introduced properly. I'm Rafe."

"I'm Martina," she says, putting on as much charm as she can. "I'm trying to convince my brother it's time to come home."

"And what does he say?" he asks in a neutral voice.

"He doesn't believe in family duty and loyalty," she says.

"I think he does, actually. I think he'd rather choose to be with a family who is loyal to him." He calmly reaches for a pancake as if he hasn't just made my day, my year, my whole fucking world.

My sister stands, switching back to Spanish. "I have to go see this lawyer guy. The plane leaves at seven, Florrie." I ignore her, and she flounces out.

I only have eyes for Rafe, and I stare at him as he tucks into his pancakes. "What did you say?" I whisper.

He puts down his fork and catches my hand.

"I said, you could have a better family than the one who manipulates and uses you."

"Could I?" Hope blossoms in my chest and I hold my breath. I look into those golden eyes that hold all the sun in my life.

"You can have me," he says. "If you want, of course, because I want—"

I shut him up with a kiss, the force of which nearly knocks him off his chair, but I don't care. I cling to him and his words, his lifeline in a stormy sea.

I'm waiting for my sister in her room when she returns from visiting Señor Bernat.

"Did you find out what you wanted?" I already know from her face that she didn't.

"It doesn't matter, anyway," she says furiously. "It'll all go to our father."

"Will it?" I ask casually. "If he was so sure of that, then why did he send us halfway across the world to make sure?"

She stops packing and faces me. I'm not usually the one getting involved in secrets and subterfuge, but I'm still a

Delgado. I think about the information Julio sent me, that I confirmed.

"I can't think what you mean," she says.

"Oh, come on Martina. I might not have a head for business like you, but I'm not stupid. I know there has to be a reason this is so important to him."

"It just is." She returns to her packing.

"Has this anything to do with the Caerus project?"

She falters but keeps packing. "How do you know about that?"

"I have my ways. I admit I bought our father's line at first, but then, when the inheritance laws were explained . . . I know that as next of kin, our father would receive at least a third of our aunt's estate. I can't believe he wouldn't have known that. So why does he need confirmation to make sure he's going to get everything?"

Martina sighs and sits down on the bed next to me.

"He's in debt."

It's the most honest she's been with me since she arrived, and she looks a little more like the sister I used to get along with.

"How much?" I ask.

"Enough to need Aunt Estrella's money."

It's a shock to hear it confirmed rather than looking at numbers on a spreadsheet. But at least I was prepared for it.

"Then why invest in a casino?" It doesn't sound like good business sense to me.

"He thinks it will make his money back. And it will . . . in time. But that's in the future. He had to secure the funds against all the properties. If he doesn't get Estrella's money, then he'll have to sell most of them."

He has the family home and a holiday cabin, but all the other properties are business blocks where he makes money in rent. It must be bad if he had to offer them up. He was always a good businessman, or so he said. I might have to rethink that belief.

"But he won't be destitute, will he? It's not like he'll lose everything?"

"No." My sister's derision irks me. "We might have to sell the lake house and downsize the family home, but we won't be homeless."

"Well, it's likely he'll get everything, anyway. I haven't heard her mention any other causes she might choose to give part of it to." I keep very quiet about the collection she gifted me.

"So you'll come home?" she asks. "Father will be pleased to see you."

"No, he won't. You're a bad liar, Martina." Her small smile confirms that I'm right; he just wants me within arm's reach.

"If you stay, then he'll stop your allowance." She repeats the same threat he gave me.

"Well, if he's in debt, it wouldn't surprise me if he was thinking of stopping it anyway." A vein in her cheek gives her away. "He *was* going to stop it anyway, wasn't he? His threat wasn't idle, but it won't make a difference whether I come back, will it?"

"No. But I wasn't supposed to tell you that." She sighs.

"Too late. I'm not going anywhere. Like Rafe said, I choose my family." I leave her to finish packing, but I can't bring myself to say goodbye; my blood is boiling too much. Instead, I go in search of those who I want to be with.

Chapter 38

Rafe

"Hey, how's it going?" Constantin pokes his head round the door of the Hollywood room.

"It's going well," I say, indicating my work laid out in front of me. "But I don't think Flo is very happy right now."

After his sister left earlier, he was in here with me for a while, but he couldn't seem to settle and I haven't seen him for the past hour. I couldn't understand most of what she said when I was making breakfast, but her tone wasn't pleasant, and Florencio was tense most of the time. Her entire visit has cast a heavy air of disquiet over the house. I feel it, and Constantin seems to as well.

"I think we all need some cheering up," he says.

"We definitely have to do something," I agree.

I close my laptop, and as we walk to the kitchen, I ask Constantin about his day. He's been down at the bar all day, going through the last of the repair work with the builders.

"Good, they're just finishing the plastering. It needs to dry for a few days and then it can be painted."

"Are you still planning to open in ten days' time?"

"Fingers crossed." He looks happy and I'm pleased for him. At the same time, a knot of worry takes root in the pit of my stomach. When the bar opens, he'll be there a lot and will probably want to stay in his own place. What will happen to us? Was I too naïve to think this could work? I dismiss the thought; we have to make it work somehow.

"So, what did you have in mind?" Constantin asks.

"Well, what do you think will cheer him up?"

"Snacks," he says at the exact time I say.

"Show tunes."

"Snacks and show tunes?" He raises an eyebrow.

"Sounds like a perfect combination to me."

"I can't argue with that," he chuckles.

I find a tray and start arranging some plates of olives, cheese, cherry tomatoes, chorizo, and serrano ham. Constantin cuts some bread and adds it to the tray.

"Shall we have wine?" he asks, holding up a couple of bottles of red.

"Naturally." The only correct answer here.

We share a look as we reach Florencio's room. The door is closed.

I have the tray, so Constantin knocks.

Several long seconds pass before the door is opened, and a very solemn-looking Florencio stands behind it. He looks so forlorn that I want to gather him in my arms and make it all better. But I have my hands full, so instead I blurt.

"Snacks and show tunes."

He frowns a little. "What?"

"Snacks and show tunes." I push the tray forward to emphasise the point, as if he hasn't already seen the tray I'm holding.

His mouth twitches slightly. "That does sound good, actually."

"And we brought wine." Constantin holds up the bottles as proof.

"Now you're talking." He opens his door wider to let us in.

When I do get to put the tray down, I pull him into a hug, feeling better the instant he's in my arms. Constantin wraps his arms around us both, enveloping us in his warmth.

"Do you want to talk about it?" I ask when we pull apart.

Florencio sighs. "I guess I always knew my family didn't really care that much for me, but to have it confirmed . . . it hurts." He rubs his chest as if easing away a physical pain.

There's the sound of a cork popping as Constantin opens a bottle of wine.

"Now that's a welcome noise," Florencio says with a smile and accepts the glass of wine Constantin holds out for him.

I flip through my phone and select "Anything Goes" from the musical. I have no great singing voice, but I try anyway, and Florencio joins in.

By the time we've drunk the first bottle of wine, we've sung our way through half the songs of *Chicago*, *West Side Story*, *Cabaret*, and *Gypsy*. The only one of us who can actually sing well is Constantin. He disappears to his room and returns with his guitar before playing a beautiful rendition of "Some Enchanted Evening" from *South Pacific* in his rich baritone.

As Constantin opens the second bottle, I try "Don't Rain On My Parade" from *Funny Girl*, but I'm no Barbra Streisand, so I just end up collapsing on the bed in a fit of giggles. Florencio throws himself down next to me and turns his head to look at me.

"This is fun, thank you," he says, and I'm pleased to see the sparkle has returned to his soft brown eyes. "But do you know what would make it even better?"

"We make Con do a *Full Monty* routine for us?" I suggest and see Constantin scowl slightly, which sets off more giggles.

Florencio tips his head back and laughs. "That would be priceless, but it's not what I had in mind." He jumps up from the bed and retrieves some of the boxes he brought back from the collection yesterday. I raise myself up as he sits back down next to me and hands me a slim white box.

"Wearing silk always makes me feel special, and I thought it might make you feel it too. I chose this for you."

I slowly prise the lid off the box and unfurl the tissue paper. I lift out a pair of shorts and a camisole in the deepest midnight blue. The silk is soft in my fingers and I instinctively hold it to my face, wanting to feel the softness against my skin.

"I . . . I've never worn anything like this," I stammer, suddenly unsure of myself.

"You're sometimes strangely hesitant for someone who wants to experience everything," he says softly and without judgement. He brushes a curl of hair away from my face, a gesture which makes my heart burst from the sweet understanding. I look down at the lingerie and run my fingers over it. What would it feel like against my body? I look over at Constantin, and he's poised, holding his breath, but his eyes are dark and swirling in a way that I've come to recognise as lust. It's the same way he looked when this was suggested in the dressing room, and a warmth stirs in my groin again.

"Okay, I'll try it on," I say and see Constantin take a breath. "What will you wear?" I ask Florencio.

He opens the lid of the box he has on his lap. It's the dark red set he first found in the dressing room, and the colour is perfect for him.

I peel off my clothes and slip on the shorts and camisole. I'm not given any time to feel self-conscious as I'm crushed by Constantin's arms, his lips devouring mine, hands running over my body. All my blood drains south, and my cock hardens from his touch. I move against him, and he shoves a thigh between my legs. He cups my arse and lifts me slightly, pulling me hard against his solid thigh as he kisses me deeper.

"You look stunning," he growls, as he disengages his mouth from mine. His eyes alight on Florencio, who is now adorned in dark red silk. With his other hand, he pulls Florencio in and kisses him just as voraciously as I still grind against his leg, his hand kneading my butt cheek. He disentangles himself and I feel the loss of the friction keenly.

"Will you dance for me?" His voice is low and husky. I don't know if my knees can hold me up enough to dance, but Florencio grabs my hand.

Constantin takes his guitar and starts a slow tango song.

I face Florencio, and as I move into a close hold, he whispers, "You're so beautiful." Before kissing me in a long, languid kiss that makes me feel boneless. I'm not sure how I'm supposed to dance now. But we move slowly, Florencio holding me expertly, and I recover my composure. We step together, back, side, pivot, *ocho*—everything I've learned so far. We've started to add in more kicks and a couple of lifts, which we incorporate. Florencio sets a different sequence, which seems to flow in a sensual way, and I get lost in each movement, in the beautiful guitar music and Florencio's arms, his eyes, and his smile.

When we come to a stop, his eyes are on mine, making me feel beautiful and special in a way I've never experienced before. I want him to keep looking like that at me forever. I want to claim it as mine.

"I want to make love to you," I whisper, and his smile widens as his answer. I walk him to the bed and lay him across it, crawling over him and settling between his legs. He looks divine, and I run my hands up his chest, pushing the silk out of the way as I want to kiss every inch of his skin. I continue up, capturing his full lips for a long kiss before working my way back down again, kissing and sucking across his rib cage. I reach the treasure trail of dark hair that leads below the waistband of the silk shorts.

"These are going to have to come off," I murmur, and he lifts so I can slide them down. Keeping hold of one leg, I press a kiss to his ankle, then trail up the inside of his leg, licking into the joint between his leg and pelvis. I run my tongue over his balls, taking one into my mouth, enjoying how he groans with pleasure. I slowly trace my tongue from the base to the tip of his cock. I lave my tongue across his slit to taste his precum before sucking in the head and bobbing up and down a few times. I pop off the end and sit back to gaze at him. The look is still there, his soft eyes and glistening lips, and I can't think of a more beautiful sight right now.

I feel a warm hand brush down my back. Constantin. I tip my head back to look up at him. I reach up and pull his head down to mine, feeling the need to kiss him too. He lifts my top up and over my head. I push my own shorts down, taking them off, exposing my arse to Constantin, and he kisses each cheek before running a tongue up my crease. I stop for a minute, enjoying his attention on my pucker.

"Fuck, what a view," Florencio breathes, and the thought of Constantin flicking his tongue in and out of my hole while I'm balls deep in Florencio is so overwhelmingly hot I nearly come from each touch of his tongue against my rim. With as much self-control as I can muster, I pull away. "Another time," I whisper. That's something to look forward to, but this is my first time, and I want to savour every moment with Florencio.

He runs his hands up my back and kisses the top of my head as I settle back on my heels. A few seconds later, he hands me lube and a condom. I rip the packet with my teeth and roll the condom over my leaking tip. I coat a couple of fingers in lube and push against Florencio's pucker.

"You don't have to." He swallows and twitches as I circle round his hole.

"Indulge me. I want to feel you," I say as I push a finger past his ring of muscle, marvelling at how tight it grips me. His breath speeds up as I push in a few times and add a second finger. He writhes, enjoying each thrust of my fingers, and when I slow down, he pushes back, desperate for more. My cock aches as I watch him, and I know I can't hold on much longer. I *need* to feel that tightness around me.

"Fuck me, *Oro*," he says with a smile. *"Fóllame."*

"What was that?" I grin. "I can't hear you."

"Fóllame!" he almost shouts, and I withdraw my fingers, wasting no time in coating my cock in lube and lining up against his hole.

He wraps a slender leg round my hip, and I push into him. Oh my. I nearly see stars with how his muscles clamp around me. I stop, needing a moment to remember how to breathe. He chuckles slightly, and in answer I go deeper, enjoying every sensation along my length until I'm up to the hilt. I can't stop my hips from moving of their own accord. I want to feel him squeeze me over and over.

"Con," Florencio beckons him over, and he moves from where he'd been watching. "I want to suck you."

Constantin bends over and gives him a sweet kiss before stripping his clothes off. Florencio shifts slightly, so his head is lined up with the edge of the bed, and Constantin kneels over him. Florencio tips his head back, and I watch in wonder as he takes him deep in his mouth, his throat stretched, undulating. It's more than I can take, and I slow down, but that makes it harder to maintain any semblance of control. I give in and drive harder into Florencio, submitting to some base urge. Constantin tips forward and snakes a hand round the back of my neck, now slick with sweat. When he finds my lips with his and kisses me, I moan against his mouth, feeling my balls tighten and draw up. I've never experienced anything as intense as the wave that washes over me as my orgasm crashes through me. Constantin holds me steady as I arch my back with one final thrust. Florencio clenches round me as he explodes all over his chest. Constantin's eyes lock with mine as he shudders down Florencio's throat. He briefly rests his damp forehead against mine as sweat drips off my hair and into my eyes. At this moment, I've never felt so connected, understood, and seen by anyone as I do with these two incredible guys. Something tightens around my core and binds my heart to them. Constantin releases his grip on my neck, and I slip out of Florencio while Constantin gets up. Florencio looks spent and I lie beside him with just enough energy to gather him to me. I pull off the saggy condom, and Constantin takes it out of my hand before grabbing a cloth to clean us up. Then he climbs onto the bed on the other side of Florencio and puts his arms round us both. As I nuzzle into Florencio, I start to understand what Constantin once told us about what being in love felt like. Right now, I'm sure I'm the happiest and most blessed man in the world.

Chapter 39

Constantin

"Wis!" I embrace my cousin warmly. It's been a few years since we were last together. Far too long.

"You're looking well, Con." He holds me at arm's length, scrutinising me carefully. "Remarkably well." I almost blush under his gaze and quickly introduce him to Florencio and Rafe.

"You look very alike," Florencio remarks, and it's true.

"We've been taken for brothers many times," Luis says. He's like a brother to me, the nearest I have anyway. He's also my closest friend and was best man at my wedding.

"You're an Otero then?" Rafe enquires, his face twisting in embarrassment.

"I am. My grandfather owns the Otero vineyards, but I wanted to set up on my own." Then, in an aside to me. "How does he know, and why does he look like that?"

I laugh. "He's wondering if he should be apologising to

you. He once researched our family for a book, and apparently he didn't portray them in a favourable light."

"Then I'm sure it was accurate." Luis laughs with me, and puts an arm around Rafe's shoulder, drawing him away. "I can tell you some dark and dirty secrets about our family I'm sure you didn't uncover."

"No, it's fine," he says, sounding relieved. "Unless, of course, you want to tell them."

"Why Wis?" Florencio asks as we follow behind where Luis is leading Rafe towards the guest cottage.

"Luis is two years younger than me, and when he was born I couldn't say Luis, I could only say Wis. Of course it stuck, so he's always been Wis to me."

Luis opens the door to the lovely stone cottage that sits separate from the main house on the vineyard. Both have amazing views, not only of the vineyard, but across the valley. We're quite high up the mountain, in the Navarre region, just across from Rioja and less than ten kilometres from the start of my grandfather's extensive vineyards. Not that I'll be going to visit him anytime soon.

"Well, here you are." He gestures to the rustic decor of the small house, and Florencio and Rafe look around the large open-plan living area, kitchen space, and a wooden staircase leading to a mezzanine bedroom. "I'm sorry, there's only one bed," he calls while giving me a shit-eating grin.

"I'm sure we'll manage somehow," Florencio calls back, and Luis chuckles.

"I'll leave you to it. Dinner is in the house at nine." He walks back past me where I'm still standing by the door, giving me a pat on the chest. "Don't do anything I wouldn't do." I roll my eyes, and as he walks the path to the main house, I hear him mutter, "Lucky bastard." I've never known my cousin to have a relationship, well, not one that lasted long enough for me to meet them, which I find sad as he has so much love to give.

"Con, have you seen this shower?" Florencio leans over the railing of the bedroom, bringing my attention back to the present. Of course I've seen it. I've stayed here many times, and I might have had one or two nice fantasies about the guys and that shower since I arranged the trip with my cousin. But I let them show me anyway, feeling their excitement.

"So, what stories can you tell us about Con?" Florencio asks over dinner. "He hasn't told us much at all."

There's not a lot to tell, and I'm trying not to dwell on the past right now.

"So he hasn't told you how he broke his collarbone then?" Luis puts down his napkin and picks up his wine.

"No," Rafe says. "He's been very quiet about it."

"That's no surprise, seeing as he was being an arrogant show-off."

"*Noooo!*" Florencio drags out the word and Luis leans forward, completely hooked by Florencio's charm.

I sit back and roll my eyes at Luis, but there's not a chance he won't tell his favourite story about me.

"My father always visited his sister in the holidays, so I spent my summers in Gran Canaria with Con. This particular year, when we were about ten . . . Well, I was. Con was twelve, and he thought he was so much more mature than me. He was grown up and a man now. There's a secluded beach on the north of the island and he said he could jump off the largest rock and onto the beach. He said he was old enough, being the man that he was. He made a big show of it, how I was too young to try it, and he was going to be fine. Needless to say, he jumped, landed, tried to roll, and broke his collarbone. I'm sure he felt like a man when he had to ride his bike one-handed all the way home and tell our parents what happened."

Yes, I remember the telling off I received, not only from my parents for being stupid enough to do it, but also from my aunt and uncle for leading Luis astray. No one seemed to care that it hurt like hell. Eventually, I got it checked out and had to wear my arm in a sling for the rest of the holiday while it set.

The next day, after a luxurious night in the *one bed*, we discover just how much fun can be had in the enormous shower. A three-way frot is possible if you have large hands, as I do, and use them both. Though I'm sure my arse cheeks will bear the marks of their nails for a long time. As if there wasn't anything else for them to hold on to. But I don't mind, and rather like the reminder every time I take a step or sit down.

After a hearty breakfast, we're treated to a full tour of the vineyard and an extensive wine tasting. Luis shows us the latest batches that are ready to be drunk, and we insist on finishing the opened bottles over that evening's dinner when we're joined by Luis's friend Jiordi. I've only met him a few times, though I know he and Luis have been friends for years. By the time I've dug up some stories of Luis and he's told some outrageous ones of our family—Jiordi joining in with a few as his father works with my uncle over at the Otero estate

—we're all fit for nothing but climbing exhausted into bed and sleeping soundly.

On the last morning, I walk with my cousin and tell him all about the bar, how the repairs are going, and the reopening plans once the final decorating has been completed over the next week. Rafe and Florencio are ahead of us, holding hands, talking, and occasionally laughing. More than once, I catch Luis looking at them.

They stop, and Florencio pushes a strand of hair away from Rafe's face. Rafe says something, and Florencio brings their clasped hands to his lips and kisses Rafe's knuckles before they continue walking.

"I wonder what it's like," Luis sighs wistfully. "To be young and so in love."

His words hit me like a sledgehammer, cracking the shell I'd constructed around us wide open. The illusion I'd formed while we'd been together, effectively cut off from the rest of the world. The one that let me believe I could be a part of their life. Now it lies broken round my feet, and I feel like an old fool. Who was I kidding? They're perfect together, just as they are. They have no need of me, and I was naïve to think so. I should've known better at my age. I said love could never happen twice, and for a while there I believed I might be wrong, but no, I was correct all along. I just wasn't following my own advice.

My skin prickles all over, and I want to pull it off like an itchy sweater, but I can't. I feel on edge and give Luis a terse goodbye. He frowns and asks if I'm all right. I'm not, but I don't tell him that. I'm sure I will be fine in time, when I've forgiven myself for making such a huge mistake. We're all quiet as we drive back to the city, which is fine as it saves me having to say anything just yet, but I know I will have to when we reach the house. I can't stay there anymore. The bar is habitable now, so I can move back.

I should have done so already, really. I've not given it enough attention, but I will do so from now, without the distractions I had no right to get involved in. What was I thinking, letting myself get swept away in the magic? I'm too old for that.

When we get back to the house, we climb out of the car. Florencio and Rafe go to enter, but I stay by the car. They turn back.

"Aren't you coming in?" Florencio asks.

I shake my head, all my carefully rehearsed words flying out of my head.

"I'm going back to the bar. I'm going to stay there tonight, and from now on."

"Of course, you have a lot to do," Rafe says, and I close the ache in my heart at his willingness to understand, to give me that leeway.

"No, I won't be coming back. He was right. You are perfect together. You don't need me."

I don't wait for a response. I don't want to hear their answer to that. I know if I look back, I might just crumble, so this is for the best. They deserve to love each other without me getting in the way and complicating things. I get back in the car and drive away, back to my bar, back to the only thing I truly have.

Chapter 40

Florencio

"What just happened?" Rafe says as we both stare at the tail end of the car disappearing out the driveway.

"I have no idea." The words die away as I recall his words, trying to make some sense of them because he wouldn't just leave us, not Constantin . . . would he? Despite the warmth of the day, a coldness forms in my core, dread pooling in my bones.

Rafe turns to me, bewildered. I want to say it'll be all right, and that he can't mean it, but in truth I don't know.

His phone rings, and he pulls it out of his pocket. Frowning, he says, "It's my dad." Before turning away to answer it.

I watch as the colour drains from his face, turning his golden features ashen.

"I'll be there as soon as I can. I'll let you know." He rings off and stands stock-still in the middle of the driveway, looking lost. I tentatively move to him, wanting to offer comfort for whatever it is, not knowing if it's something he'll want. As soon as I get close, he pulls me to him and I hug him tightly as he burrows his head into my shoulder. It takes several minutes before he lifts his head enough to rest his chin on my shoulder.

"My mum's in the hospital. She collapsed. I need to go home."

"I'm so sorry. Do they know what's wrong with her?"

I feel the slow shake of his head. "They're running tests."

He pushes back a little so he can look at me.

"I'm sorry, Flo. I need to book a flight."

I swallow back the panic that threatens to overwhelm me, the one that makes me want to scream that it's unfair he's leaving too. Instead, I say, "What can I do to help?" His small, grateful smile wrings my heart dry.

I'm not much help. I just trail after him, unwilling to let him out of my sight as he reserves a seat on the next flight out, books an Uber, and then packs up his notes and laptop from the Hollywood room. I sit on his bed as he stands in front of his case, randomly throwing things into it.

When he's zipped it up, he sits next to me and takes my hand, interlacing our fingers.

"I'll be back, Flo."

I want to cling to him, beg him to promise me he will. But this isn't about me, he has his own worries for his family, and I don't want him to make promises he can't keep, so all I say is, "I'll be waiting."

He gently touches my cheek and pulls my head round, giving me a sweet, sad kiss. I ignore the fear that this might be the last one and swallow past the lump in my throat, finding the strength to say.

"You go. I hope your mum will be well."

"Thank you. I'll call you," he says as his phone buzzes that the Uber has arrived.

And so, for the second time in under two hours, I watch a car drive away, taking with it a man that I love.

I want to believe that Rafe will come back, but I noticed he said he needed to go home. I can't shake the feeling that being back in England will feel like home to him, and he'll forget me, us, and what we have been building here.

In reality, we've built nothing but a house of cards, blown away by the wind.

In the end, everybody leaves me.

I make it back to my room and curl up into a ball. Only then do I let the tears I've been holding back spill over and I don't stop until the coverlet is soaked and I fall into an exhausted sleep.

Chapter 41

Rafe

I sit and hold her small hand in my own, and the only sound is the soft beep of monitoring machines. It feels surreal to be here watching my mum lying in a hospital bed, when only a few hours ago I was walking through a vineyard in Spain.

My dad is taking a break. He's been here for hours already and hasn't left her side since she was brought in.

There's still no news, since the doctors say they're still waiting for the test results. I will them to hurry up.

I sent a text to Florencio as soon as I landed, but I haven't heard anything back. I don't know about Constantin, and I can't think about what happened right now. I don't have the capacity to unpack what he said and try to work out what went wrong. I can only focus on the lifeless form in front of me. Dad says she said she wasn't feeling well earlier in the day, but when she went into the kitchen to get a drink after refusing my dad's offer of help, she collapsed.

She's been unconscious ever since and the only problem

they could immediately find was a high temperature. They've given her something to help bring that down, but said they can't do anything until they know what they're dealing with.

At one point, a nurse enters and changes her IV drip. He gives me a smile but doesn't say anything.

I let go of her hand and place my head on the bed. I'm exhausted and just need to rest for a minute.

I become aware of fingers tangling in my hair, and for a second I think it's Florencio. he likes to wake me up by running his fingers through my hair and placing soft kisses on my cheeks and nose. It's become a game to see how long I can keep my eyes closed, feigning sleep to get more kisses before he realises I'm awake. But the kisses don't come, and I blink my eyes open, remembering that Florencio is hundreds of miles away. That must mean the fingers . . . I peel my face away from the bed and turn my head to look at the kind eyes and weak smile gazing back at me.

"Mum," I croak, wiping the dried drool from my face. "How are you feeling?"

"Terrible," she rasps, and closes her eyes for a minute before opening them again.

"Let me find Dad," I say. He's just outside the door, looking like he's aged a decade. When I tell him she's awake, his shoulders lose their visibly hunched appearance. As he passes me to go to her, he gives me a hug, the first I remember him giving me since I was a boy. I hug him back and then go to track down a doctor or nurse to tell them she's awake.

While the nurses bustle around for a few minutes, my dad updates me that they found she has a virus and have started some antiviral meds.

"Why didn't you tell me?" I ask, upset that I didn't know.

"Because you were fast asleep. You look like you needed it too. I let you stay sleeping and would've told you as soon as you awoke, but I guess she woke first."

I watch him look over and give her a tender smile, loving that they still have so much affection for each other.

Eventually, we're allowed back to her bedside. I want to hug her, but I don't want to hurt her so I squeeze her hand instead. Then I give my parents some time alone for a few minutes while I step outside and call Florencio. I'm desperate to hear his voice, but there's no answer. I leave a message, but not being able to talk to him causes a small knot of anxiety until I realise that time seems to have no meaning in places like hospitals and it's three in the morning.

As my mum is out of immediate danger and we have to wait until the doctors give us an update, we head home to rest, eat, and get a change of clothes.

I stand in my childhood bedroom. I haven't stayed in it since I moved out years ago. At first, I had my own apartment, and then I shared one with Loretta. When she left me I gave up the apartment, which was rented, and put most of my effects into storage. Not that there was much. I brought a few boxes here, but didn't stay as I was headed to Spain straight away. It no longer feels like home. Living with Loretta didn't feel like home either. I thought it did at the time, but it was all part of the dream I was allowing myself to be led into. Home is where you feel comfortable being your authentic self, where you're surrounded by love and support. I know now that I've never felt at home the way I have been for the last few weeks. I think of the memories we've already made and the ones we still have to make.

I fall into the narrow bed and manage to sleep for a few hours despite however long I slept at the hospital.

When I wake up, the first thing I do is reach for my phone. There's a reply text from Florencio, which eases the knot in my chest, and I call him.

"Hey."

"Hey."

"How's it going?" he asks.

I fill him in on the progress, even though it's still early stages, and how I'll be heading back to the hospital soon and will update him later.

When I ask him how he is, he's subdued, and hasn't heard anything from Constantin.

"I'll be back as soon as I can," I tell him.

"Good. I miss you." He rings off, and I hold the phone in my hand for a long time before I work out that his tone sounded like he didn't believe me.

Chapter 42

Constantin

"You've painted that spot three times already," Alena says, and I turn to scowl at her.

"Just pointing it out, boss." She's the one person I can stand to be around right now, so it's a good job she not only doesn't care that I'm grumpy and surly, but is happy to come and help me finish getting the bar ready to open next week.

But she's right, I've painted the same area of the wall. I throw the roller down into the tray and reach for a cigarette.

She raises an eyebrow, and I know what she's thinking, but I don't need her judgement making me feel any worse about myself right now. I had all but given up smoking, but found myself reaching for them more and more over the last few days.

During the day, I've made sure I've kept busy—painting, cleaning, and sorting not only the bar area but my apartment as well. As soon as I wake, I throw on some clothes and get to work. Alena has started bringing me food, but I have no appetite, so half of it doesn't get eaten. When I do eat, it's usually only because she's standing over me. I work until I can't do any more and then I knock back a couple of drinks to numb my mind so I can sleep.

Anything to keep myself from thinking, because if I go down that route, I fall into a pit of self-loathing and embarrassment. I can't believe I didn't wake up sooner. But my jagged heart was awakened, and I followed the siren's call even though I knew it was a foolhardy idea. I had no right to lust after two younger men. Nobody has a relationship like that. It's bizarre and I'm disgusted with myself, so I don't allow myself to think, and I don't look at myself in the mirror. I don't need to see my mistakes reflected back at me.

I know I'll be able to get over this because it was never real in the first place. It was just a fairy tale, and I needed a dose of reality and my bar to let the memories fade. I just need to ride it out. I've had the love of my life, Valery, and I feel ashamed that I might have denigrated his memory by getting carried away in a delusional fancy. Love never strikes twice, you only get one chance, so I know this will pass. But what I don't understand is why every time I wake up, I feel worse instead of better, and my heart feels like it's turned to ash.

Chapter 43

Florencio

I sign my name on yet another document that Señor Bernat puts in front of me. This is to set up my own secure storage at the bank. There have been several documents, signing over ownership of most of the art that hangs on the walls of the mansion. I don't know much about them, and I'd usually ask Rafe as he has far more knowledge of art than I do, but he's not here. No one's here. It's just my aunt, Juana, and myself, and it feels empty.

Apparently, on paper, I'm now very wealthy. I've craved financial independence all my life and now that I have it, it brings me zero joy. I wander listlessly around the house, trying to avoid areas that bring back memories, which are pretty much all of them. Instead, I spend more and more time with my aunt, reading to her and talking with her, but even she grows weary of my melancholy.

I've spoken with Rafe a few times, and while he says he's coming back, each time he feels more distant—more English

—which is a ridiculous thing to say. I don't know whether he noticed, but from being with us so much, he'd started speaking English with a Spanish accent. Now it's fading every time he calls me, and that makes me sad in a way I can't describe. It's like every time you look at a picture, the colour fades, making it look more translucent. That's only one of the layers of emotion I'm experiencing. I hover between anxiety that he's going to forget me and sadness that he won't want to come back. Then there's the huge part of my heart that Constantin has ripped out and left bleeding. I didn't even know I loved him too until he left.

I knew the moment I fell for Rafe; it hit me like a freight train when we were in Park Güell. It was the day when everything looked brighter and tasted sweeter and I knew I would do anything for him, even if that meant letting Constantin in. I liked Constantin a lot, but I didn't think I was in love with him. I was expecting another huge impact, but nothing came. There was no big revelation. My love for him is more subtle, it's grown gradually, like ivy taking possession of a house, entwining its roots into the brickwork. I didn't notice how much it had become symbiotic with my soul until he tore it all away.

I walk into the kitchen, usually my happy place, but I can't calm myself by cooking. What's the point? There's no one to cook for. I miss seeing Rafe burning pancakes as I distract him with kisses, or having them try to steal empanadas when they think I'm not watching. The conversations we've had over the many meals we've taken together. What was it all for, if I'm left feeling like this? I stare uselessly into the refrigerator, trying to remember what I came in for. Something to eat? No, that can't be right. I'm not hungry. Maybe just some coffee then.

I force myself into the ballroom and make myself dance, partly because I need to exercise so I can keep supple, but I'm hoping that moving my body will unlock some of the heaviness I'm feeling. Going through the varied practice routines does help to a certain extent, but the memories crowd round me as soon as I stop. Constantin at the piano, his soulful dark eyes watching Rafe and me dancing. Beautiful, sweet Rafe in my arms, always trying his best, and his joy when he gets something right. It's too much and I can feel the tears welling up again. I thought I was done crying, but it seems the tears aren't done with me. I sit on my bed, my arms gripping a sweater Rafe left behind. Like I have every night, I bury my head in it, inhaling the scent of him.

My phone rings and my heart jumps a little as I see it's Rafe.

"Hey," I say as I answer it.

"Hey, Flo. Baby, I'm coming home."

Chapter 44

Rafe

After getting off the phone with Florencio, I feel a lot more settled. The turmoil of the last few days has left me feeling jittery and being able to make plans is calming. My mum was discharged yesterday, and apart from being weak, she's doing well. It turns out the virus had affected her so badly because she had an unknown iron deficiency. Now they've diagnosed her, and she's getting treated for that as well. She just needs to rest but isn't in any danger. I want a couple more days to make sure she really is on the mend before heading back to Spain. I know I've only been there six weeks, but I love the city, and it feels a lot more like home to me than England.

I don't know what the future holds. I need to make plans and discuss them with Florencio, because apart from the fact he doesn't want to go back to Argentina, I don't know what he wants to do.

And then there's the massive ache in my heart called Constantin. I haven't even begun processing what he means by what he said and did. I couldn't take it on board when I found out about my mum, so I put a plaster over that part of me, and now I'm scared to rip it off. I live with the dull pain that's constantly with me, carrying it around like a cumbersome bag I can't put down anywhere.

Whilst I've told my parents that I want to go back to Spain, I haven't told them about Florencio and Constantin. I think it's time they knew, and I honestly have no idea how they'll take it. It's a big change from marrying—and then not marrying—Loretta. They've only just got over the shock of all that.

I seek them out in the living room.

"Mum, Dad." I wipe my hands down the front of my jeans and take a seat opposite them. "I know I haven't turned out the way you wanted."

My mum puts down the book she's reading and my dad the newspaper.

"Whatever gave you that idea, love?" my mum asks.

"Like, I didn't go into law like Dad or become an accountant, but I became an author instead. I'm sorry to disappoint you."

"Do you really think that? That we're disappointed? We wanted you to have a steady career so you didn't have any worries . . . financially," my mum says, looking worried.

"We're so proud of you, son, of what you've achieved," my dad chimes in. Oh! I really had no idea.

"You could've said so!" That comes out stronger than I meant it to, but I still have to break the bigger news to them and my nerves are a little stretched. "Sorry, sorry." I run my hands through my hair.

"No, we're the ones who are sorry, love."

"Are you?" My mum beckons me over. I sit next to her on the couch and tuck myself into her side in a way I haven't done for a long time.

"All we want is for you to be happy, and I'm sorry if we gave you any impression that we were disappointed in you. I guess we were cautious about how happy you'd be as an author, and we didn't want to see you struggle."

I can almost understand their twisted logic, but it still hurts that they never told me they were proud of me.

"I thought all these years you didn't approve and just wished I was doing something else, but you know I could never be happy being a lawyer or something. Not that there's anything wrong with it." I glance at my dad, but he's smiling.

"We know, love. Well, we do now, anyway." My mum rubs her hand up and down my arm.

"There's something else I need to tell you," I say hesitantly. "And it might be a shock so I'm a little nervous."

"As long as you're happy, Rafe, that's all we want for you."

Well, we shall see how far that extends. I take a deep breath.

"When I was in Spain, I met someone."

"Oh, that's nice, love," my mum says quickly.

"Mum, hear me out please, it's not what you think."

"Oh, did you get married? I mean, after the whole debacle with Loretta—"

"Mum! Please?" I ask, and she stops. "No, I'm not married, nor likely to be."

"Oh."

"Will you let me explain?" I need to make sure I don't have any further interruptions, as I want to make sure I can explain everything.

"Yes, of course. Sorry."

"Well, I actually met two someones in Spain, at the same time, and we're all together." I don't want to complicate the issue with Constantin, especially as I refuse to think he would just leave us suddenly, and I want my parents to understand.

"But they're both guys. We've been living together for the last few weeks."

I'm met with silence. I guess they need to process it.

"Two guys?" my mum asks, at least it's not hysteria.

"Yes, Mum."

"Are you happy?"

"Very much so."

"Then we're happy too." She side-hugs me, and I lean into her, relief and love for her easy acceptance almost overwhelming me.

"Thank you," I whisper, and she tightens her hold.

"We're happy for you." She pulls back slightly and looks pointedly at my father. "Aren't we Reggie?"

I turn to him. I'm not sure what I expected, but it certainly wasn't the bemused expression he has plastered on his face. I should be thankful it's not disgust.

"Aren't we Reggie?" she repeats a little louder.

"Yes, of course." He still seems tickled by the idea. "How do you?" He makes a series of hand motions. "You know?"

"Reggie!" my mum shouts, and I can't stop a giggle from escaping, as it was pretty much my first question too. "Go and make us all a cup of tea," she orders him and he obeys. "I'm sorry about that. We can have a nice cup of tea, and you can tell us all about them."

I breathe a sigh of relief, which is very short-lived.

"But *how* do you?"

"Mum!"

I take a deep breath before I open the door to the office. When I first started out with Helen, she didn't have her own office, but now, with her impressive roster of authors, I guess it's become more important for her. I called her a couple of days ago to set up the meeting, something I feel I need to do before returning to Spain.

"Rafe. How lovely to see you." Her greeting is overly friendly, which grates on my nerves slightly.

"Helen," I say before I sit down in the chair offered.

"You're looking very . . . European." Helen always was the master of conveying what she means while pretending to be pleasant, and I see nothing has changed.

"Que maleducada," I utter under my breath, amusing myself that I can swear so easily in Spanish. But out loud I say, "It comes from living in Europe." I enunciate the word deliberately. She narrows her eyes and sits back.

"You've changed," she says icily. Yes, I have. I'm no longer going to allow myself to be pushed around. I can stand my ground. Love, respect, and support can do that for a person.

"And you haven't," I reply, proving her point. But I haven't come here to do anything other than terminate our agreement, so I remove the letter my father helped me draw up last night and place it on the desk in front of us.

"I don't have a lot of time as I have a plane to catch." It's not true—I don't leave until tomorrow—but I want her to know I am going back. "But effective immediately, I'm no longer in need of your services. You've been paid up to the end of the month."

She looks at it but doesn't take it.

"How does it suit you to write the biographies of decrepit old stars no one's ever heard of?"

"Very well, thank you." I chuckle, not allowing her to bait me. I see her nostrils flare as she finally realises she can no longer affect me.

"It won't sell," she sells peevishly.

"We'll see," I say, rising from my chair. "But it's not your problem anymore, is it?"

I don't bother saying goodbye. That she didn't use the Sloan Kennedy card raises her very slightly in my estimation, but only slightly. Helen, Loretta, Sloan, they're all part of my past now, and I allow any last hold their influences have on me to be borne away on the breeze as I stroll to my next appointment, one I'm much more looking forward to.

I glance up at the impressive stone facade of the building. It's a gentleman's club. It oozes old money and looks as tight-lipped as the secrets it no doubt keeps. Not so long ago, the thought of entering a building like this would have intimidated me, but I've spent weeks living in a large mansion surrounded by almost priceless artworks and antiques. I think I can hold my own.

I say my name to the concierge on the door and am shown to a small room that looks like a library. The books make me feel at ease. The concierge announces my name, says he'll arrange tea, and withdraws.

A dark-haired man who had been staring out the window turns round. He's about my age and height, but I'm struck by two things: first, his pretty eyes framed by tortoiseshell glasses, and second, he appears to be very nervous. Then he starts talking.

"Thank you for coming, Mr Alderson." He crosses the room and holds out his hand, which I shake. "I hope you don't mind me asking you to meet here." He gestures round the room. "It's my father's club . . . Well, I suppose mine too, but I don't have an office yet, and I thought it very amateurish to invite you to my house, or rather my parents' house, as I don't have one of those of my own yet . . ." He stops with a grimace.

"I assume you're Noah Ellington?" I enquire, as he hasn't introduced himself, but I don't really need to ask as he talks exactly like his email.

"Urgh, yes, sorry. I'm not good at this, but I want to be. Good at it, of course."

"Greeting people?" I'm teasing him slightly, but I like him, and I think some gentle teasing might help him calm down a little.

"That bad, huh?" His shoulders lower as he lets out a breath, and he looks so glum that I think I might have gone too far. The door opens, and a waiter comes in pushing a trolley. We both watch him as he transfers a tray onto a low table between several wingback chairs in front of an unlit fireplace, before going away again as soundlessly as he entered.

I look back at Noah. "Shall we try again?" He brightens considerably to show me a slightly less nervous smile.

Once we both have a cup of tea and are ensconced in the very comfortable wingback chairs, I ask Noah to tell me a bit about himself. I learn he was privately educated, studied at Oxford for an MA in World Literature, but has just returned to complete his Masters in publishing.

"Up to now, my job has been working for a dealer in antique books. I'm good at it. I like hunting down rare editions of books and attending auctions."

"Then why do you want to be a literary agent?" I ask, sensing a but.

"The books I deal in are all by dead authors. I'd like to get to know some living ones."

I let out a genuine laugh and decide I like Noah very much.

"Why me?" It's an honest question, and it looks like the nervousness that the last few minutes of chatting have managed to dispel is going to creep back.

"I hope you don't mind that I contacted you," he starts. "But I would really like to represent you with your current project."

Now he does have my attention.

"How do you know about it?" I haven't told anyone about it except my parents . . . and of course Helen.

"Well, we were at an event a while ago, for my course and with some people in the industry. Your agent was there, and whilst she didn't mention any names, she was telling people what to do when your authors 'go rogue' as she described it. Then later, I overheard her say one of her authors was trying to ask her to sell a biography of a nobody. Her exact words were, 'I mean, who's ever heard of Estrella Winters?'"

I can't help scowling at the indiscretion of my former agent, but somehow it doesn't surprise me, and only adds weight to the belief that my earlier action was the correct one. But that's not what interests me here.

"And you have?"

"Oh, yes. I know she's not as widely well known as the Hollywood stars, but I dealt in some vintage books recently, photographs of the stars from the forties to the sixties. She appeared several times in those."

I'm impressed, but I'm still not connecting the dots.

"How did you know it was me if Helen didn't mention me by name?"

"Ah, this is where I might have overstepped the mark, I'm afraid."

I sit and wait for him to continue, and with a slight intake of breath, he does.

"Our fathers. I think they like to talk about us, and as we're both in books, so to speak, I think it gives them some common ground. Your father mentioned it to mine, who told me. I put two and two together with what Helen had said and, I'm sorry to say, I begged him to ask for a contact for you." He wrinkles his nose and makes a slight grimace. It is indiscreet, and my dad is a lawyer so he should know better. But now I know he's proud of me, so I can imagine him mentioning it to Noah's dad with some pride. It fills me with a warm glow, and so I can forgive him.

I look around the room, remembering where I am, and wonder how much business is done, how much has been won and lost, on a chance word or a name dropped here and there in the right ears. It's the way things are conducted behind the closed doors of gentleman's clubs and it seems apt that this is where he set up the meeting.

"Well, indiscretion of former agents and the gossiping of our fathers aside." His face relaxes and his eyes brighten at that. " What makes you think you can sell this book?"

He reels off a list of potential publishers, some I'd never heard of, who could be interested in the biography, and not for the first time since we met, I'm impressed by him.

"So, would you consider taking me on as your agent, at least for this book?" he finishes. I am very tempted, but I don't want to rush into it. I want to step away and have time to consider all my options.

"I'd like to think about it, if I may?"

"Thank you." He gives a relieved smile. "Now, would you like to stay for lunch? They have an excellent restaurant here."

I have no doubt about that.

"You don't have to woo me with lunch," I say teasingly.

"If I was going to do that, I would have opened with it," he quips and I laugh. "I'm asking because I like you."

"Then thank you, I accept." I have a feeling Noah and I are going to be good friends.

Chapter 45

Constantin

The work on the bar is going well. Everything is starting to come together . . . except for me, where it's all falling apart. I feel like shit and I know I must look the same as Alena pulls a face every time she turns up for work. But I don't have time for that, we're just two days away from reopening the bar.

It's been rebuilt, redecorated, and cleaned. Today's job is to unpack the storeroom and see if there are any last-minute items that need to be ordered.

We work hard for hours, lugging and emptying crates and refilling the fridges. Putting the bottles back on the shelves and giving all the glasses another clean.

I also do a stocktake and tidy the storeroom back to some sort of order. It's hot work, and by the end of it I'm sweating. I lift my T-shirt to wipe my face.

"*Urgh*, boss. When did you last shower?" Alena's lip curls in disgust as she walks past me.

I don't actually remember. Am I that bad? I lift an arm and sniff. Okay, she has a point.

She turns around and faces me. "I'm going to say this as your friend and because I care about you. Go have a shower, put on some clean clothes, and take the night off. We're nearly ready to open, and you need a rest, or you'll not be fit to reopen on Friday. I'd like to tell you to sort out whatever's put you in this funk, but I doubt you'll listen to me. You have a tendency to stick your head in the sand, and I hate to see you like this."

Her expression is soft, and I know she really does care. I'm lucky to have her as a friend. She's also right, I could do with a shower and clean clothes. As for sticking my head in the sand . . . yeah, well, let's not dwell on that one. I push myself off from leaning on the bar.

She backs off a little and puts her hands up. "Woah, if you're coming in for a thank-you hug, can we postpone it? I like you but not that much."

A laugh escapes me, the first for several days.

"Thank you, Alena. I guess I needed that."

"You're welcome, just please look after yourself, Con. I'll see you tomorrow," she says before leaving me alone in the quiet of the bar.

I let the water run over me, turning it up as hot as I can stand. I stay under the shower for a long time, convincing myself that I really did do the right thing. "It's for the best," I mutter to myself for the umpteenth time. It's almost become a mantra to me.

When I'm dry, I go in search of a clean shirt, which isn't that easy, but then half my clothes are still up at Estrella's house. The rest, well, I'm surprised they haven't made their own way to the washing machine. I gather them all up into the laundry basket—I'll sort them later—then open the closet and find at least something half decent to put on. My eyes catch sight of the wooden box and I pull it out. Yes, a reminder of Valery is what I need right now. Memories of true love, not a crazy infatuation. I sit cross-legged on the bed, and opening the lid, I start pulling out the photographs and treasure within.

I thumb through the pictures and relive the memories and good times, feeling the familiar ache, the long-settled grief that sits behind my ribs. I can bear it better now, almost welcome it. It's an old friend, something I know the extent of. It can hurt me sometimes, and I've let it bring me down, but I know the depths it can reach. I know its limits.

Other images start inserting themselves into my well-worn pattern. That day with Rafe at Castle Montjuïc when he looked both vulnerable but so also like the brightest star in the universe. Florencio and his breathtaking honesty and feisty fun. Watching them together . . . and being a part of them. A large tear lands on the photographs I'd stopped looking through a while ago. I wipe it away and put down the stack of pictures. This is like nothing I've felt before. It snags on every breath, like fresh barbs waiting to dig into me when I close my eyes. It hurts to breathe, it hurts not to breathe. I'm caught in its thorny web, and every time I try to pull myself out, I get ensnared deeper. Its hooks pierce my skin, the pain burrowing in bone deep. I have no idea of the limits of this and until I find out, I know the only way I can cope.

First, I light a cigarette to steady myself, and then I reach for the bottle and pour a drink. A detached part of me is disgusted that I started keeping alcohol next to the bed again, but I pay it no heed as I try to numb myself. I pick up the photographs again, trying to get back onto safe ground. As I pack them back in the box, I find a letter. It's open so I must have read it, but I don't remember it. It's Valery's handwriting.

· · ·

My Dearest Con,

It saddens me that I won't be there for your best years, to share them with you side by side, but we don't make this world, we can only live in it, and I've had my time. I couldn't ask for a better person to spend my short time with. Thank you for every minute.

But now, however, I want you to put yourself first and find someone to share that huge heart of yours with. As you read this, I can almost hear you saying that lightning never strikes twice. It used to amuse me, but now I fear you will believe it and use it to not let yourself love again. I know I've told you this, but I also know you're stubborn and won't listen to anyone. I thought if I wrote it down, one day you might have need of it.

Please look out for love, Con, and if you see it, grab it with both hands and don't let go. Don't become a martyr to my memory, because I know in a heart as big as yours there will always be a corner for me.

Love,

Valery

I knock back the drink and pour another. My phone rings and I ignore it, but as soon as it rings off, it starts again.

"What?" I snatch it up and answer it.

"Con?"

"Wis." I let out a long breath.

"Are you all right?"

I ignore his question and ask tersely, "What is it you want?"

I hear his sharp intake of breath at the other end. He didn't deserve that from me, but I'm past caring.

"I was going to wish you luck for the reopening."

"Thank you," I manage through clenched teeth.

"How are those lovely guys of yours?"

"They're not *my* guys," I grind out.

I hear a slightly exasperated sigh. "Con, what did you do?"

"What makes you think *I* did anything?"

"Because I know you, Con, and if anyone was going to fuck it up, it would be you."

"Well, I rather think it was you," I spit.

"What the hell did *I* do?" Luis' voice is incredulous.

"You said they were perfect together, and what the hell did they need me for?"

"I did not say that!" he almost shouts down the phone. "Yes, I said they were perfect together, but I didn't say they weren't perfect for you as well. Don't go adding your narrative to my words and blaming me. I've always said you should stop moping and get back out there. It's you who's always got his head up his arse. Fucking hell, Con, I'd give my right arm for half a chance at one go at finding love, but you have it right in front of you again and throw it away. You need to take the chances you get in this world."

"Valery said as much."

There's the briefest of pauses. "Valery?"

"He wrote me a letter before he died. I'd forgotten about it, but I've just found it. He said I would be stubborn."

"I always said he was wise. You didn't deserve him."

"Ouch!" That was really below the belt. It's only because he's my cousin and best friend that I don't hang up on him.

"Tell me that isn't so right now." Luis is still pissed at me. "Tell me I'm wrong, Con."

The coil of my core that's been tightly wound for the last few days springs free and unravels. I let out a deep sigh. I finally allow myself the truth—that I want nothing more than to be back with Rafe and Florencio.

"I've really fucked this up, haven't I?"

"I'll say you have." Luis doesn't pull any punches, but it's what I need right now.

Dread floods through me. It might be too late.

"What do I need to do, Wis?"

"What you do best, Con." This time, his voice is softer. "And good luck."

I stand, and picking up my glass, I pour the rest of my drink down the sink. I throw my cigarettes in the bin. I know exactly what I have to do.

Chapter 46

Florencio

I pace the house again, the way I have been doing most of the morning. It's become a route, from the lobby through the halls to the ballroom, out onto the terrace, down into the kitchen and back. There's no point sitting still, I can't settle long enough to do anything. Rafe is arriving very soon.

Last night we talked on the phone for a long time, longer than we have since he had to return to England. Afterwards, I had the best night's sleep I've had since he left. This morning, I cooked some empanadas for him, the first meal I've prepared that hasn't been just heating something out of a tin. But now, as the time inches closer to when he's due to arrive, I'm like a nervous horse, skittish and jumping at my own shadow.

My heart constricts when I hear a car on the driveway, and then suddenly he appears like a golden vision. I almost knock him over as I leap at him, and he drops his bags to clasp me tight.

I kiss him long and hard, tears of relief and joy running down my face.

"Niño de oro," I breathe when our lips part. "I thought you weren't coming back." I kiss each part of his face between every word, and still, it's not enough.

"Flo, baby," he whispers. "I'm sorry. I won't leave again."

"Baby?" I noticed this has slipped in a few times.

"Well, you call me *niño,* and I'm older than you, so surely you must be baby . . . but in truth, I like it," he says, a smile lighting up his face.

"I love it," I say, tucking my head into his shoulder. "I've never been anyone's baby before."

He holds me tight in his arms, and my world, which has been spinning out of control, finally starts to slow enough for the nausea to subside, but it's still off-kilter.

I allow Rafe enough time to get to his room and start unpacking before I bring up the elephant in the room—or rather, who definitely *isn't* in the room.

I sit on his bed and hold a pillow to me, hugging it for comfort.

"What are we going to do about Con?"

He pauses in his unpacking. "Still nothing from him?"

"No. Why didn't he want us?" It comes out as a wail.

Something twists in his face, and he looks like he's about to crumble. Rafe climbs onto the bed and lies next to me. His eyes are wet, which accentuates the gold flecks in them, lending them a fragile beauty. He looks up at me.

"Flo, I don't understand it," he says. I let go of the pillow and lay beside him. He reaches out and traces my face with his fingers.

"I love you, Flo, in all the ways Con described and more. I hated every minute of being away from you. But while half my heart is full like a meadow of blooming flowers, the other half feels empty and desolate." He pauses, and I catch his hand in mine. Turning it over, I press a kiss on his wrist. *He loves me, he loves me,* rings through my brain.

"I remember the exact moment I discovered I was in love with you," I whisper, trailing kisses across the palm of his hand. "That day in Park Güell, the realisation hit me so hard I nearly fell over."

"I thought you just stumbled." He smiles at the memory.

"That was me falling for you," I murmur, leaning down to kiss his beautiful lips.

"I'm sorry," he says when I release him. "This is all my fault. I wanted to taste everything, sample the world. If I hadn't—"

"No." I stop him. "At first, I might have been reluctant to want to share you. I won't lie about that." I see his brow crease slightly that he might have caused me pain, and I want to kiss it away. "But I liked Con, a lot. So it was my decision to let him in. That grew in a different way. There was no arrow to the heart, but it was more like a nurtured plant. And now . . . and now . . ." I gulp, trying to stop the tears that have never been far from the surface all week. If I let them go, it's going to be ugly. "Now it feels like I'm missing a limb. And all the time, I keep thinking I should have told him how I felt— like I should've told you. Maybe then he wouldn't have left." I press my eyes shut and lie on my side. Rafe shifts slightly to lie facing me. As I open my eyes, he touches his forehead to mine. We just look at each other, our sadness mingling in a combined grief. Neither of us moves, not willing to break this moment, not knowing what to do next, or how to move past this.

Then Rafe blinks. "Do you hear something?" he whispers.

I strain, listening carefully, and hear the unmistakable sound of a guitar and a voice I'd recognise anywhere.

We sit up, trying to work out where it's coming from. Rafe makes it out of the door a fraction before me, but it's neck and neck down the stairs as we race through the house and wrench the front door open.

Constantin is standing there with his guitar, singing Enrique Iglesias's "Somebody's Me."

He finishes the song and takes a deep breath. His face is creased like he's in pain.

"That was my apology song. I'm . . . I'm so sorry. You two are so good together and I thought . . . you would be better off without me. That you don't need me. But *I* need *you* and if it's not too late . . ."

Rafe goes to move, but I catch hold of his arm. Anger mixes with the relief that Constantin wants to come back.

"You're going to make me beg, aren't you?" Constantin asks.

"It's very tempting, but it's not about that, Con. Right at the start of this relationship, we agreed to communicate. So we didn't get hurt. That wasn't just about who could kiss or fuck who, it was about *everything*. And you hurt us, Con, in here." I thump my chest for emphasis. "You should've talked to us. If you had doubts, you should've said something instead of running away."

"Yes, Wis said I stuck my head up my arse."

"Well, he's right. You hurt us all. I don't know, Con. I don't know if I can go through that again."

His face drops as he takes in what I'm saying. But if he wants to come back, he has to fight for this. *For us*.

"I'm so sorry. I fell into an old pattern. I know that's not good enough. I can see that now. Please let me back. Please. I promise you both it won't happen again."

"You'll talk to us first?"

"Absolutely."

I don't know if I want to kiss him or hit him for what he's put us through, but he looks so forlorn that I just go to him and put my arms around him. Rafe joins me and clings to us both.

"Con," I say against his chest. "You know I hate you right now. I love you, but I also hate you."

His answer is to wrap his warm, strong arms around us both and say, "I hate me too right now."

My heart is pounding in my ribcage, the swell of emotions too much. It's like a buildup of electricity that needs discharging, the same way lightning needs to strike the ground. Constantin explained his actions, and whilst I understand them, I'm still not ready to forgive him, not just yet. I expected to feel whole again, but I'm too keyed up. I look over at Rafe and he still wears a slightly bewildered expression, like he's still processing.

"Con, I think you need to apologise more."

"I—" he starts, and I place my fingers against his lips.

"Not like that."

He tilts his head at me, and I see his eyes darken as he catches my meaning. He grabs my hand and one of Rafe's and leads us inside, kicking the door shut and pulling us up the stairs with him. I direct them into my room.

I shut the door, and he pushes me up against it.

"I'm sorry," he utters in a low, gravelly voice before he kisses me. Then he lines Rafe up next to me, muttering the same words before he kisses him as well.

When he draws back, he frowns slightly, swinging his head between us.

"See, this is the problem. How can I choose?"

"You never have to," I say, dropping to my knees and taking the decision out of his hands.

I unbuckle his belt and pull down his jeans to release his cock, watching it bob in front of me. "I thought I was apologising," he chuckles slightly.

"You will," I say before taking as much as I can into my mouth in one go. He returns to kissing Rafe as I ply my tongue to him, enjoying the little twitches his pelvis makes under my touch.

I pop off him and stand, knowing exactly what I want. I peel off my T-shirt and instruct Constantin to finish getting undressed. I kiss Rafe and then explain it to him, checking in with him that he's all right with it.

"Fuck yeah, I want to try that," he says, pulling his own T-shirt off and undressing.

I find some lube and condoms and toss them onto the coverlet.

Then I lead Rafe to the bed and ask him to kneel up. I kneel in front of him, and we kiss. I grab his arse and pull us closer, so we're pressed chest to chest, our cocks grinding against each other. I know I'm doing this mostly to give Constantin a show to prove to him just what he'd be missing. I hear him groan, and look over at him fisting his own cock. I smirk at him, and he gives me a dark, lustful look. He gets the message that he understands, but as punishments go, it could be a lot worse. I return to kissing Rafe senseless, enjoying him trying to find some friction against me.

I lie back on the bed and pull Rafe on top of me. He kisses down my chest, but he doesn't waste too much time, feeling the urge as much as I do.

He gives my cock a couple of long, slow sucks before sitting back on his heels.

He turns his head to flash a smile at Constantin, who

comes over and kneels behind him, kissing the back of his neck.

Rafe picks up the condoms and passes one to Constantin. I see him murmur against Rafe's neck, who nods. I love how he cares and checks in with Rafe—consent is sexy.

Constantin runs his hand down Rafe's back and pushes him forward, so he leans over me on all fours. I take the condom packet off him and open it, sheathing him as Constantin does the same to himself. I pop open the lube, squirting some into my hand before taking Rafe's cock and slowly running it down, up, and down, watching him relax as Constantin lubes his fingers and gently preps him. I enjoy seeing how much he loves this, and he's soon thrusting into my hand before pushing back onto Constantin's fingers. Constantin withdraws and coats himself with more lube before lining up with Rafe's hole.

"You ready, *precioso*?" Constantin murmurs and Rafe nods. Constantin presses forward slowly and a smile forms on Rafe's face.

"Wow, that feels good," he whispers, and I smile with him as I know exactly what he means. Constantin bottoms out and stops for a minute, letting Rafe get used to the feel of him before gripping his hips and giving a few slow thrusts.

I lean up and give Rafe a quick kiss before I get on my knees and back up to him. Feeling his cock against my entrance, I push back, taking all of him in one go.

"*Unnngh*," Rafe lets out, and I huff a laugh. Then Constantin starts to move, and I feel the power of his thrusts transfer through Rafe and into me. I brace my forearms and let them pound into me. It's glorious and I give in to the motion. Feeling the delicious way he nudges my gland elicits a deep moan. Rafe pecks kisses across my back and a warmth builds in me. Only now does my brain settle, and my body feel grounded and wholly connected to those I love. I turn my head to see Rafe twist his body to kiss Constantin, then he leans down to capture my lips too.

Rafe shudders as he comes first. The force of it as he pegs my prostate once more forces me over the edge and I nearly collapse in ecstasy. Constantin holds on to us both for a couple more thrusts before he plasters himself to Rafe's back —also spent.

He withdraws from Rafe, as I slide off him and crumple onto the bed. Rafe crashes down beside me, panting.

"Holy fuck, that was incredible." He laughs and whoops with joy. I catch his euphoria and laugh with him. Constantin cleans us up and crawls up the middle of the bed. We both snuggle into him as he puts an arm round each of us.

"Am I forgiven yet?" he whispers into my hair.

I look at him with a sly smile. "Maybe."

Chapter 47

Rafe

"How do I look?" I ask Florencio as I adjust my collar in the mirror.

"Good enough to eat," he replies, but sadly we don't have time for that. Though he still comes to stand behind me and puts his arms around me, resting his head on my shoulder and looking in the mirror with me—him in a dark red shirt, his favourite colour and one that looks so good against his skin, and me in midnight blue.

"We both look good enough to eat, and if we're lucky, that might just happen." He smiles, and I turn my head to kiss him.

"Did Con say anything about the surprise he's arranged?"

"Not a thing. Not to me, at least."

"Do you think he'll come?" I glance at my watch.

"He will be here. If he isn't, he knows what'll happen." He gives me a feral grin in the mirror.

"You were so good at making him apologise the other day. After that song, I was ready to jump into his arms."

"Your beautiful spirit, sense of forgiveness, and willingness to see the good in everyone are some of the many things I love about you. But we needed to make sure he understood because I'm not joking, I cannot go through that again," he says, turning me round and kissing me properly.

Just then, we hear the beep of a car horn and make our way down to the lobby. Constantin is near the door, which is standing open. We look through it to see a huge black limousine.

"I thought we could do this in style," Constantin says.

"I love it!" Florencio exclaims.

Estrella and Juana appear from the other side of the house. Estrella looks stunning in periwinkle blue, and Juana looks beautiful in a green dress, which makes a change from the plain clothes she normally wears that she calls her uniform.

"*Señora*, your carriage awaits," Constantin says with a flourish. "Ladies, are you ready?" He goes over to them and offers each of them an arm, escorting them both out to the waiting car.

Florencio and I follow right behind. We're ready to take Estrella for her day out.

"How's everything at the bar?" I ask Constantin as we settle into the car, fully aware that it's the grand reopening tonight. We said we should change the day to take Estrella out, but Constantin was adamant about keeping it the same as he had another surprise.

"We're as ready as we can be. Alena is more than capable of handling the opening, and we'll be there later. There's also the band and Anton."

We drive out to the Museu Nacional d'Art De Catalunya

first, where Estrella spends some time looking up at the huge building and the cascading waterfall.

Then we drive past the Casa Vicens and to Park Güell.

Estrella tells us tales of times when she used to visit often. How she wasn't sure about the Gaudi designs at first, but has grown to love them over time.

Estrella won't be able to walk around the park, but she wants to visit the dragon steps one last time.

Florencio and I walk with Estrella and Juana. Constantin follows slowly, as if he finds each step a struggle.

"What is it?" I ask when he catches up with us.

"This was a place that Valery and I came to a lot." He looks down at his feet. "This was pretty much the exact spot I proposed to him."

"Oh, I'm sorry. We shouldn't have come, Con."

"It's fine. He wouldn't want me to be upset about it. He'd say I was a sentimental fool. I have my memories, they'll always be there, but I'm ready to make new ones." He places an arm round each of us, and we stand there together, looking across the city.

Back in the car, we travel to the Eixample district, past the roof like a dragon's back of Casa Batlló to see the Sagrada Familia. I haven't visited it yet and am excited to see the huge building. Construction started in 1882, and over a hundred and forty years later, it's still not complete. I look up at the passion façade, but it's impossible to take it all in with just one brief visit, so I vow to come back again.

"I've watched this grow ever since I arrived in this city," Estrella says as we walk through the apse where hundreds of stained-glass windows throw their colours onto us. "It takes a lot of vision to start something that you are never going to see finished, a lasting legacy that it will take generations to build. And yet no one ever said no, let's not bother. If something is worth building, it's worth taking the necessary time to make sure it's the best it can be." She takes Juana's arm and walks slowly back to the limo, leaving us all staring after her and then looking curiously at each other.

We make our way to the old town, passing the parabolic arched doorways of Palau Güell and on to the Cathedral. Only Juana and Estrella go in, while Florencio, Constantin, and I walk in the shady cloisters.

"She's saying goodbye to everywhere, isn't she?" Florencio's voice is strained.

"I think she is," Constantin agrees. "It's like she's visiting each of her old friends in turn."

"She's the only member of my family I actually like. I don't want her to die." Florencio gulps and I pull him in for a hug.

"None of us do, baby," I whisper, and we stay like that for a long time.

Estrella, though, looks very cheerful as we get back into the car, and Florencio manages to smile even if he is not his usual bubbly self.

We pay a visit to Cafè de l'Òpera, a restaurant Estrella was a frequent visitor to, and she's greeted effusively by the owners who lament that they haven't seen her for several years. She's treated like royalty as they show us to a private room and bring tapas and drinks.

The day gives over to evening as we make our way back into the limo for the short journey to Constantin's bar. Neither Florencio nor I have seen it since the day the ceiling collapsed, and I'm keen to see how the repairs have gone. It also feels special as it's the place where we first met each other. I reach for Florencio's hand as the limo stops at the end of the alleyway. Constantin has talked several times to Alena on the phone, but he assures us all is well.

Constantin goes on ahead as the rest of us walk together to the bar. When we get to the door, Constantin opens it.

"Señora, welcome to La Casa De Valery," he says, and ushers us inside.

I'm struck by how it looks. It's the same and yet very different. It still has the wooden dance floor to one side, and half wood-panelled walls. The sign behind the bar is neon, but that's not the only change. The walls are brighter, and most of the old pictures are gone. Instead, hanging on the walls are most of the photos from the Hollywood room. Photos of Estrella and all the stars she met. It's beautiful and gives the bar an elegantly classical feel.

My eyes are finally drawn to Estrella, who is standing in stunned silence. Then I notice Sofia and Señor and Señora Bernat. I don't recognise the rest of the people in the bar, but it's clear Estrella does because she turns to Juana.

"You did this for me?"

Chapter 48

Constantin

Watching Estrella's face when she realises she's surrounded by friends and acquaintances was worth the mad frenzy over the last thirty-six hours. I was only too happy to help when Juana approached me yesterday morning with the idea and I made the reopening night an exclusive event.

"Now who do you think cares enough?" I ask Estrella as I escort her to a table next to the dance floor.

"Touché." She gives me a glittering smile as she sits.

I return to Florencio and Rafe.

"It looks amazing," Florencio says.

"Thank you."

"I'm impressed. The party is a great idea." Rafe adds.

"Well, that was Juana, really. She's the one who pulled everyone together. I just provided the venue. Here, I have a table for us." I direct them to an empty table.

For the next few hours, we drink and eat and watch as Estrella holds court amongst people she hasn't seen for a long time. I can see she's in her element and how she would've been an amazing hostess.

I seek Juana out as she comes to the bar. "It's a good thing you've done for her," I tell her.

"It's the least I can do. She's been a good employer. More than that, really, she's also a good friend to me."

After a while, I signal for the band to start playing and a few of the guests get up to dance. I go to help Alena with the bar and see Rafe and Florencio get up to dance together.

I go over to the piano, which survived the ceiling crash very well, only requiring a retune.

"Ladies and gentlemen, in honour of our special guest tonight, I want to play for you 'Esta Noche De Luna.'" There's applause and I start to play. Señor Bernat rises and offers his hand to Estrella to dance and I continue playing, including the song of her name. Eventually, she begins to tire, and in the early hours of the morning, the limo takes us all back to the house.

I find the guys on the terrace, leaning on the balustrade and looking out over the lights of the city. I put a bottle and three glasses down on the wall.

"What's this?" Florencio asks.

"Champagne."

"Is there something to celebrate?"

"I thought we could celebrate us," I say.

"Okay, I'm listening." Florencio turns and hoists himself up to sit on the wall. Rafe joins him.

"This has been a truly incredible summer, and whilst it hasn't been easy with my bar, it did mean that I got to know you both. If I hadn't, I would still be the same sad, broken, and lonely bar owner I was before. You've brought a light into my life I thought I lost a long time ago. Rafe, you opened my heart, and Cio, you filled it with joy."

I stop and take a breath.

"I was wrong before when I said you don't get a second chance at love, and I ignored the signs for a long time. I thought it was a stupid infatuation, the fancies of an old man. But when I left—for which I will always be sorry—it hurt. It hurt *so* much. Even then, I tried to ignore it, but I couldn't."

I pause and swallow.

"What I'm trying to say is I love you, both of you. Which I know should be crazy but it isn't, it's amazing, and when I'm with you I feel like a whole person again."

I'm out of words and I wait, holding my breath. I watch as they look at each other and smile.

"Well, I think that is something to celebrate," Rafe says, and I breathe a sigh of relief.

Florencio passes me the bottle and I open it and pour it into the glasses, handing each of them one.

Rafe takes a sip and puts his glass down on the wall. He pulls me close, and I stand between his legs. He puts his arms around my shoulders and leans in, kissing me.

"Con, I love you too. That was never in doubt."

I answer him with another kiss, pushing against his teeth until he lets my tongue in so I can deepen it.

When we part, he gives me a sweet smile.

"By the way, my parents are looking forward to meeting you both."

"You told them about us? Both of us?" I ask.

"I did," he says, looking quite smug.

"How did they take it?"

"Surprisingly well, actually. And yes, they want to meet you so . . . they're flying over next week."

"Next week? No, I don't think I'm ready for meeting the parents next week!" I take a gulp of champagne, regretting it almost immediately as I end up choking.

Florencio is giggling, and I glare at him. "It's all right for you, you're pretty and young! Fuck, I'm like an old bear. Do they know how old I am? Fuck, do they?" Panic starts to set in, and I appeal to Rafe, but he looks amused.

"Yes, they know," he says easily, taking a casual sip of his drink. "But bear? Yes, it suits you. What's bear?"

"*Oso*." Florencio supplies. "*Oro* and *oso*. It's perfect."

"I said you were going to be trouble," I tell him and he gives me a feral grin, the one I love so much.

I look between them.

"Does anyone feel like dancing?"

Epilogue 1

Florencio

Two months later

"Hola Padre." The first time I see my father in four months is in the church for the funeral.

His returned greeting is cold, but I expected nothing less. He took my decision to stay in Barcelona badly, which, considering I'm now not costing him anything, is surprising. Constantin seems to think it's more that he no longer has any control over me, and I think he's probably right.

We exchange a few words, but in the end, we have nothing to say to each other, and he's certainly not travelled all this way to see me. With my sister, it's a bit easier, but not much. Again, I'm no longer a resource to be exploited, and that suits me. My father's manner couldn't be more different from Rafe's parents, who came to visit a few weeks ago. They were warm and welcoming, and we all got on really well, though I think Rafe was more amazed than anyone that they were so accepting of our relationship.

Although I knew it was going to happen—after all, it was why I was sent to Spain in the first place—Estrella's death was a shock. Although we saw her getting weaker and more frail every day, her spirit remained as indomitable as ever and I was lulled into a belief that she would live forever.

When she was taken to the funeral home, either Juana or I stayed with her, keeping vigil. For the most part it was a quiet, contemplative time, which helped me come to terms with her passing, but at other times there was a steady flow of visitors paying their respects. Those who attended the party we gave her two months ago and many others who had heard the news.

After the funeral, which I'm pleased to see is well attended as it seems she was well liked despite her seclusion in later years, we follow in procession to the cemetery. Estrella's wishes were that we would all gather back at the house afterwards, where Sofia has made some food for the guests.

Rafe, Constantin, and I are still staying at the house, though we have talked extensively about what we will do next. Mostly along the lines of renting somewhere until we can buy a property. Constantin still has his place above the bar, but he's reluctant to move back or invite us to live there with him. He says that now he's been living separately from the bar, he feels like having a bit of distance from it helps him to not overwork. I think this is just half the story and there's more to it than that, but I don't mind. Having a new place that is just wholly ours is a good idea.

I spend some time thanking the guests and learning some stories about Estrella I hadn't heard before. Word gets round that Rafe is writing her biography, which is now largely complete, and he is soon commandeered by those who want to hear more or who want to tell him some snippet of gossip they know.

I'm taking some air on the terrace, thankful to be away from everyone for a few minutes, when my father appears.

"Are you still keeping up this nonsense of staying here, then?"

His manner irks me, though it's a question and not a command for once.

"I have a life here now. More than I ever had in Argentina."

"But we are family and it's your duty—"

"No!" I say vehemently, the sharpest tone I've ever taken with him, which stops him in his tracks. "Family are people who love and support you, who you trust and have shared values. I'm not sure you've ever been *family* to me."

I'm done talking with him and make my way back to the guests. As I pass him, he says, "You'll be vacating *my* house immediately."

Even if he inherits every last euro of my aunt's money, the house is held by the estate until probate is granted and I have permission to stay until then, so at best a power play of words. I don't bother answering him and instead seek Rafe and Constantin, suddenly needing my true family close.

Most of the guests have left when Señor Bernat seeks me out.

"This is unusual, but your father has requested to see the will. I cannot refuse him, but I need you to be present. You two as well." He directs the last to Rafe and Constantin. We all exchange curious glances but follow the lawyer to my aunt's office. My father is already there, accompanied by my sister. Juana is sitting in a corner, trying to make herself as unobtrusive as possible.

Señor Bernat takes a place behind my aunt's desk and takes a document out of his case. I've come to respect the lawyer over the last couple of months as he has handled the setting up of the bank storage for me, as well as arranging the sale of a couple of pieces of art.

I take a chair and Rafe and Constantin sit next to me. My father gives us all a glare.

"Why are *they* here?" my father demands. Señor Bernat looks at my father over his glasses, ignoring him, and looks back down at the document. I can't help but admire him.

"I have here the final will of Miss Estrella Delgado, which was created and authorised by the correct notaries." He then says a date, which was just over two months ago.

My father makes a noise, and again, Señor Bernat looks at him. When my father doesn't say anything Señor Bernat begins reading,

"In accordance with the inheritance laws of Spain, I leave one-third of my estate to my nephew, Antonio Delgado."

Señor Bernat glances up and then back down to continue reading.

"I leave a third of my estate to my grandnephew, Florencio Delgado." My mouth goes dry, and I seek Rafe's hand as he's closest. I can't believe she would leave me anything after being so generous with her collection and her art. My mouth goes dry, and my heart starts pounding.

I dare not look at my father.

"Of the remaining third of my estate, of which I may dispose as I wish. I leave one-third to my grandnephew Florencio Delgado, one-third to Juana Garcia." I hear a sharp intake of breath, and I steal a look at Juana, who has her hands over her mouth.

"One-sixth to Rafe Alderson, and the remaining sixth, along with my Steinway piano, I leave to Constantin Marin."

Everyone is frozen in stunned silence as Señor Bernat folds the papers and then opens his case. He takes out further documents and lays them out on the table.

"I have made copies for you so you can read them at your leisure. I will, of course, be handling the disposal of the estate." He rises and my father jumps up, shouting.

"This has to be a mistake. I should get everything."

"I think you'll find that everything is correct, Señor Delgado," Señor Bernat says, unruffled by my father's outburst.

I stand and turn to Rafe, who still looks stunned, if not a little puzzled. He stands slowly.

"Why would she leave me anything? I hardly knew her?"

I have no answer as I have no idea why she left me, according to what Señor Bernat's just read out, the bulk of her estate. Except that she was a canny old woman who did whatever she wanted. I look over to where Constantin is hugging a very shocked-looking Juana and ushering her over to us. I hug her too. She has tears running down her face, and she's overwhelmed with emotion.

My father comes over and says venomously, "Whatever it is you think you're playing at here, you won't get away with it."

I stand up straighter, the first time I've ever done so in my father's presence, and look him in the eye. "I want you to vacate *my* house immediately."

Epilogue 2

Rafe

Two years later

Every time the plane's wheels touch down on the runway, I get an overwhelming sense of home.

After a month away, I'm more than glad to be home. The book tour has been successful but exhausting. I'm not going to complain, though. Estrella's biography was a huge hit here in Spain, the UK, and surprisingly, on the other side of the water. The decision to take Noah on as my agent is one I've never regretted and have often been extremely thankful for. He managed to get the biography into markets I'd not thought of, and on the back of its success, was also able to sell the Blackwater series to a major publisher. It's the tour for the first book in the series that I've just finished.

I text the chat I have with Florencio and Constantin as soon as I'm off the plane and receive texts back. A typically loud one—all in capitals—from Florencio makes me giggle so much I get funny looks while waiting in line for customs. A more sedate one from Constantin, saying he's caught up with something at the bar, but he'll be back as soon as he can . . . and a curious "start without me" message, with a peach emoji.

Alena manages the bar now so Constantin can concentrate more on playing with the band, which is his first love. She also rents the apartment above, taking over when Constantin properly moved out.

I call an Uber to take me to the apartment we bought together eighteen months ago. We own the whole building, but rent out the other apartments, reserving the top floor for ourselves.

"*Oro!*" Florencio shouts as soon as I'm through the door, followed a second later by his physical form as he jumps into my arms and covers my face with kisses.

"I missed you, baby." I kiss him back, trying to devour his mouth in one go. Yes, I've definitely missed his lips.

A delicious smell hits my nostrils. "Flo, have you been cooking?"

"*Cariño*, of course I have. You probably haven't eaten properly in weeks."

I laugh. I've eaten very well, but for some reason, Florencio thinks it's not real unless he's cooked it. He doesn't need to cook for a living so he does it for fun, though he will still help Sofia, whom we see often, if she asks. We also visit Juana, who bought herself a beautiful villa outside the city and lives in a quiet but happy retirement. Florencio also teaches dance lessons, holding them in the bar before it opens. But mostly, we dance together. I've improved a lot in two years, and we've made a name for ourselves that brings people to the bar. We even took part in the first tango festival held this year, which was a lot of fun.

"Oh! Hold on, I need to turn the oven down." He rushes

off in the same whirlwind he arrived in. Before I pick my bags up, I do what I always do when I return home. I stand in front of the photograph in the lobby and say a silent thank you. The photograph, taken on Estrella's night out, is of her, me, Florencio, and Constantin. We all look happy and it's the only one of us all together. It was the first picture we hung on the wall when we moved in.

The apartment is a huge open-plan space, covering nearly the entire top floor of the building. The whole side has floor-to-ceiling windows with an amazing view across the harbour. In the centre is a dance floor where the Steinway stands to one edge. On one side is a dining area leading to a large kitchen space where Florencio is bustling around being busy. On the other side is a cosy living area and den with a huge screen TV. A few rooms lead off, mostly the cloakroom, a bathroom, and my office. There's a steel and glass curved stairway to a mezzanine floor, where our bedroom is. It has a huge bed, dressing rooms, and a bathroom with a shower plenty big enough for us all.

We all had a say in decorating it and whilst we mostly agreed, there are distinctive touches from each of us in the decor. I start unpacking, and Florencio brings me a coffee, which is very welcome.

"Thanks, baby," I say, taking it from him. "What did Con mean by his message?"

Florencio sashays up to me. "He wanted to give you a special welcome home. Said we had to take care of you . . . if you're not too tired?"

His voice is warm and silky, and I can already feel my cock taking an interest.

"I'm never too tired for you, baby."

"That's good then." He starts slowly unbuttoning my shirt, pressing kisses to my chest. I hiss as his mouth finds my nipples, and he takes one in his teeth, tugging gently before giving the same attention to the other. When I'm undressed, he peels off his own clothes and leads us to the shower. He won't let me do a thing myself and I just stand under the hot water as he massages shampoo into my hair. He reaches for my shower gel, giving it a deep smell, and murmuring "*Mmmmm,*" before pouring it out and smoothing it all over my skin. My body responds to his touches and strokes as he's spent hours mapping it out, the same as we have for each other. He washes himself and then turns off the water. He even towels me dry, only allowing me to distract him with kisses.

When we're dry, he leads me to the bed and pushes me to lie on my back before climbing on top of me, straddling my hips.

"You're beautiful," he says.

"So are you." I smile at him, and he grins at me before attacking my mouth with kisses that leave me breathless. He licks and sucks his way down my chest and ribs. He wriggles his way backwards until his mouth hovers just above my cock, which is rock hard and leaking precum.

He locks eyes with me, making sure I'm looking as he stretches his lips round the head, his tongue flicking over the tip and dipping into my slit. I keep watching as he slowly takes me deep, teasing me with his tongue until I'm moaning with pleasure. He knows how to take me right to the edge, until my back arches and I want to thrust into his throat, but he doesn't let me, holding my hips down instead.

"Well, isn't that a welcome sight and sound?" Constantin's rich voice precedes his body as he appears in view behind Florencio.

He crosses to me and kisses me, open-mouthed and fierce, claiming me.

"Welcome home, *precioso,*" he says when he releases me.

"Hey." I smile at him, not capable of any more words.

Florencio lifts off my cock, his lips glistening. Constantin tips his head back and kisses him, too.

"I'll be right back," he says, pulling off his T-shirt as he heads to the bathroom. Florencio lies down beside me, and I turn on my side so I can kiss him, trailing my fingers over his perfect skin.

Constantin is back in double-quick time, rubbing his hair with a towel, his erection jutting out.

He watches us for a minute before grabbing some lube from the dresser and kneeling on the bed. I go to move, but he says, "No, stay on your side."

He lies down and lifts one of my legs, draping it over his shoulder. He tilts his head and licks across my taint, seeking my hole with his tongue.

"Oh, I've missed your arse," he whispers before he circles my pucker, nipping and teasing until I can't stand it anymore, and I push against him, desperate to have his tongue inside me. He thrusts a few more times before he withdraws, leaving my hole clenching the air. He moves to his knees and coats himself with lube. Lifting my left again, he kisses my ankle before resting my leg across his thigh. My other leg is in front of his knees, so he's sideways to my entrance. He glances at me, checking in. I nod. I'm ready.

He pushes in slowly, letting me adjust to him, taking his time. I can't help letting out a satisfied moan.

"That's it, you're doing so good," he murmurs, his voice and words causing me to push back onto him.

He gives a gentle roll of his hips, and I groan. It feels so good. He looks down.

"Damn, the visual of this is fucking awesome. You look so good taking my cock, *precioso*."

"Let me look." Florencio shifts position so he can see. "Wow, that looks good." He turns to me, his eyes shining.

"Look at you, swallowing my dick in your tight hole.

You're so good, taking all of me, gripping me tightly, *muy bien, precioso*," Constantin purrs, knowing praise turns me on, that I love being filled by him. Every thrust pegs my prostate, and I start to lose control. My cock aches and I reach for it.

"Oh, no you don't," Florencio says, pulling my hand away. "That's mine."

He settles in front of me and resumes his previous ministrations.

"This is perfect, *precioso*. Does this feel good?" Constantin strokes his hand up and down my leg. I lose myself, being so completely full of him while Florencio sucks my soul out. Warmth blooms in my lower back and my legs start shaking.

"That's it. Beautiful. Let go. Come for me. Shoot down Cio's throat while I fill your arse with my cum. You're doing so well, *muy bien*." Constantin keeps up his crooning, which pushes me over the edge. I come with a jerk, my orgasm blooming through me and stealing any sense of time. I'm barely aware of Constantin exploding into me, or of him sliding out and resting my leg down, or even of him cleaning me up. As Florencio crawls next to me, I reach for him, and he crawls into my arms, giving me a gentle kiss.

Constantin curls himself round us both and encircles us with his arm.

When he presses a kiss to the back of my shoulder and tells me how good I am, I practically purr.

Nothing before has ever felt so much like home, and I'm looking forward to spending the rest of my life with the men I love.

Get ready to be seduced by dance…

It's Not Strictly Ballroom
Order here: **https://books2read.com/jwballroom**

Darcy has been training for the National Ballroom Championships all his life. When his chances of competing are dashed he asks his best friend Nick to step in.

Nick's feelings towards Darcy are already getting deeper, will dancing together complicate things? Can an all male couple win the Championships?

It Takes Three To Tango
https://books2read.com/jwtango

It was the need to shade from the hot sun that sent me down the shadowy alley shortly after midday.

It was the desire to slake my thirst that made me enter the small bar with the curious name and the soft music.

It was the hypnotic voice of the singer and the sensuous movements of the dancer that kept me there until after midnight.

What brought me back the next day I have still to discover, and yet here I am, book unopened on the table as I sit sipping coffee and trying not to contemplate the disaster that is my life.

Dance Dirty With Me
https://books2read.com/jwdance

A re-telling of the classic Dirty Dancing but MM style.

Are you ready to fall in love with Johnny and Baby all over again?

Meet our heroes in a Sixties English seaside resort for this coming of age classic

Larchdown Valley Series

Check out the complete Larchdown Valley series - you might not want to leave...

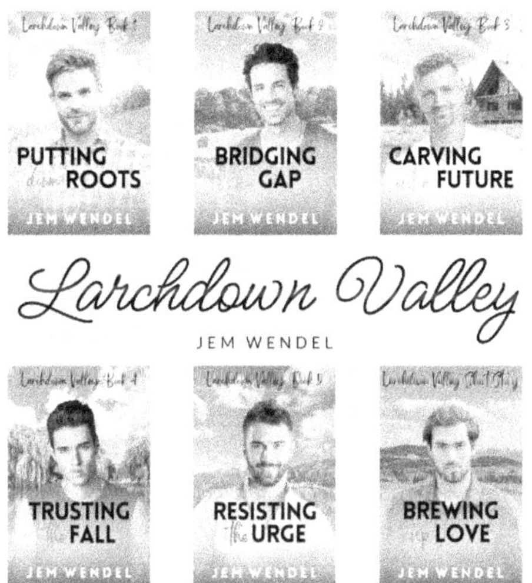

Find them all here - https://jemwendel.com/larchdown-series-information

Book 1 - Putting down Roots

Book 2 - Bridging the Gap

Book 3 - Carving out a Future

Book 4 - Trusting the Fall

Book 5 - Resisting the Urge

Short - Brewing up Love

Short - Blooming for You - download for FREE - https://BookHip.com/WSDTCQL

Acknowledgements

This project would never have been possible without the support of some incredible people.

First of all I need to thank my bookwriting bestie Hinsel Meyer, who without her constant support and messages half my words wouldn't get written I appreciate you daily. On top of that she taught me a lot of Spanish - many of the words naughty!

Big thanks to Nini Alfonso for putting up with my endless questions on Spanish language, culture, names and everything else when I dropped her a messages with - I have a question . . . Also thank you for reading and providing enthusiastic feedback, it helped keep me going through the harder times.

Huge thanks (which are truly inadequate) to Stephanie who alpha reads, creates my graphics, videos, book covers and lets me get on with writing.

Thanks to Jenn Green and Sam Buckley for knocking my rough vision into a readable form and Wren, Michelle and Ami for beta reading and proofreading.

I also want to thank my Street team who have shown their support by sharing and promoting this book.

Thanks also to the members of my readers group for their enthusiasm and support.

And final thanks to you the reader for picking this up and giving my guys a chance.

About the Author

Jem Wendel is a British author who lives on the East Coast. She survives on gallons of tea. She loves history and is never happier than when wondering round a stately home or castle. She has been writing since she was old enough to hold a pen and as well as novels, has published several short stories and magazine articles.

When she's not writing she is usually hanging out with her rescued dogs and horses and mule.

She specialises in M/M romances that are sweet, low angst with heat and a HEA.

Stay in Touch

https://linktr.ee/jemwendel

Come and join my readers group - www.facebook.com/
groups/jemwendelsgems/